Tales From The German
German
Volume II

by

C. F. Van Der Velde

Double9
BOOKS

Tales From The German
Volume II
by C. F. Van Der Velde

ISBN: 978-93-68096-12-2

Published by

DOUBLE 9 BOOKS

2/13-B, Ansari Road
Daryaganj, New Delhi – 110002
info@double9books.com
www.double9books.com
Tel. 011-40042856

ABOUT THE AUTHOR

Carl Franz van der Velde was a German author renowned for his contributions to historical novels. Born on September 27, 1779, in Wrocław, Poland, he was part of a Huguenot family with a rich cultural heritage. His father, Johann van der Velde, served as a Stempelrendant, while his mother, Beata Rosina van der Velde, provided a nurturing influence. His upbringing in a historically significant region likely inspired his fascination with historical narratives, which became the hallmark of his literary career. Van der Velde's works often captured the essence of medieval and early modern Europe, weaving tales of love, betrayal, and social dynamics with intricate historical detail. He is remembered for his ability to blend compelling storytelling with a keen sense of history, offering readers vivid depictions of past eras. His life was cut short at the age of 44, as he passed away on April 6, 1824, in his hometown of Wrocław. His legacy endures through his novels, which continue to offer insights into the complexities of human nature and historical change.

CONTENTS

THE LICHTENSTEINS

A TALE OF THE TIMES OF THE THIRTY YEARS WAR

BY

C. F. VAN DER VELDE

CHAPTER I

On christmas-eve, in the year 1628, Katharine, the wife of the merchant Fessel, of Schweidnitz, was standing in her large back parlor, with her infant upon her arm, arranging with feminine taste, upon a long table covered with a snow-white cloth, the Christmas gifts destined for her husband, her children, and the other members of her family.

At a table in the corner, sat the book-keeper, Oswald Dorn, giving the finishing touch to a miniature manger, which he had ingeniously constructed for the children of his employer. He now placed a beautifully painted angel, cut out of isinglass, in the side of the manger in which the infant Savior lay, for the purpose of indicating the celestial mission of the heavenly messenger by its transparent brilliancy. He gave yet another satisfied look at the well executed work, and then approached Katharine, who had, meanwhile, spread out an infinite variety of useful and agreeable presents, articles of dress, pieces of coin, books, toys, &c. She was now distributing to each one his portion of cakes, sweet biscuits, sugar animals, gingerbread, apples and nuts, with just impartiality. In deep thought, the book-keeper took from the table two figures formed of Schweidnitz gingerbread. They represented two of Dr. Martin Luther's enemies, Tetzel and Eck, in their official robes, disfigured with the heads of animals. The names inscribed on them left no doubt whom they were intended to represent. Dorn examined the caricatures with an ominous shake of the head. 'Do not give these ill-shaped things to the children,' said he. 'Believe me, it is not well for them to be so early taught to make war upon opinions which they do not understand. Mockery and derision are bad aids to the holy cause, and the hand, which grasps filth to throw at an adversary, is itself the first soiled. The bitterness, with which the struggle for truth and spiritual freedom has been carried on, has already spread enough of suffering and misery over Europe. Let not the demon of sectarian zeal intrude itself into the nursery.'

'You take every thing in the same earnest and serious way,' jestingly answered the friendly Katharine, laying the caricature figures aside. 'Who that heard you would suppose you had bravely drawn your sword for the new faith yourself? The red scar upon your forehead contradicts your words.'

'You are right,' cried Dorn with emotion. 'I have wielded the sword for the new faith. A bold captain of daring robbers, I have achieved many a deed of arms under this pretext; but daily do I pray to God to pardon me for it!'

He hastened away. The reverend Johannes Beer, who had entered the room unnoticed at the commencement of this conversation, looked after him with astonishment, and then asked the hostess: 'that young man talks very strangely--may he not be a papist in disguise, sent into this house as a spy for our destruction?'

'By no means!' cried Katharine with zeal. 'You know, my worthy sir, that he was wounded fighting for the Augsburg confession, and during the two years he has dwelt under our roof, he has constantly evinced so true an attachment for us, and such a noble zeal against the tyranny of the pope, that I would answer for his honesty with my life.'

'You judge of others according to the goodness of your own heart!' cried the parson. 'Believe me, in the iron times in which we live one cannot be too cautious. One Judas was found even among the apostles. Many a one who was a Paul for the pure evangelical doctrines has fallen from the faith, and now rages an angry Saul against his former brethren. The devil has once more become wholly devilish, and the anti-christ again goes about like a roaring lion seeking whom he may devour. The emperor, incited by the monks, has determined to effect a counter reformation in Silesia; and already in Glogau, the Lichtensteins, 1 those terrible men of blood, who convert by fire and sword, are raging in a furious and shocking manner.'

'Ah, reverend sir,' complained Katharine, 'we have invited you to share our joys and partake with us of the festival of our Lord; but by repeating such dreadful news you will embitter all our enjoyments, and convert our christmas supper into a mourning feast.'

'It is the duty of a faithful pastor,' said the clergyman, 'to frighten away the sleep of safety into which we are rocked by ease and selfishness. Our good Schweidnitz will also have to suffer in its turn. Have they not already taken from us the honorably purchased church of the cross, and the church of our dear lady of the woods? Have they not already forbidden us the service of God in the church of the Holy Ghost? They will surely take the earliest opportunity to do the same with St. Stanislaus and St. Wenceslaus. Various suspicious signs and tokens have lately been seen. As I was observing the stars last night, with my colleague Glogero, the constellations were very ominous; and about midnight a fearful sign arose in the heavens from the north. A large red ball of fire described a flaming arch from the edge of the horizon to the zenith of the parish church, where it burst with a powerful explosion. It indicates the near proximity of great danger to our religious liberties.'

During this speech so prophetic of evil, Katharine, with a happy feminine tact, contrived to forget the threatened troubles amid the little cares of the moment, and proceeded to ignite the innumerable lights of the christmas-trees, and those placed in the little manger for the purpose of illuminating its interior. The brightness of day was diffused through the large room, which awaked the child upon her bosom, and it smilingly stretched out its little hands toward the joyous light.

'See how my little Johannes is delighted,' said the mother to the gloomy man. 'Careless of the threatening future, he enjoys the present. Does not our holy bible say, 'unless you become like little children you shall not enter into the kingdom of heaven!' Therefore leave the portentous future to the wise guidance of God, and be happy with us to-night, for once, like this harmless child. Above all, be silent in my husband's presence, respecting your bad news. He has been very anxious and dejected for some days, and I shall be much grieved if anything occur to render us unhappy this evening, to which christians of all denominations look with general joy as the anniversary of their common origin.'

One of Fessel's apprentices now opened the door. 'My master directs me to say to you,' cried he, 'that you may immediately commence the distribution of the presents, before it is too late. He has yet much to do in the counting-room. Two important letters have arrived. He will come to you at the earliest moment possible.'

'That is not at all pleasant!' sighed Katharine, as the messenger disappeared. 'There can be no true family festival where the master of the house is missing. Nevertheless, my husband is right! If I delay much longer, the supper will be spoiled and everything will be in disorder.' She rang a bell which stood upon the table. A distant shout of children answered the noisy summons. She rang a second time, when the shouts came nearer, and a joyous tumult arose at the door of the room. She now put down the bell, and looked pleasedly toward the door, before which the whispering, laughing and tramping band awaited the third call.

'They must wait a little,' said Katharine, smiling, to the clergyman. 'It seasons the pleasure, and is a wholesome lesson for youth, when early taught.' The holy man nodded assent to the pedagogical artifice; but meanwhile the mother's heart began to yield, and impelled Katharine's hand toward the bell.

The third call now sounded, when the door burst open as if at the explosion of a petard, and the four children of Fessel, two vigorous boys and two lovely girls, stormed into the room, surrounding and dragging their favorite, the book-keeper, along with them. After them followed the clerks, apprentices, servants and maidens, who modestly arranged themselves in a row near the door until their places were pointed out to them.

The children precipitated themselves toward the richly laden table like a rushing stream, recognizing the portion destined for each with a searching and rapid glance. 'I will draw this against Wallenstein!' screamed the wild Martin, brandishing a little sword that he found among his presents. 'A bible and a bunch of quills,' cried the intellectual Ulrich, holding them up: 'now I will write against the papists like the noble Hutten, whose name I bear. 'Alas, the poor maidens who can never be married!' cried both of the girls, bringing two waxen nuns to their mother.

'Beloved children!' said the clergyman, pressing them all to his heart. They tore themselves from his arms and broke out in a simultaneous shout of astonishment and joy upon observing the miniature manger. Then as if beside themselves they ran, tumbling over each other, to their mother, the clergyman and Dorn, thankfully showing and praising their several presents.

'Will you not look at your christmas present, master Dorn?' asked Katharine of the book-keeper, who kept himself apart in serious silence.

He turned toward the designated place with a melancholy smile, and as he cast his eyes upon the rich present, a complete and splendid dress-suit with a full complement of the finest linen, he turned again with deep emotion to Katharine, who was pointing out their places to the rest of the household.

'This is too much, madam Katharine,' he cried. 'How may you thus favor the stranger beyond the children of your house?'

'The stranger?' asked Katharine resentfully. 'In our hearts it has been a long time since you were so, and we should much regret to have you consider yourself one. Believe me, we are sensible what a faithful companion and assistant my husband has acquired in you, and that every thing we can do for you is but honestly discharging our obligations.'

'Ah, see, master Dorn, you also have got a sword!' cried Martin, holding up this essential part of the dress of a burgher in those times, which lay by Dorn's present.

Dorn suddenly approached the boy and taking the magnificent sword from his hands gazed upon it with secret pleasure. At length he could no longer resist the desire to draw and try the temper of the blade.

'You are not angry,' asked Katharine, 'that a lady should presume to arm you? Really your old sword with its hacked hilt and notched and rusty blade, would not have become your new suit.'

'You have done well, worthy lady,' said Dorn, proving the blade by pressing its point against the floor and bending it in every direction. 'The old sword had indeed become dear to me, like an old friend who had always remained true in times of necessity and danger; but I never reflect upon the deeds I have performed with it without shuddering. It seems to me that it is possessed by an evil spirit which impels my hand to deeds of blood against my will, and I therefore do not like to touch it. This has as yet drank no blood, and, so help me God, I will preserve it unstained unless I am compelled to draw it in defence of the hearth where I, a friendless stranger, have been so hospitably received.'

'Or in defence of religion,' added the parson.

'The true religion, most worthy sir,' answered Dorn, 'needs not the aid of the sword!'

The reverend man had already opened his mouth to refute this bold proposition, when the master of the house entered with a clouded countenance, holding two open letters in his hand. He briefly greeted the parson, gently put aside the children who gathered about him in their noisy joy, and handed one of the letters to his wife.

'From your mother, at Sagan,' said he; and while she proceeded to read it with visible terror, he drew the book-keeper to a window.

'I have a sudden and disagreeable business for you,' said he to Dorn. 'The terrible Wallenstein conducts himself in his new dukedom with a tyranny almost unheard of among christians. He has determined to send all the orphan sons of burghers of Sagan to the school he has recently established at Gitschin. Those whom he has found in the place, have been forcibly sent to Bohemia. Their property and relatives are held answerable for the absent. As you already know, my mother-in-law's nephew, young Engelmann, is at present studying at the gymnasium in this city; and the tyrant has thrown his uncle and guardian into prison until the pupil shall be forthcoming. No other course remains, but to send the poor boy home as soon as possible; and, that he may, in these dangerous times, reach Sagan with safety, it is my wish that you would accompany him. When there, you may also be able to assist me in another affair. I have loaned a thousand gilders upon the two houses of the joiner Eckebrect. My debtor now informs me that the houses are among those the duke has caused to be demolished for the purpose of opening a better view for his palace. Nothing has yet been said respecting indemnification. I therefore wish you, while on the spot, to obtain all the information you can upon the subject.'

'I am very willingly at your service,' modestly answered Dorn. 'When shall I set out?'

'Did I not fear the sin of keeping you from church on christmas night,' said Fessel, 'I would beg of you to start this very evening. Sagan is distant, and old Engelmann is a very worthy man, whose release from prison I should be glad to effect as soon as possible.'

'The performance of duty is God's service!' cried Dorn. 'I will go immediately and prepare for the journey.' He left the room, followed by the boys, who lamented the loss of their best christmas enjoyment in his departure.

'Your book-keeper is indeed no papist,' said the parson to Katharine after a long pause; 'but there may also be some doubt of his Lutheranism; for he appears to sustain the doctrine of good works. He may be tinctured with Calvinism.'

'If he were, he would still be our protestant co-laborer and brother in Christ,' answered Fessel in the name of his consort, who was busily reading.

'Calvin, Zuinglius, and the pope--all are heretics alike!' grumbled the parson.

The weeping Katharine now folded the letter, handed it to her husband, and in a soft, submissive voice asked him: 'What have you decided upon, Tobias?'

'I wished to advise with you upon the matter first, my Kitty,' he answered, in a friendly manner. 'They are your nearest relatives who now seek a refuge with us, and I would not willingly leave them in the claws of those fiends; but at all events their coming would increase your domestic cares, and I know not whether you would like to have your mother and sister reside in the family.'

'As I know my beloved ones,' she joyfully answered, 'I have only relief, consolation and joy, to expect from them; and, if my opinion is to decide the matter, I beg you with all my heart to have them brought here.'

Dorn now entered the room in his traveling dress, with his rusty sword by his side. He was followed by Martin and Ulrich, and the young Engelmann with his traveling bag in his hand, much grieved at being compelled to leave his dear Schweidnitz for a strange school where he was unknowing and unknown.

'The carriage is ready,' said the book-keeper. 'I come to take my leave, and ask if you have any further commands for me.'

'I have yet one more request, my dear friend,' answered the merchant. 'A captain of Wallenstein's body guards is quartered in the house of my mother-in-law at Sagan, who plays the duke of Friedland on a small scale in the quiet residence of the widow; and, what is still more unfortunate, woos the favor of my sister-in-law after the fashion of a wild Tartar. She very naturally rejects the monster, who has already served under four different masters, has four times changed his religion, and is now, by accident, a catholic; but the refusal has brought her no relief, and he only, who knows how much a bad man may afflict a family upon whom he is quartered, can imagine what the poor women must suffer. On this account they wish to leave all behind them and flee to me at Schweidnitz; and after having delivered up your scholar, you can bring them with you on your return. This writing may serve as your credential.'

'I beg of you to be especially careful that you suffer no injury on the way from the marauding soldiers, who render the public roads unsafe,' said Katharine with anxious solicitude.

'I take with me my faithful old battle-companion,' said Dorn, striking the hilt of his sword with a glance in which all his former military spirit shone forth. 'Do not be concerned for me, madam Katharine. We have a hard frost--I shall let the horses travel at a round pace--and with God's blessing, I will be here to partake of the christmas supper, which I should have eaten now, with you and your dear relatives on new year's eve.'

He raised the sorrowing children, whom even the ingeniously constructed manger could not console for his departure, one after the other to his lips, bowed to the others, disappeared with his protégé, and the wheels of his carriage were soon heard rattling over the hard-frozen ground.

CHAPTER II

It was the evening of the third christmas holiday. The snow-flakes were merrily whirling about out of doors; and in a well warmed room at Sagan sat the merchant's widow, Prudentia Rosen, with her daughter, the lovely Faith. Both of them were industriously winding the fine spun thread upon the twirling spindles. The impudent captain of the guards had planted himself in the matron's armchair, at the table, and was afflicting the poor women by a recital of his terrible warlike deeds, while he emptied the silver goblet standing before him, and directed love-glances, which made him look even more disagreeable, at poor Faith, who, sighingly and reluctantly replenished it from time to time.

The servant announced a stranger who wished to speak with madam Rosen alone.

The widow rose to go out in obedience to the summons; but the captain sneeringly observed that as she could have no motive for a secret interview with the stranger, she could give the required audience in his presence.

The widow nodded to the servant, with a slight shrug of the shoulders at this new exhibition of insolence. The latter immediately ushered in a young man, who greeted the ladies with modest friendliness, and the captain with cold courtesy.

'I am the book-keeper of your son-in-law,' said he. 'I have the honor to hand you this letter as my credential, and to inform you, that, if agreeable, yourself and daughter can accompany me to Schweidnitz to-morrow morning.'

'How? You wish to leave Sagan now, madam Rosen?' asked the captain, angrily stroking his red beard.

'Family affairs render this journey unavoidable,' answered the widow, with quiet firmness.

'You must arrange the matter otherwise,' blustered the ruffian. 'Your most imperative duty is to remain here and provide for the comfort of those who are quartered in your house.'

'Do not be anxious on that score, captain,' answered the widow. 'Every thing will be furnished that you need in my absence.'

'Then go, in the devil's name, where you please,' cried the captain; 'but, that my comfort may not be disturbed, your daughter remains behind to discharge the duties of hostess.'

'Give yourself no uneasiness, madam Rosen,' said Dorn, consolingly, to the terrified woman. 'If you are not by the duke of Friedland's command a prisoner in your own house, the captain will let you go without requiring a hostage.'

'How is that?' cried the irritated captain, viewing the young man from head to foot. The latter quietly returned his measuring glance, whilst the beauteous Faith timidly raised her eyes from her spindle, inwardly delighted with the fearlessness of the interesting stranger.

'You are a fine fellow,' said the captain with a malicious smile; 'well-grown and strong; and your bold behavior is very becoming. You would make a good trooper. Come, do me justice to the health of our most gracious emperor.'

'We must become better acquainted with each other, captain, before we drink together,' answered Dorn, politely declining the goblet.

'Do you slight my proffered courtesy,' growled the captain; 'or do you belong to the rebels, that you refuse to drink the emperor's health?'

'Drink!' imploringly begged the timid Faith, and, vanquished by the glance which accompanied the request, the youth seized the goblet and cried, 'May God enlighten the emperor and teach him the true way to promote the welfare of his subjects!'

'Bravo, comrade!' cried the captain, as the goblet was drained. 'You will never regret having entered the emperor's service. I pledge you my word that you will be a corporal in a month.'

'What mean you by that?' asked Dorn with surprise. 'The idea of entering the emperor's service never once came into my head.'

'You jest!' cried the miscreant. You have drank to the emperor with a captain in the imperial service, and by that act have become a soldier.'

'Is it possible!' cried Dorn. 'Can you so prostitute the emperor's name as to use it for so low an artifice?'

'Not a word of opposition, fellow!' said the captain menacingly. 'You have consented to take service under the standard of his imperial majesty, and must abide thereby.'

'I am a free burgher of Schweidnitz,' said Dorn; 'what right have you to hold me?'

'What right! what right! blustered the captain, striking the floor with his sword. 'Here is my right, which is valid through all Europe.'

'I warn you, captain,' cried Dorn, 'to be cautious how you take a step which may disgrace you without accomplishing your purpose.'

'That we shall see!' said the captain; and, going to the door, he threw it open and cried, 'Orderly!'

A gigantic guardsman came clattering up the steps, stooped to enter the room, and then, straitening himself up like a tall pine, thundered, 'Here!'

'Take this recruit to the guard-room,' commanded the captain, 'and deliver him over, on my account, to the officer of the day. He may as well be put in uniform and sworn to his colors this evening as tomorrow.'

The colossus stepped up to Dorn, pointed to the door, and in a very insolent tone commanded, 'March!'

Dorn hurled him back with great force, and drew from his pocket a sealed document which he held up to the view of the captain. 'My commission as captain in the royal Danish service,' said he, 'protects me against the honor of serving under you. The duke of Friedland shall satisfy himself of its authenticity to-morrow. To me you must make reparation, upon the spot, for this personal outrage. Have the goodness to follow me to the door.'

The captain, who, like many a bragadocio, hid the ears of the ass under the skin of the lion, stood utterly confused before the angry youth, in whom he had very unexpectedly found his match. At length he motioned his orderly to retire. 'It is not possible for me to accept your invitation to-night; but early in the morning we will speak further upon this matter,' said he with constrained courtesy to Dorn, and immediately left the room.

'We shall not be able to start before noon, in this way,' said Dorn, with some little vexation. 'Meanwhile, have the goodness, madam Rosen, to pack the best and most necessary articles which you may wish to take with you, to-night.'

'Ah, that would prove a fruitless trouble, my dear sir!' exclaimed the widow. 'The captain is now highly incensed, and I believe he would strike the horses dead before the carriage, sooner than let us go.'

'I trust some one higher than he can be found here,' said Dorn. 'When matters come to the worst, I can speak to the duke himself.'

'God preserve you from that!' cried the widow. 'He is indeed a passionate, tyrannical man, who will not tolerate even the sparrows upon his roof. He directly hangs every one who makes the least opposition to him. He strung up a poor apothecary's apprentice for making too much noise in his neighborhood with his pestle and mortar, and a poor child because it cried in its mother's arms.'

'I nevertheless doubt not he will suffer me to live,' said Dorn, with a smile. 'I have seen the white of his eye at Dessau, and was not frightened. Therefore dismiss your fears and pack up as quick as you can. I shall start at one in the afternoon to-morrow. I have promised your daughter to be in Schweidnitz on new-year's eve, and will keep my word.'

He was about to take his leave; but the widow held him fast by both his hands.

'No,' cried she, anxiously, 'I will not let you go. I thank God for sending a manly protector to my house in these evil times, and should die with fear if compelled to sleep alone under the same roof with that monster, now that he is irritated. No, you remain with us. My daughter shall prepare the little guest-chamber for you, and I will mix your evening draught.'

'I would not be troublesome to you,' said Dorn, 'at a time when your house is already occupied by other guests.'

'It is, indeed, and by those who are uninvited and unwelcome,' sighed the widow. 'But for that very reason I would add a welcome guest to the number, that I may know whether I am yet mistress of my own house.'

In obedience to a nod from her mother. Faith, with blushing cheeks and downcast eyes, took a light to show the guest to his chamber. He followed her through the Gothic building, up one flight of steps and down another, through crooked passages, until they reached a small, but neatly furnished chamber, in which was a snow white bed. While Faith removed the flowered damask covering, filled the shining pewter ewer with fresh water, and hung a towel near it, he was occupied in observing the beautiful form of the lovely blonde, whose graceful motions, employed for the promotion of his comfort, were for that reason rendered doubly charming.

'Perhaps I render you an unwelcome service in taking you from this place, fair maiden?' said he, by way of beginning conversation.

'How can you think so, sir?' quickly replied Faith. 'I thank my God and yourself for my release.'

'Well, one cannot always know,' said Dorn, jestingly. 'The heart may often have attachments in a place otherwise particularly disagreeable.'

'If I thought you alluded to the captain,' said Faith, with some asperity, 'I could become angry with you, in the first hour of our acquaintance.'

'He is not, indeed, a very fascinating suitor,' continued Dorn; 'but there nevertheless may be in the city of Sagan, some slender rosy youth, who has eyes for so beauteous a maiden.'

'I know none here for whom I could have eyes,' answered the maiden, quickly, and immediately became somewhat alarmed at the traitorous emphasis she had laid upon the word *here*.

'Not here, but elsewhere?' asked Dorn, seizing her delicate white hand.

'These bold questions come from the evil customs of your hateful military profession,' said Faith, endeavoring to withdraw her hand. He suffered her to regain it only by slow degrees, letting but one rosy finger out of his hand at a time, while his pulse was becoming greatly accelerated by the soft, caressing touch. His eyes sought and met hers, which looked kindly upon him, not with the sun's consuming fire, but with the mild chaste light of the friendly moon.

'So you have not yet loved, charming Faith?' he earnestly asked, holding fast the last little finger of the imprisoned hand.

'What a question,' whispered she, turning away from him. 'I am scarcely sixteen years old.'

'Then the first silver-tone is yet to be drawn from this untried 'harp of a thousand strings;' O, how happy,' cried the youth, 'will be that artist who shall one day succeed in awakening its thrilling music!'

Faith suddenly exclaimed, 'Good night, captain!' The farewell bow released the yet imprisoned finger, and the delightful vision disappeared.

CHAPTER III

When Dorn opened his eyes the next morning, a corporal and six halbardiers were standing before his bed.

'Dress yourself quickly,' commanded the corporal. 'I am ordered to bring you before the duke.'

Having soon become satisfied that no opposition was, in this case, to be thought of, Dorn obeyed. As he and his guards were passing through the streets, he saw many things which went to prove the arbitrary power of the man before whom his own emperor and all Europe were then trembling. Notwithstanding the misery and suffering produced by the war, he saw whole rows of houses which had been repaired, newly painted, and splendidly furnished, that the city in which the Friedlander dwelt and governed might present an agreeable appearance to the eye. The beautiful flocks and herds of the city, driven by weeping burghers, were making their way toward the gates, having been expelled because their continuance in the city was inconsistent with the dignity of a capital. The work of demolition was yet going on in the vicinity of the palace, and more than fifty houses were lying in ruins. To all of Dorn's questions, however, the corporal had but one answer:--'the duke wills it.' They had now reached the castle. The corporal conducted Dorn through the crowd of halbardiers, footmen and pages, to the ante-chamber of the audience-room, where fifty of the body guards were on duty. Two Silesian noblemen, ambassadors to the duke from Leignitz and Oels-Bernstadt, were here waiting in patient humility to learn if the dictator would please to grant them an audience.

At length one of the duke's counsellors came out of the audience-room, and with insolent hauteur beckoned the Leignitz ambassador, who reverentially approached the proud knight.

'What you have delivered to my lord in behalf of your province,' said the counsellor, with contemptuous disrespect, 'he will take into consideration and communicate his pleasure to your duke at the next assembly of the princes. Your complaints against the troops are not deserving of consideration. The soldier must have something for his trouble and toil. In that respect, my lord has far heavier and more just complaints against your duke. The latter has put a man to death who wished to take service in our army.'

'The culprit was a subject of our duke, and a wilful murderer,' answered the ambassador. 'He was executed in accordance with the right and in pursuance of the judgment of the court of Aldermen of Leignitz.'

'No court of justice,' continued the counsellor, 'may presume to punish any one who claims the Friedlander's protection. My lord directs you to say to your duke, that he must send him two hundred infantry from his own troops as an indemnification, or the heads of a dozen of the Leignitz nobility shall be answerable for the neglect.'

The Leignitz ambassador retired with a deadly paleness, and the messenger from Oels-Bernstadt was beckoned to approach.

'Duke Wenzel,' said the counsellor, in a cutting tone, 'has ventured to hang same soldiers of count Terzky's regiment.'

'As robbers taken in the act,' interposed the messenger; 'in obedience to the orders of the generalissimo himself, to keep the high roads safe, and punish all convicted criminals.'

'Terzky has written to him,' continued the counsellor, without noticing the interruption, 'that he has ordered the same number of the prince's counsellors to be hanged, and that he has already set a price upon their heads. Thereupon lord Wenzel immediately complained to the emperor, and the complaint, as was proper, has been transmitted to my master, who has decided upon the affair. He directs it to be announced to your master that he approves and will sustain the acts of count Terzky, and to give an example to the Silesian princes generally, the principalities and baronies of your master will be confiscated and divided among those soldiers who have merited them by their services. With this message you are at liberty to depart.' He turned his back upon him and with a haughty step returned to the audience-room. The messengers departed in speechless sorrow, and at that moment a corporal conducted two well dressed ladies into the ante-chamber. They were closely veiled and weeping bitterly. Another corporal led a bound Wallensteiner, with wild, staring eyes, blue lips and bristling' hair, through the ante-chamber into the audience-room. The ladies now looked up, and, perceiving Dorn, quickly removed their veils. He instantly recognized his hospitable hostess and her lovely daughter.

'My dear Faith!' cried he with tender compassion; but the corporal rapped him upon the shoulder, and whispered to him, 'silence, if you have any regard for your neck. Without the duke's permission no word must be uttered here.'

A deep and awful silence now prevailed in the ante-chamber, broken only by some plaintive tone which occasionally reached them through the double doors which separated the two rooms. An angry voice suddenly cried within, 'let the brute be hanged!'--'That was the duke,' whispered one of the soldiers to another. The doors opened, and the delinquent was again led through the ante-chamber by his companion. 'God be merciful to me!' stammered he, as he staggered onward and disappeared.

Again a deep silence, again the doors of the audience-room opened, and the counsellor cried out, 'the Dane, with the two gentlewomen!'

'Forward!' commanded each of the corporals, and with a firm step Dorn walked into the hall, supporting the almost fainting females.

A tall haggard man, with a dreadful sternness in his yellow face and small twinkling eyes, frightfully expressive of anxiety, a magnificent plumed hat upon his short red head, a black velvet Spanish jacket decked with the stars and chains of various orders, an ermine-trimmed, dark violet-colored velvet mantle upon his shoulders, was standing by his gilded armchair before a table, at which three counsellors and a Jesuit were seated. Six barons and the same number of knights, stood in files by the wall in respectful silence, that the behests of the all-powerful noble might be followed by instant execution, as the deed follows the will, or thunder the lightning. Behind the arm-chair stood the well known captain of the life guards, who met the entering group with a smile of Satanic triumph.

With the majesty of a prince of the lower world, the duke advanced to Dorn, looked at him with his little piercing eyes as though he would interrogate his soul, and in a gruff repulsive tone asked him, 'Danish captain?'

'By virtue of this commission,' quietly answered Dorn, handing the document to him.

The duke glanced through it, gave it back to him, and said, 'a prisoner of war, then!'

'When count Mannsfeld was driven through Silesia by you,' answered Dorn, 'I was left in Oels severely wounded. I there found a charitable merchant who had my wounds healed and afterwards took me with him to Schweidnitz. Tired of the trade of war, I have remained there for the last two years, and served my benefactor in the capacity of book-keeper. Under these circumstances, I leave it for your sense of justice to decide whether I can be considered a prisoner of war.'

'Or spy?' asked the duke.

'My free passport remains with the commandant of the city,' answered Dorn.

'What was your object in coming to head quarters?' asked the duke.

'To bring a scholar from Schweidnitz,' answered Dorn, for your school at Gitschin, and to take back to Schweidnitz my employer's mother-in-law and her daughter.'

'Prove it!' cried the examiner.

'Send to the merchant Engelmann,' said Dorn; 'who must have left his prison last evening; and Madam Rosen must yet have the letter which she wrote to Schweidnitz and which I brought back to her as my credential.'

'Here is the unlucky letter,' sobbed the trembling widow, handing it to the duke on bended knee.

He took it, read, and turned towards the captain.

'We have your portrait here,' said he; 'not flattered, but well drawn. Did you know the object of his coming here?'

The captain replied only by stammering some unintelligible words.

'He wished to prevent their departure,' said Dorn.

'To know and keep silence, is called lying!' observed the duke, with anger. Then to Dorn, 'you have, however, abused the emperor!'

'That is not true!' cried the latter with vehemence. 'He drank the emperor's health with the captain!' cried the trembling Faith, encouraged by her anxiety for the youth. 'I and my mother are witnesses, and because he drank the emperor's health, the captain pretended that he had enlisted for a soldier.'

'Shame upon you!' thundered the duke. 'Has a lord who has all Europe for a recruiting ground, need of such miserable devices?'

'Here is a heretic conspiracy,' cried the captain, 'planned for my destruction. This woman is secretly a Lutheran, together with her daughter. Already have I twice watched their stolen attendance upon the preacher of Eckensdorf. For that reason they have called the Mannsfelder here, that he may take them to heretical Schweidnitz, where they can practise their idolatry undisturbedly; and because, out of zeal for the true faith, I wished to prevent their heathenish abominations, I am calumniated by the apostate women and their accomplice.'

'Heap not new insults upon us,' cried Dorn, forgetting in whose presence he stood. 'You know that you yet owe me satisfaction for those of last evening. You promised indeed to meet me this morning; but you preferred to rob me of my liberty and the ability to punish you for the outrage you committed, by false charges.'

'Mannsfelder! Mannsfelder!' exclaimed the duke, secretly delighted with the boldness of the warrior; 'We also are yet here!' and turning to the captain, he asked; 'What have you to say to this accusation?'

'Challenged and not appear!' cried he, as the captain stood mute, with frightfully flashing eyes. 'A Friedlandish captain! Announce yourself to the officer of the day as under arrest, and immediately afterwards seek for your discharge. You can no longer serve under Wallenstein!'

'Yet the captain's information with regard to the secret church-going of these women may well deserve some consideration,' remarked the Jesuit, rising.

'A soldier should be no priestly spy,' angrily answered the duke. 'I am the emperor's generalissimo; but not his inquisitor. What care I about the catechisms of his subjects. They may believe what they like, provided they but give what they should. I adhere to my decision.'

With a devout sigh the Jesuit again seated himself; and, in despair at the rebound of his last arrow, the captain left the hall.

With a kindness which strangely suited his stony face, the duke now stepped directly to Dorn and slapped him upon the shoulder. 'You are laconic and resolute,' said he, 'I like that; and moreover I must have seen this face somewhere.'

'Perhaps on the Elbe near Dessau,' answered Dorn.

'Right!' cried the duke. 'You are the officer who held the last entrenchment with such obstinacy. I liked you, even then. Will you become a major in my regiment of life-guards? I shall conclude a peace with Denmark at the earliest opportunity, and so your Danish commission need be no hindrance.'

'To the true hero the truth may be fearlessly spoken,' said Dorn. 'I cannot fight against my conscience.'

'I regret that any obstacle deprives me of your services,' said the duke. 'I would very willingly do something to oblige you. Ask some favor of me!'

'I have only to ask you,' said Dorn, 'to permit me to depart immediately for Schweidnitz with these ladies, and also your permission to take back with me the poor boy whom I tore from his friends in obedience to your commands.'

'Well, take the whole baggage, comrade,' said the duke beneficently: 'and a prosperous journey to you! I will cause the necessary papers to be given you.'

The duke kindly nodded permission to retire, and Dorn led the ladies from the hall.

'A happy escape from the lion's den!' sighed the matron with a lighter heart, as she turned her back upon the palace.

What may not one accomplish who is a man in the fullest sense of the word!' cried the enthusiastic Faith, pressing Dorn's hand to her heart.

'I know not,' said Dorn pensively, 'whether I shall have especial reason to rejoice at the turn the affair has taken or not. It just now occurs to me that the dismission of your persecutor from his quarters in your house, removes the evil which impelled you to leave Sagan, and that you may not now wish to accompany me to Schweidnitz.'

'O! we have on many accounts long desired to visit our Katharine,' said Faith with great earnestness. 'Our house can never remain long free from this detestable quartering, and who knows how the next may conduct himself! Besides, I fear the captain now as much as I did before. He has lost the power of tormenting us, and his bread into the bargain. He will soon be released from the guard-house, and a bad man, however insignificant may be his situation, has the power to injure with the will!'

'My daughter's zeal,' smilingly interposed the matron, 'saves me the trouble of explaining my reasons for wishing to go with you. Let it suffice, that we ride with you to Schweidnitz.'

CHAPTER IV

At Schweidnitz, on new year's eve, the Fessel family were gathered around the well lighted and richly covered table; but no one had an inclination to eat; for Dorn, the idol of the house, was still absent, and anxiety for her beloved relatives saddened the countenance of the affectionate Katharine.

'I thought master Dorn would have kept his word better,' cried the impatient Martin, striking the empty seat which had been placed near him for the expected traveler. 'The supper will soon be over and still he is not here.'

'He will yet be sure to come,' said the confiding Ulrich. 'God grant it,' sighed Katharine. 'A carriage! a carriage!' cried the listening daughters, running to the window. 'It is father's horses!' they shouted. Out ran the two boys, overthrowing their seats with a tremendous racket; and, as if there had been a wager among the four children, which should first break their necks, they all rushed out of the door and down the steep stairs.

'Welcome to Schweidnitz, my dear mother!' joyfully cried the master of the house from the window, to which he also had hastened.

'Has my sister come with you?' asked the anxious Katharine, running to the door. The children had already let down the steps of the carriage, and madam Rosen with her daughter hastened to meet their expectant friends. The cloaks and wrappers soon fell off, and mother and daughters were clasped in a mutual embrace.

'Happily redeemed from the prison of the hateful Holofernes?' asked Fessel, affectionately greeting his mother-in-law.

'After great trouble and anxiety,' answered the widow, drawing a long breath, whilst the attentive Katharine was busily relieving her of her superfluous traveling garments.

'Had you not sent us so bold a knight,' said Faith playfully; 'to rescue us from the terrible giant, we should have been at this moment sitting in Sagan, listening to the insupportable boastings of the monster.'

'Where is the valiant knight, that I may thank him for his good service?' asked Katharine.

At that moment Dorn entered the room, leading the young Engelmann by the hand, and surrounded by the four children of the house.

'How! Do you bring the boy, also?' asked the astonished master, warmly embracing his book-keeper.

'He has permission to remain and pursue his studies here,' answered Dorn. 'Here is the Duke's consent in his own hand-writing.'

'You must understand the black art,' cried the overjoyed Fessel. 'I should sooner have expected to remove the everlasting hills from their foundations than to move the Friedlander from his purpose.'

'I could not, however, save your property,' said Dorn. 'The houses already lay in ruins, and all applications for indemnification are rejected by the ducal court.'

'I am sorry to lose the capital,' said Fessel; for I had already built a fine speculation upon it; but you have saved my dear friends, and so in God's name let the guilders go. Now seat yourselves and relate to me circumstantially how this eighth wonder of the world has been accomplished.'

They placed themselves at table. Dorn obtained a seat near the charming Faith; and, as among a swarm of bees, narrations and corrections, questions and answers, praise and astonishment, fear, anger and laughter, so buzzed about the table that the business of eating was scarcely thought of.

'Thank God we are finally here!' remarked madam Rosen, reaching her goblet of Hungary wine to the book-keeper, for the purpose of touching his glass. 'My best thanks,' said she with emotion, and at the same time gave an intimation to Faith to follow her example.

'Thank me not so much, dear madam,' said the youth with a pensive air, while touching glasses with the blushing maiden; 'else I shall have my whole reward in thanks.'

'And in consequence lose the courage to ask for a dearer one,' jested Katharine, who had noticed the glance he gave her sister.

'We are so merry to-night!' cried Fessel's youngest daughter, the little Hedwig, 'cannot you let us have the play of the light boats now, dear mother? You promised it to us on Christmas eve; which, by the by, was passed sadly enough.'

'Yes, yes, the light boats!' shouted the other children, clapping their hands.

'Well, bring the large soup-dish,' said the mother, who could refuse nothing to her youngest daughter; 'but be careful not to spill the water.'

'Glorious, excellent!' cried the children in chorus. Hedwig flew out of the room; the other children produced wax candles of various colors, and began cutting them into innumerable small pieces; while Faith, Dorn, and young Engelmann, were instructed to divide the walnuts, of which the table famished an abundant supply, in halves, and neatly to extricate the kernels without injuring the shells.

'I know not if you are acquainted with this play of the Silesian children,' said Fessel, laughing, to Dorn. 'It was omitted by us last year, in consequence of my wife's illness. It is a solemn oracle upon matters of love, marriage, and death. The children, however, do not trouble themselves about the serious signification; but only take pleasure in the movements of the boats and in splashing the water.'

The door now opened, and little Hedwig stepped into the room, with the large dish full of water in her hands, with a solemn and consequential air, and deposited her burden upon the centre of the table.

'Now put the lights in the boats,' commanded Martin; 'we have prepared enough of them.' A small wax taper was placed in each shell, projecting like the mast of a boat.

'Who shall swim first?' asked Elizabeth, lighting the tapers in two of the boats.

'Mother and father!' cried the others, and the shells were placed in the platter near each other, when they moved forth upon the clear liquid surface with a regular motion, and burning with a steady light, until they reached the opposite side where they quietly remained.

'We are already anchored in a safe haven,' said Fessel to his beloved wife; 'and in the quiet enjoyment of domestic happiness, we can have no wish to be restlessly driving about upon the open seas.'

'Ah, may God grant that the troubles of the times reach us not in our safe haven and rend our bark from its fast anchorage,' cried the true-hearted Katharine with timid foreboding.

At this moment the light in one of the boats began to hiss and sputter, and after flashing for an instant was extinguished, amid exclamations of sad surprise from the children.

'What does that forbode?--to whom does that boat belong?' asked Katharine, smilingly.

'That is not decided,' eagerly cried Ulrich; 'and the whole oracle is invalid.'

'Elizabeth filled the boat with water by her awkwardness, when she started it,' announced Martin, who had been investigating the causes of the accident.

'Every event in life must have had its cause,' said Fessel with more earnestness than the trifling accident merited. 'If this portends the extinguishment of the light of life in either of us, I pray God in mercy to grant that mine may be the first to expire.'

'Say not so,' tenderly replied Katharine. 'Our children would lose in you their only stay. Their mother would be more lightly missed, and the strong man would better bear the sad bereavement than weak and helpless woman.'

'Why this earnest and deep-meaning conversation on new year's evening?' said madam Rosen, half angry. 'Come, children; go on more briskly with your play and give us something pleasanter to think about.'

'Who comes next?' asked Elizabeth.

'Honor to whom honor is due,' laughed Hedwig. 'Cousin Faith must swim now.'

'But she must herself decide with whom,' said Fessel. 'I have not been at Sagan for some years, and know not who has made himself most agreeable to her.'

'Indeed, I know not whom to name to you,' said the maiden with a low tone and hesitating manner, blushing deeply for the untruth which thus escaped her lips.

'Then we will take master Dorn for the occasion,' cried the obstreperous Martin, whose natural boldness was increased by the wine he had tasted; 'he is constantly giving Faith such friendly glances!'

'It shall be so,' shouted Ulrich; 'and they shall have the handsomest tapers. Choose your own colors; here are red, and green, and white, and variegated.'

'Red for Faith and green for me,' quickly cried Dorn, silencing the maiden by a gentle pressure of her hand under the table, as she was about to make some objections.

'They must not, however, start together from the shore,' said Ulrich. 'Well, do you set the red ship on that side and I will place the green one here,' answered Martin; 'and then they may seek each other if they wish to come together.'

Brightly burning, the little barks swam towards each other for a moment; then, both floated to the edge of the platter and remained motionless, at some little distance apart.

'Master Dorn is too indolent!' cried Martin, throwing a nut-kernel at the green skiff to urge it towards the red; but it only reeled to and fro, without removing from its place.

'Insufferable!' cried Dorn. At that moment the water became slightly agitated, and both skiffs left their stations at the side for the open sea.

'Faith has jostled the table!' cried the falcon-eyed Hedwig.

'I--no--I wish to hinder their meeting,' stammered the confused Faith.

'Did you really jostle the table, dearest maiden?' asked Dorn, his hand again seeking hers.

'Ah, ah, my daughter!' reprovingly exclaimed madam Rosen, and amid the exclamations of the children the two skiffs met in mid ocean, while a gentle pressure from Faith's hand gave an affirmative answer to the bold question of the youth.

The joy of the children, which the grandmother's remonstrances only increased, was every moment becoming more bold and noisy. Without aim or object a crowd of lights were now set afloat in the mimic ocean, and apple cuttings and bread bullets flew like bombs among them, causing immense damage and innumerable shipwrecks. 'It is enough!' cried Fessel, the disturbance becoming excessive, and moved his chair from the table. A respectful silence succeeded the wild tumult. The children dutifully arose, folded their hands with a serious air, and Martin said grace with decent solemnity.

The mistress of the house now invited her beloved guests to retire to rest; that they might sleep away the fatigues of the day; but the children, who had again become as noisy as ever, and had not the least inclination to sleep, strongly opposed the movement.

'It would be fine indeed,' cried Martin, 'if we should have no writing of notes.'

'Pray, pray, dear mother!' entreated the flattering and constant petitioner, Hedwig. 'You well know that you promised me, if I filled a writing book without blotting, that I should be indulged with writing notes, on new year's evening. My last writing book is without a spot, and you must now keep your word.'

'Children are the most inexorable creditors,' said Fessel, directing little Ulrich to bring the writing materials from the counting-room, while the table was being cleared.

'This is a strange remnant of the old heathen times,' explained Fessel to the book-keeper, who looked inquiringly at him. 'It is a form of new year's congratulation, and an oracle at the same time. You write three several wishes upon three slips of paper, which you fold and give to the person who would try his fate. These wishes may be, honors, offices and success in business, to the men,--chains, bracelets, and new dresses, to the women,--agreeable suitors to maidens. All place the notes they have received under their pillows, and the wish contained in the one which is first opened on new year's morning shall be fulfilled in the course of the current year.'

'I always take great pleasure in this sport,' said Katharine to her mother; 'my husband is always so anxious to fulfil his oracle and to present me what is wished me in the note I open.'

'There comes Ulrich!' screamed the children, as he entered, heavily laden, and deposited his burden upon the table. The notes were prepared, and the whole family were soon seated around the table, moving their pens as assiduously as if an instrument was to be drawn for securing religious liberty. Amidst the scratching of the pens, which were very awkwardly handled by the younger children, and therefore made the more noise, arose the admonitions of the father to sit erect, and of the mother not to bespatter themselves with ink; which admonitions were obeyed just so long as they were heard. Meanwhile Dorn was sharply watching the paper upon which Faith was writing; who, as soon as she became aware of it, covered the writing with her little hand and whispered to him: 'If you watch me, you will get no packet from me to-night.' He discreetly drew back and began writing his notes.

Fessel now strewed sand upon his last note, enclosed it with the others and gave the packet with a kiss to his Katharine. The children snapped their pens to the infinite damage of the well scoured white floor, for which their grandmother very properly scolded them. Dorn handed his packet to the beauteous Faith, who hid hers in her bosom, strenuously asserting that she could think of nothing to write.

The clock now struck the midnight hour, and a peal of bells from the tower of the city hall greeted the new year.

'A happy new year! a happy new year!' shouted the children, springing from their seats; and the impetuous Hedwig proposed to open the notes directly, as the new year had already commenced; but Fessel interposed his decided negative and commanded them to defer it until the actual rising of the new year sun.

Amid the noise and confusion of the thousand new year congratulations, Dorn once more approached the lovely Faith.

'Must I enter upon the new year without one kind wish from you?' he pensively asked. She looked at him with embarrassment and irresolution. At that moment she was called by her mother who was already standing in the door. The startling call helped her to come to a decision, and, suddenly drawing the packet from her bosom and smilingly placing it in Dorn's hand, she hastened after her mother.

Long did the youth hold the much coveted packet pressed to his lips. 'How much earthly happiness,' said he to himself with deep emotion, 'have I destroyed in my military career. Do I indeed deserve that love should crown me with its freshest wreaths in a land I have helped to lay waste?'

Dorn, who had retired late and awoke betimes with the interesting little packet under his pillow, found himself at an early hour leaning against a window in the family parlor, and engaged in examining a delicate little note. While thus occupied, Faith, impelled by a similar restlessness, entered the room. As she perceived him whose image had embellished her dreams, an enchanting blush overspread her delicate face, and her beautiful blue eyes beamed with love and joy; but when Dorn, enraptured at the encounter, affectionately tendered her the congratulations appropriate to the new year's morning, changing her mood she turned away from him with feigned displeasure and exclaimed: 'Pshaw, captain! I am angry with you. You have wished me two horrible suitors.'

'Before I undertake to exculpate myself,' said Dorn, 'only tell me which you drew from the packet.'

'The duke of Friedland,' stammered the embarrassed maiden with downcast eyes.

'Look me directly in the eye!' cried Dorn, seizing the hand of the unpractised dissembler. 'Did you really draw no other name?'

'Ah, let me go,' she murmured, her confusion and maidenly timidity rendering her still more charming.

'You do not once ask what wish I have drawn!' said Dorn, holding up his note.

'Who knows whether you would tell me the truth,' answered Faith.

'Have a care,' cried Dorn. 'The suspicion can only spring from a consciousness that you have deceived me, and that is not fair. I will set you an example of ingenuousness. You wished a poor mortal to choose among three daughters of heaven. Love, Hope, and Faith, were inscribed upon your three notes. My good genius helped me to the best choice. Love I already had deep in my heart from the moment I first saw you; Hope visited me last evening; and I only lacked Faith in the certainty of my good fortune. I drew it with this note.'

'A gallant officer well knows how to convert trifles into matters of importance,' said the maiden, repelling the persevering youth. 'I wrote the three names for you, merely in jest, Faith, Hope, and Charity, because they follow each other in the calendar.'

'Only for that reason?' asked Dorn in a tender tone, throwing his arms around her slender waist. Endeavoring to push him gently back with her right hand, she dropped a note which Dorn caught up and read before she could hinder him.

'Victoria!' shouted he. 'You have drawn my name, as I have drawn yours. Who can doubt now that we are destined for each other? Obey the friendly oracle, dear maiden, and become mine, as I am yours, in life and death.'

He embraced the lovely creature more ardently, while she, no longer able to withstand the solicitations of the youth and the pleadings of her own heart, sank on his bosom, and exclaimed in low accents: 'Thine, forever.'

CHAPTER V

'Well, really, master Dorn, you begin the portentous new year upon which we are entering in a very worldly manner,' cried a reproving voice behind them. Faith shrieked with terror that those blessed moments should have had a witness, and fled from the room. At the same time Dorn, displeased at the awkward interruption, turned suddenly round and stood facing the parson, who viewed him with severe and reproachful looks. 'Is it well,' at length said the angry preacher, 'to seduce the inconsiderate sister-in-law of your brother and benefactor into an amorous intrigue?'

'You are right, reverend sir,' answered Dorn; 'that would be to do him foul wrong; but to seek the honorable love of a maiden whom I hope one day to lead to the altar as my beloved wife, appears to me to be well, and is not forbidden in the holy scriptures.'

'You wish to espouse the maiden, then?' said the parson; 'that is quite a different thing, and I take back my censure. In that case my office imposes upon me another sacred duty. The maiden is how under my spiritual care, and I must be answerable to heaven for her religious principles, which might be perverted by an unbelieving husband. I have become doubtful of you, from your own conversations, and therefore, as a called and ordained servant of the word, I ask you, are you an orthodox Lutheran christian?'

'You would find it very difficult to justify that question before the great author of your reformation,' answered Dorn, moodily. 'Know you not how peremptorily he forbade the professors of his doctrines to designate themselves by his name?'

'You wish to evade my question!' cried the parson, feeling the sting, but endeavoring to conceal the smart.

'That is not my custom,' said Dorn. 'I will never deny that I adhere to the doctrines which were first promulgated in Switzerland, and have thence spread throughout the German empire.'

'As I feared!' cried the parson. 'A Calvinist, or perhaps even a Zuinglian! and you wish to take a wife of the Augsburg faith?'

'Why not?' asked Dorn. 'That God who has disposed my heart toward the maiden, will not be angry that I choose her as my companion for life.'

'I much doubt whether you can have and keep a true heart for one who is of a different faith,' said the parson, shaking his head.

'God, who is eternal love, pardon you for the doubt, reverend sir,' said Dorn with emotion. 'It is a sad consideration, that contentions about unimportant dogmas and forms so frequently divide christians who should stand united against the common enemy. It would be dreadful if the feeble chains by which you are yet fettered, after throwing off those of popery, should bar the way between two innocent individuals, whose souls have become united by the bonds of holy love.'

'Unimportant dogmas and forms?' repeated the parson.

'I consider them so,' answered Dorn. 'Adhering to the words of Christ, we celebrate, in the Lord's supper, only a holy remembrance of the Savior; while you, by virtue of the same words, find therein a mysterious presence of his body and his blood. You ornament your churches with pictures, of which practice we disapprove. Are such differences really sufficient grounds for the quarrels and contentions which the followers of both confessions continue to wage against each other with such reprehensible bitterness?'

'You wilfully overlook a principal point,' said the parson; 'the almost insurmountable partition wall which your Calvin has raised between you and us. I mean your monstrous doctrine of election. *Aliis vita æterna, aliis damnatio æterna præordinatur!* How can you reconcile this declaration with infinite love and eternal justice?'

'I willingly give up these doctrines to your disposal,' answered Dorn; 'for they have never formed a part of my creed. Even Calvin himself stated, that he had some scruples whether predestination could be reconciled with God's wisdom, the rock upon which this doctrine has always foundered.'

'I take this concession for all it is worth,' said the parson; 'but I cannot pass over your assertion, that our difference upon the subject of the Lord's supper is a contest *de lana caprina.* Because your presumptuous reason cannot comprehend the declaration of our Savior, 'this is my body,' you wish to strike it out of the bible; but this we cannot permit; because we cannot give up one tittle of God's word, and because the communion solemnity falls to the ground when the mystery becomes robbed of the wings which bear it up to heaven. If, however, you take away from the holy scriptures all that is not clear to you, nothing will remain but a good sensible book, but with no high revelation which can only be received by pious faith. If you can see nothing in the sacrament of the Lord's supper but a remembrance of its founder, you need not partake of the bread and wine. Without this *medium* it would be impossible for us to forget our Lord and Master.'

'Sensual man,' answered Dorn, 'needs sensible signs as symbols of spiritual things. To be reminded of the author of our religion is to be reminded of his doctrines; and as he established this solemnity and consecrated it to the remembrance of himself on the evening before the death with which he sealed his doctrines, so must it, according to *our* creed, be deemed sacred--must soften and purify our hearts, and inspire us with devout and holy resolutions, which is the important point in question for you as well as us. We consider the *mystery* unnecessary, and we have the voices of the earliest churches with us, as the transubstantiation doctrine of Paschasius Radbertus, from which yours but very little differs, was first heard of in the ninth century.'

'For a book-keeper and ci-devant military officer you are deeply learned,' remarked the somewhat excited preacher.

'My early religious education,' answered Dorn, 'was superintended by a well informed, clear headed Bernardine monk, who afterwards, like myself, went over to Zuinglius's belief. I may thank him that I at least know what the point in dispute is,--a knowledge which, alas, is needed by many thousands of our brethren in the faith.'

'I supposed something like that,' said the parson. 'But I interrupted you. Proceed with your pretended refutation of my arguments.'

'Excuse me from answering further,' modestly replied Dorn.

'Because you cannot answer them!' exclaimed the parson in imaginary triumph.

'These controversial battles,' calmly continued Dorn, 'have been too often fought in vain for me to hope that we can be brought to agree. I have not endeavored to defend my doctrines; but only to show that a difference in creeds need not divide hearts. I abide by my tenets; but I believe that you also may attain salvation with yours. Believe you the same of mine, as I doubt not you do, and we can readily co-operate for the advancement of the good cause. The remaining topics of difference are not essential. Here it only concerns us, setting aside the creeds of men, to hold the doctrines of Christ as the true teachings of God's holy word, and by them so to govern our minds and actions that we may win the approbation of a good conscience, a serene dying hour, and a merciful judgment. That, in my opinion, is the true, living, christian faith; and whoever has it is our brother in Christ, whether he calls himself Lutheran, Calvinist, Zuinglian, or even catholic.'

'My God! you are then not even a Zuinglian!' angrily exclaimed the parson. 'This despicable toleration of all opinions is godless indifference, behind which naturalism and deism conceal themselves. Were you an intelligent and confirmed heretic, the argument might be continued; but you are nothing but an *eclecticus*, who seeks in christianity just so much as suits his purpose, and throws the rest aside!'

'Paul said, 'prove all things and hold fast that which is good,'' interposed Dorn.

'I am well satisfied that you do not desire to know any thing of the true faith,' continued the parson; 'and yet it is the only foundation of our religion. Know you not that Christ himself has said, 'he that believeth not shall be damned?''

'If you could convince me,' angrily remarked Dorn, 'that Christ intended those words to mean what intolerance would construe them, I would become a heathen from this moment, and joyfully take my portion in that hell in which the noble Socrates and just Aristides are burning.'

The parson started back with a shudder. Dorn checked himself and continued in a subdued tone; 'Be not alarmed, reverend sir, at my audacious words. My belief is not so bad as you fear. Would to God all christians had it, and then much less of tears and blood would be made to flow. Now repeat to me, quickly and peacefully to end our strife, that which Christ pronounced to be the chief commandment of God.'

'Thou shalt love the Lord thy God with all thy heart, and thy neighbor as thyself,' said the parson.

'Even thine enemy!' added Dorn. 'How much more then those who only differ from us in opinion! Here you have my profession of faith, and I trust in God that I shall be able to stand before him at the last day with it.'

'You confound ideas,' cried the vexed parson. 'You speak of christian ethics, and I am reasoning only of the articles of faith.'

'Devised by men!' said Dorn. 'I hold the chief point to be the observance of the system of morals taught by Christ. Do not you also?'

'No!' emphatically exclaimed the parson after a short pause.

'No?' asked Dorn with some surprise. 'The divine doctrine that we must live devoutly to die happily, not the substance of our religion! Ah, my dear sir, it was your cloth, and not your head or heart, which dictated that negative. You are too good and too intelligent not to be of my opinion.'

'Ah, do not press me with such *argumenta ad hominem*,' said the parson with excited but not unfriendly feelings. 'In point of fact there can be no disputing about matters of faith. It must come from within, and cannot be derived from without. Nevertheless I do not for that reason give you up. A time will come when you will be no longer satisfied with cold syllogisms, and you will then seek a refuge in the open maternal arms of the true faith, in which only you can find peace. Until when, only let your conduct be as fair as your speech, and I shall at all events hope that the maiden will not have made a bad choice. One thing, however, you must promise me with hand and word. Urge not upon your future wife your unbelief, or half belief, or whatever else you may choose to call it. Cause her not to waver in her own, which she has imbibed with her mother's milk. Yet more than the strong and self-relying man does weak, delicate and suffering woman need a steadfast faith. You would rob her of a belief, which is capable of sustaining her in the hour of sorrow and trial, and give her nothing in return but cheerless and disconsolate doubt; which would be an exchange unworthy of the magnanimity of a man.'

'In this case you are for once wholly right, my worthy friend,' said Dorn: 'and I promise you *with this handgrip*, by God and my honor, to do as you require. Now let a lasting peace be concluded between us. When we hereafter meet above, as I firmly believe we shall, when the scales shall fall from our eyes, when we shall clearly see what we perceive but dimly here below, then shall we as surely be one in knowledge as we now are in feeling, and side by side before the throne of the father of all men shall we unite with full hearts in the song of praise to the one true God.'

'So may it be!' cried the parson, pressing the youth's hand and leaving the room with visible emotion.

CHAPTER VI

In the forenoon of the 20th January, 1629, a joyful bustle prevailed in Fessel's house. The floors and steps were carefully swept, strewed with a beautiful yellow sand, and adorned with evergreens. A large fire was crackling in the kitchen, before which the spit was turning, and pots and stew-pans were steaming. The diligent housewife, notwithstanding the ready assistance of her mother, had her hands full of business; her two daughters, who insisted on being employed, hindered more than they aided her; and the sons who, with their cousin Engelmann, had just returned from school, raced about the house like wild animals, practically illustrating the *'Dulce est desipere in loco,'* which they had that day construed in their class. In short, it was the betrothing day of the beauteous Faith and Fessel's new partner in business, master Dorn.

The interesting pair had just returned from the church, where, in pursuance of a good old custom, they had made their mutual engagements in the presence of their God, and commended themselves to his protection by pious prayer. In the house-door they encountered their brother-in-law, who was returning from the city council-room, where his attendance had a short time before been required. He was, however, unusually pale, returned but brief thanks for the joyous greeting of the lovers, and silently mounted the stairs with a slow and dull motion, as if he had been troubled with asthma.

'In God's name, my brother, what has happened to you?' cried Dorn, returning from the kitchen, where he had left his fair companion.

'Dark clouds are beginning to overshadow our horizon,' answered Fessel, with anxious concern. 'Colonel von Goes has arrived, and demands permission to march through the city with seven squadrons of the Lichtensteins.'

'Goes!' exclaimed Dorn, becoming paler than his brother-in-law, and covering his face with his hands.

'What is the matter with you?' asked the astonished Fessel. 'Do you know so much evil of the man?'

'From the knowledge I obtained of him during my military service,' answered Dorn, making an effort to command himself, 'I may pronounce him a good soldier, and a man of honor; but he adheres to the catholic faith with ferocious zeal.'

'We are under no obligation,' continued Fessel, 'to admit troops within our walls, except upon the especial command of his imperial majesty....'

'You will not do so on this occasion!' exclaimed Dorn with fearful vehemence. 'You will render the people of your city miserable if you open your gates to these dreadful protectors. They have given a specimen of the manner in which they treat protestants, at Glogau.'

'What can we do?' said Fessel, shrugging his shoulders. 'The honorable council have a great inclination to admit them, and for that purpose hastily called some of the most respectable burghers to the town-house, to give their opinions as to what answer should be returned to the request. We honestly stated to the gentlemen what we expected of them. The colonel then remarked, that he hoped we would not show such disrespect to the imperial troops, as to compel them to take a wide circuit round the city in the present cold state of the weather. He then proceeded solemnly to swear and protest, that he only desired a passage through the city, and a brief rest for the refreshment and recovery of the frozen. Indeed, he said he would have no part in God's kingdom, if any citizen were injured in consequence of the granting of his request.'

'For God's sake, trust not to that oath,' begged Dorn.

'If the colonel be a man of honor, as you say, wherefore not?' asked Fessel with surprise.

'Have you forgotten that horrible saying, *hæreticis non est servanda fides*?' cried Dorn. 'No time is to be lost in averting the evil. The council is still in session. I will accompany you to the town-house, and ask leave to address them upon this matter. Schweidnitz must not open her gates to these hordes. They certainly can show no mandate from the emperor, and if the worst come, we have walls and ditches, and strong burgher hands accustomed to the use of arms, to defend our dearest treasure, religious freedom.'

During this conversation, he had with eager impetuosity drawn his brother-in-law towards the door. There they heard the distant notes of a march from trumpets, clarions and kettle-drums, and the confused murmurs of a crowd reached them from the great public square.

'We are too late,' sighed Fessel. 'The music comes from the direction of the Striegauer-gate. The Lichtensteins are already in the city.'

'Then may God by some miracle give the lie to my fears, and Goes keep his word!' cried Dorn. 'I anticipate dreadful scenes.'

Fessel opened the window and listened to the music, which at first appeared to approach, but afterwards sounded fainter and fainter as if receding. 'Do you hear?' said he to his distrusting brother-in-law, 'you owe an apology to the worthy colonel for your suspicions. The troops are already passing out by the Nieder-gate.'

'God grant it may be so,' sighed Dorn, placing himself by Fessel's side at the window. 'I am not yet satisfied of the fact, however.' Both continued listening to the last dying tones of the march.

'How the ear can deceive one!' said Fessel. 'It now seems to me as if the music were again approaching.'

'I fear it does not deceive you this time,' answered Dorn significantly. At that moment a cry of fear and anguish arose along the main street, and the worthy serjeant-at-arms of the city council was seen breathlessly running toward the town-house.

'Whither with such haste?' cried Fessel to him from the window.

'God be merciful to us!' cried the serjeant. 'The soldiers have made a halt at the Nieder-gate, have relieved and dismissed the burgher guard there, and, turning to the left about, are now marching up the main street.

'That indeed does not look much like passing through the city,' sighed Fessel, closing the window. 'It rather indicates an intention to take up permanent quarters here.'

'For the purpose of proselytism!' cried Dorn, despondingly. 'Now God be merciful to me! For if these villains insult our women, I shall die no natural death.'

He hastened forth, while Fessel remained standing at the window awaiting the event in silent sadness.

The music of the Lichtensteins sounded nearer and nearer, and soon their banners, muskets and halberds came waving and glistening up the street, and in serried ranks the troops came marching into the public square. 'Halt! order arms!' was now echoed by the commanders. The muskets and halberds rattled upon the stone pavement with a dull crash, the music ceased, and the silent and motionless soldiers remained standing by their arms. Only a malicious smile, which played upon their dark faces, and the restless and inquisitive movements of their twinkling eyes, gave them any appearance of being aught but lifeless statues.

Katharine and Faith, pale as ghosts, followed by their mother, now burst into the room. The children, naturally excited by these unusual occurrences, crowded in after them, to get a better view of what was going forward.

'Have the Lichtensteins turned back?' simultaneously asked or rather shrieked the three women, as Fessel directed their attention to the human masses in the public square. 'My end has come,' groaned the matron, sinking down upon a seat. The children hastened to the window, and in their innocent ignorance right heartily enjoyed the view of the brilliant uniforms, splendid standards and glistening arms of the soldiers.

'Children,' said Fessel calmly, 'lamentations and complainings cannot help us. Let us not, in the present emergency, lose our presence of mind, which in times of misfortune is the greatest misfortune. I will go to the compting-room, and as far as possible during the short time that remains to us, place my property in safety. My Katharine will hastily collect the most valuable of our things, and conceal them in the under cellar. I will afterwards see what course is required for our personal safety. My mother and sister-in-law must meanwhile prepare for the quartering of the soldiers. As a well conditioned merchant, and a warden of the evangelical church, I may expect that a full share of them will be assigned to my house.'

'It is fortunate that we have a repast already provided for them,' sighed Katharine, seeking, among a bunch hanging at her girdle, for the key of the plate closet.

'Provided for the betrothal-feast of our good sister!' said Fessel, compassionately caressing the cold cheek of the maiden. 'Poor child! they will leave you little enjoyment of it to-day.'

'Only see!' cried little Hedwig at the window, 'the officers are all crowding around a tall stately chief, and our alderman Newmann is standing near him with uncovered head and a great number of slips of paper in both hands.'

'The tall officer is the colonel,' said Fessel to them by way of explanation, 'They are drawing tickets for their quarters.'

'My God!' suddenly shrieked Faith, who had stepped to the window, and flew back to the remotest corner of the room.

'What is the matter with thee, sister?' asked the sympathizing Katharine, hastening to her side.

'It is all over with us,' sighed Faith, pressing her little hands upon her beating heart. 'One of the officers suddenly stared wildly up towards the house. I saw his face but for an instant, and it was partly shaded by his plume; but I recognised it so certainly and with so much alarm that I could not help screaming. It was childish, I know. Pardon me that I frightened you so needlessly. How could this man come here at the present time? and what a fool I was instantly to fear the worst!'

'Of whom do you speak, my daughter?' asked the anxious widow; and, as Faith was about to explain, Dorn rushed into the room.

'Save yourself!' he cried. 'Your persecutor, the broken captain of dragoons, now commands a company of the Lichtensteins, and is endeavoring to get your brother-in-law's house for his quarters. His hellish object is obvious, and he may be expected here every moment.'

'Then are we all lost,' groaned the mother.

'Not yet,' said Katharine, with calm self-possession. 'Listen to my proposal. These soldiers cannot stay here forever. While they remain, mother and sister can conceal themselves in the dry vault back of the cellar, whose opening in the garden is concealed by the thick grove of yew-trees. We can pile up boxes and casks before the door, and every evening convey to them provisions and consolation.

'The captain shall be told,' interposed Dorn, 'that you fled from Schweidnitz the moment you heard of the approach of the Lichtensteins. God reward you, Katharine, for the lucky thought.'

'You will accompany us in our hiding place, beloved sister will you not?' asked Faith.

'Shall I take my husband and children into your circumscribed retreat?' smilingly asked Katharine; 'or could you really and in earnest ask me to desert the dearest objects on earth to me? Nor is there any reason why I should. You have a sufficient cause for concealing yourself, having offended a bad man who would probably improve the first opportunity to avenge himself. I am only threatened with the same misfortunes every family in the city must expect, and with God's help I must endeavor to bear them.'

'She is entirely right,' decided the mother.

'My noble wife!' cried Fessel, embracing his courageous and confiding spouse. At the same instant Hedwig, who was still at the window, cried: 'There comes a hateful red-bearded officer directly towards the house, with a whole troop of soldiers behind him.'

'Then indeed there is no time to be lost,' said Dorn, hurrying the mother and daughter from the room. 'Farewell!' cried the women to each other. 'God's angels protect you!' said Fessel, proceeding to the door, at which the Lichtensteins were loudly knocking.

CHAPTER VII

At the head of the table, which had been beautifully adorned for the betrothal-feast, the red-bearded captain had seated himself in terrible majesty. Desiring, for the present, to appear unusually gracious, he had invited the heads of the family and their children to take places at the table. The hospitality so kindly extended to them in their own house by a stranger, imparted no especial pleasure to those invited. The children had formed the heroic resolution of not eating a morsel, merely to show their dislike to the detestable red-beard. Fessel looked with a gloomy brow directly before him; while the faithful Katharine forced herself to introduce and sustain the conversation, that a want of occupation might not give the fiend leisure for evil thoughts. Four arquebusiers guarded the doors, and in every part of the house arose the boisterous songs of the converters, who were revelling with Fessel's choicest wines.

'We are satisfied,' said the captain; and, emptying his goblet, he took off his military cap, murmured some words in a low voice, crossed himself, again put on his cap, and then, with feigned affability asked: 'So, your mother-in-law left you last night, Herr Fessel?' and as the latter answered affirmatively, he further asked: 'And her daughter, little Faith,--did the good woman take her with her?'

'Certainly!' stammered Fessel, who was not altogether prepared for this close examination.

'Strange!' said the captain, extending his goblet to the lady of the house to be replenished. 'How a man's eyes may deceive him! As I was standing with the other officers before the house three hours since, I would have sworn that I saw the little Faith standing at that very window.'

'It was probably me whom you saw, captain,' interposed Katharine. 'You must have observed that I resemble my sister very nearly.'

'Possibly!' observed the captain with a still more hateful smile. 'You had, indeed, at that time, a rose-colored band in your blond hair, and now you have brown locks and a black plaited cap. However, that is not so very strange. Women's toilets often produce much greater transformations.'

At this moment a violent outcry was heard from without. Fessel hastened from the room, and soon returned with his eldest apprentice, who was profusely bleeding from a wound on the head.

'What is the matter?' asked the captain, addressing himself to the wounded man. 'How dare you thus disturb me while at table?'

'By your leave, captain!' said the apprentice, with confidence; 'your sergeant has robbed me of all the money I had about me, and then beat me over the head with his sword because I had no more to give him. It was proper that I should complain to you in order that you might take measures to punish the outrage.'

'You did not know how to behave yourself properly, my son,' said the captain. 'My people are always kind and harmless as children to all who are complaisant towards them, and give them every thing they desire. Go and have your wound dressed, and be more careful another time.'

'Is that all the satisfaction I am to get for my injuries?' asked the apprentice, irritated by the pain of his wound, and still more by the captain's contemptuous answer.

The captain's eyes flashed like two baneful meteors. 'Satisfaction!--injuries! How dare you, a damned heretic, use such words in my presence? vociferated he, starting from his seat. You ought to thank God that my sergeant did not cleave your head asunder. Pack yourself hence, if you do not wish that I should complete the work he began.'

He grasped his sword, the young man sprang beyond his reach, and Katharine, in soft and soothing tones, besought the savage to be pacified; but the last link of the chain, by which his natural brutality had hitherto been restrained, was now broken; the wild beast in human form was let loose, and yielded only to the most savage impulses.

'Do you suppose, vagabonds,' roared the fiend, 'that we have come here to keep strict discipline and to wait quietly for what you may please to dispense to us? We are come to chastise you for your heresy, which is a revolt alike against God and the emperor. We are come to convert you to the true faith; and if your stubbornness will not suffer our object to be accomplished by fair means, you are given over to us as a prize, with your property and lives, bodies and souls, to be tormented by us to our heart's content, until you are brought to repentance and an abandonment of your abominable opinions, or sink in despair.'

'No, captain,' cried Fessel, with manly firmness; 'that is not the will of our emperor, and I should consider it treasonable to believe your scandalous assertions. Nor was that the condition upon which we admitted you within our walls. From your colonel's own mouth have I heard quite a different speech, and I shall go and ask him if he is about to give the lie to his own words.'

'First go to your own chamber as an arrested prisoner,' said the captain, with a smile of contempt; 'until I have had you tried for your rebellious speech. Lead him forth!' commanded he to the guards. 'Lock him up, watch him sharply, and if he attempts to escape shoot him down.'

'Eternal justice, judge and avenge!' cried Fessel, as the soldiers dragged him away.

'Mercy!' implored his faithful wife, clasping the captain's knees; but the latter disengaged himself from her, put the children, who pressed around her, out of the room, drew Katharine to a window, and in a low voice said to her, 'you see that I can be either good or bad as you would have me. Upon you alone it depends how I shall further proceed. Therefore answer me honestly and truly, where is your sister?'

'She fled last night,' answered Katharine, with calm firmness; 'to escape the horrors which threaten us. Whither, I do not consider it my duty to inform you.'

'This is fine!' exclaimed the captain, grinning like a Bengal tiger when his keeper compels him to show his teeth. 'I like to know how people feel towards me. I now go to my colonel, and you shall soon hear from me again.'

He departed, and the children, again rushing in, embraced their mother with loud lamentation. Katharine sank upon her knees, and her children with her, and, raising their eyes and hands towards heaven, with a bleeding heart but nevertheless with confidence, the pious woman prayed in the words of the royal psalmist: 'Why art thou cast down, O my soul? and why art thou disquieted in me? Hope thou in God; for I shall yet praise him for his countenance who is my help and my God.'

The boisterous sorrow of the children subsided into gentle weeping, and from every lip was heard the loud, believing, joyful, amen!'

CHAPTER VIII

Some days later, Katharine was sitting with her children at the close of day and exerting herself to read by the fading twilight a letter of consolation which her imprisoned husband had thrown to little Ulrich. The door was cautiously opened and a soldier in the Lichtenstein uniform hesitatingly entered.

'Do not be alarmed,' whispered he, as they shrunk from his approach. 'I am Dorn, and have smuggled myself into the house in this disguise, that I might bring you consolation and see for myself how you were situated. Your mother and sister are in health and safety, and send kind greetings to you. Nor need you be anxious on your husband's account. I am certain that it is better for him to be in confinement than to be free and expose himself to the outrages to which every hour gives birth, and do things in moments of passion and excitement which would only make matters worse. Should his situation become more critical, I shall always be near him.'

'In God's name, master Dorn, what is to be the end of all this?' anxiously asked Katharine.

'A city full of catholics,' answered Dorn with a bitter smile. 'The count of Dohna has arrived to-day. That is a sufficient reason for fearing the worst. From a renegade, who expects to win the principality of Breslau by his tyrannical fury, nothing is to be hoped.'

'Then God help us!' sobbed Katharine, wringing her hands.

'By means of our arms, if it cannot be otherwise,' said Dorn, with energy. 'I have carefully avoided encountering your worthy guest, because I well know that one of us must in that case remain dead upon the spot, and that would little help you in any event; but, if it becomes necessary, I will strike the devil to the earth and free you from him.'

'No,' anxiously entreated Katharine; 'no murder on our account.'

'That is man's work, dear lady,' said Dorn. 'No woman can reason upon the subject. Every one must act according to his conscience. It will be well for me and him if the necessity does not occur.'

A gentle and afterwards a more decided knock was heard at the door. A voice asked, 'are you alone, madam Fessel?' and directly the pale and bleeding face of parson Beer peered into the room.

'How pale you look! what has happened to you?' cried the frightened Katharine.

'My face bears the marks of the converting zeal of the imperial apostles,' answered the parson with suppressed anger. 'Most terribly do these Lichtensteins deal with the servants of the word. I have escaped with less injury than some of my brethren. Me they only misused and smote with their side arms, because I preached the truth to them with the sharp fire of the spirit which had come upon me. I heed it not, and even consider myself honored by the blows I received; one of which came near making me a martyr. My worthy associate, Bartsch, was much more shamefully treated, and my blood boils and foams when I think of it. That they hustled, abused and plundered him, might be passed over; but the hellish crew, adding to these outrages the most shameful scorn and mockery, compelled that man of God to dance before them; himself, his wife, and children to dance, like the infatuated Israelites before the golden calf. For which the reprobates will one day be compelled to dance to the howlings of damned spirits in the everlasting fire prepared for the devil and his angels!'

'How goes it with the poor citizens?' asked Dorn, for the purpose of diverting the attention of the zealot from the occurrences which had so excited his anger.

'As might be supposed, very badly,' answered the parson. 'The counter reformation may be said to have dated its commencement from the arrival of the terrible Dohna. The soldiers are quartered only upon the protestants, to whom they say, 'the moment you go and confess to the Dominican or Franciscan priests, and bring a certificate of the fact, that moment we will leave you and go elsewhere.' When the poor people have been thus oppressed until they can bear it no longer, they become frantic and repair to the priests for the certificate of confession. The tormenting fiends then leave them and are distributed among such of their neighbors as yet hold to the true faith, and treat them in the same manner, until they, overcome by the weight of the burthen, also go, like Peter, and deny their lord and master in the churches of their adversaries. In this way we clergymen have each sixty men quartered upon us, and the aldermen the same number. Burgomaster Yunge has already over a hundred men to provide for, and if the apostacy extends much further, the last true believing christian of Schweidnitz will have the whole seven squadrons of converters collected in his own house.'

'Why do not the wretched people flee and abandon house and home, property and sustenance?' asked the excited Dorn.

'So they would have done, by thousands,' answered the parson; 'but the converters will not let them go. The citizens are kept prisoners in their city, and every householder is confined to his house. The gates are closed, and each family is guarded by those who are quartered upon it. In vain have some of our wealthiest citizens offered to give up all their property with the promise never to ask for it again; in vain have others sought death rather than a continuance of their sufferings. That is not the object of our oppressors, whose only answer to all our prayers is, 'you must embrace our faith.'

'I have heard enough,' cried Dorn, with bursting rage. 'Say no more, or, unable to restrain my wrath, I shall strike some of the hounds to the earth and thereby bring my life to a sudden end. Farewell, Frau Katharine,--I return to my hiding place; but shall not be far off, and most joyfully will I lay down my life, if need be, in defence of you and yours.'

He strode forth,--the parson stepped to the window, through which the bright moon was pouring its silver light, and, while watching Dorn's retreating steps, convulsively pressed his hands across his breast and gave frightful utterance to the following imprecation: 'Thy hand shall find all thine enemies, Thy right hand shall find them that hate thee. Thou wilt melt them as in a furnace when thou lookest upon them; the Lord will consume them in his anger, fire shall devour them. Their seed wilt thou destroy from the face of the earth, and their names from among the children of men.'

'God preserve us, reverend sir,' interposed Katharine. 'How can you offer up such a horrible prayer? Rather should you remember and imitate the forgiving spirit of our Savior when he prayed; 'Father, forgive them, for they know not what they do!'

'Father forgive them, for they know not what they do,' he tremblingly repeated after her, his anger rebuked by the divine sentiment, and submissively raised his eyes toward the exhaustless source of love and mercy.

CHAPTER IX

The next morning Katharine was sitting in her closet, with her infant at her breast. Over its rosy cheeks rolled the mother's tears in quick succession. Her other children were pressing around her, like chickens who seek to hide themselves under the mother's sheltering wings, and all were tremblingly and silently listening to the cries of lamentation which occasionally arose from the neighboring dwellings, evincing the activity of the tormentors.

The clattering of spurs was heard at the door, which was immediately thrown open, and the captain entered the room, accompanied by a file of soldiers.

'I am now satisfied!' cried he. 'I have subjected your cook to a sharp examination. You have more food prepared daily than is necessary for the family. Dishes are secretly conveyed away full and returned empty. I am therefore satisfied that your relatives have not departed; but are yet in the city, perhaps in this very house, and my duty requires me to insist on their immediate appearance, that they may become participants in the reformation which we bring to this deluded city.'

'I have nothing more to answer upon that subject,' said Katharine with firmness.

'No?' asked the captain, grating his teeth. 'Will you bring me a certificate of confession?'

'Not to all is given such greatness of mind as to enable them to change their faith according to the emergencies of the moment,' said Katharine, with a bitterness which the unworthiness of the tempter forced from her naturally mild heart.

'Still scornful!' growled the captain. 'The cup now runs over. To the cellar with this brood of young heretics!' thundered he to his soldiers, who immediately forced the children from the room. 'My children!' shrieked Katharine, making an effort to rush after them; but the captain dragged the unhappy mother back.

'The sands of mercy have run out,' he exclaimed; 'and the hour of vengeance approaches. It is now no longer question of the runaway girl. I have torn from my heart my sinful passion for the heretic, and have to do only with you and your heterodoxy. I give you an hour to consider whether you will return to the bosom of the mother church. If you then obstinately choose to adhere to your erroneous belief, I will probe your breast yet deeper, and by all the saints I swear to you that I will find your heart.'

He left the room. 'Preserve me from desperation, O God!' cried Katharine, pressing her infant to her bosom and sinking powerless to the earth.

CHAPTER X

When she awoke she was sitting in a chair with her slumbering babe in her arms, and before her stood, with weeping eyes, an old Franciscan monk belonging to the city convent, upon whom she stared with wondering and uncertain glances.

'Calm yourself, dear lady,' said the old man in a friendly tone. 'The cowl I wear may be doubly hateful to you in this heavy hour; but it covers a heart that feels kindly and truly for you. I have heard of your sufferings and have come to bring you succor. I have not forgotten the kind attention and care I received in your house when, six years ago, I came here from Breslau as a mendicant lay brother, and fell fainting before your door. There were indeed hard-hearted Lutherans who chid you for your charity and said you ought not to trouble yourself about the beggarly papist priest,--but you answered that it was your christian duty to succor a fellow christian. That was a noble sentiment, and has ever since remained engraved upon my heart, and I have daily offered up my prayers that God would bless you for it through time and eternity. It is true that by some of my brethren this prayer for a heretic has been considered sinful; but I have answered them, 'Solum de salute Diaboli desperandum,' and that it may please the Lord in his mercy to bring this good woman one day, if even upon her death bed, into the embrace of the only saving church.'

'May God reward your love, my good father,' said Katharine with a feeble utterance. 'A kindly human heart is always deserving of respect and esteem, even though it wander in error.'

'I came not,' answered the monk, 'to hold a controversial discussion with you. My only wish is to warn you of what must necessarily and absolutely be done, if you would save your mortal body, to say nothing of your immortal soul. You must know that it is the irrevocable determination of the emperor that all the protestants in his hereditary dominions shall return to the true faith, and for that sole purpose has he sent his troops to this city. It is true that these soldiers conduct themselves here in a manner which no true catholic can justify, and should one of these so called *converters* stray into my confessional, he would have a hard time of it. But so it is, and I, a poor feeble monk, have no power to avert the evil. The Jesuits, who hold the emperor's heart in their hands, might and should have prevented it; but they have kindled the fire and poured oil thereon. Wherefore I say, yield to the times, for they are dangerous. Without a certificate of confession your tormentor will not leave you--he dares not, even if he would. I bring you the necessary certificate. The urgency of the moment will not permit a formal confession, and you therefore need only subscribe to these articles. You can send your certificate to count Dohna, and receive in exchange for it one from him, which will relieve you from the presence of these soldiers.'

'Excuse me!' cried Katharine. 'In the faith in which I have lived, will I also die. I cannot subscribe.'

'How now, so good and yet so stubborn!' exclaimed the reverend father. 'At least read what you are required to subscribe, before you refuse. After reading it, you can subscribe or not, according to the dictates of your own judgment. These sacred truths must, I should think, be capable of striking the pure springs of true knowledge from the hardest heart.'

Katharine ran her eyes rapidly over the articles. As she came towards the close, she read aloud. 'I swear, that through the intercession of the saints I have now become converted to the catholic religion.'

'Place your hand upon your heart, reverend father,' cried she, springing up, incensed, 'and then say upon your sacred sacerdotal oath, shall I not be guilty of perjury, if I swear that what I do out of fear of an earthly power, is done through the spiritual effect of the intercession of the saints?'

The monk silently folded up the paper.

'You see there can be no help for me,' said Katharine with humble resignation. 'Leave me, therefore, to my fate, and take with you my heartfelt thanks for your good intentions.'

'You are a very obstinate woman!' said the monk, with evident and deep sympathy. The longer his eyes rested upon her pale, pious and suffering face, the more his sympathy increased, until at length, amid a flood of gushing tears, he cried, 'I know that I commit a deadly sin, but I cannot do otherwise. Take the certificate, which alone can put an end to your sufferings.'

'How! without confession or signature?' asked Katharine with astonishment.

'I have given to my God the offering of a long life,' cried the old man with vehemence, 'full of heavy privations and hard struggles. He will now, therefore, be a merciful judge to me, and after long and severe penance will pardon me for once lending the aid of my holy office for the purpose of deception. Yet, should I even incur his everlasting anger, I cannot do otherwise. I cannot leave my benefactress to be persecuted to death, even though I may one day be compelled to enter the dark valley of the shadow of death, without absolution. Take the certificate.'

'God forbid!' said Katharine, tearing it in pieces, 'that I should rob you of your soul's peace and disturb the tranquillity of your dying hour. Nor would my own conscience permit me to accept your offer. Every use which I should make of this paper would be an act of apostacy from my own faith; if a hypocritical use, so much the worse. 'Be not deceived, God is not mocked.''

'Woman, thou art more righteous than we!' cried the monk, with deep emotion; and, covering his head with his cowl, he departed, weeping audibly.

CHAPTER XI

The infant was still slumbering upon Katharine's bosom. The door was again thrown open and the captain entered, this time without attendants, bolting the door after him.

'The hour is past,' said he with a demoniac smile. 'Have you a certificate?'

'No,' answered she, and at that moment the child in her arms awoke and cried for its nourishment. 'Poor thing,' said she, bearing it towards an alcove.

'Where are you going?' asked the captain, seizing her arm as though he would crush it in his ferocious grasp.

'To nurse my child,' answered Katharine. 'You cannot wish that I should do it in the presence of a stranger!'

'You shall not nurse your child!' cried the captain, forcing it from her arms. 'It shall not imbibe heresy with its mother's milk.'

'What would you with my child, horrible man?' shrieked Katharine, rushing upon him.

'There it shall lie,' said he, putting it upon the floor.

The poor infant uttered the most lamentable shrieks.

'For God's sake, let me go to my child!' exclaimed Katharine. 'It is dying.'

'In that case I shall have saved a soul to heaven,' answered the captain.

'You cannot be a man!' cried the miserable mother. 'You must be satan disguised in the human form.' Convulsive spasms seized her. Her eyes closed, her lips became blue, and her senses fled.

Some one knocked loudly at the door. 'Are you here, Frau Katharine?' asked a voice which the captain recognized with terror.

'Back!' cried the sentinel without. 'The captain is with the lady.'

'The captain! and she answers not, and the child is screaming!' exclaimed the same voice, with wild alarm,--and powerful blows thundered upon the door.

'Back!' again cried the sentinel, and immediately afterwards, with the exclamation, 'Jesus Maria!' a heavy fall was heard near the door, which now flew in fragments. Dorn rushed into the room over the body of the wounded sentinel, who lay groaning upon the floor, with a drawn sword in his hand. The captain sprang to meet the intruder, but shrunk back, pale and trembling, the moment he recognized him.

'Cut him down from behind!' cried he to his soldiers who now came rushing into the room.

'Down to hell!' thundered Dorn, thrusting the captain through the body. With a frightful death-cry he fell to the earth, and Dorn threw down his bloody weapon, 'I am your prisoner,' said he, with imposing dignity, to the soldiers, and took the child from the floor. 'Call the maidens to take care of the mother and infant, and then lead me to your colonel, to whom I have something of importance to say.'

Hardly knowing what they were about, the astonished and confounded soldiers obeyed the bold youth. With loud cries the maidens rushed in to assist their adored mistress and quiet the screaming infant. Dorn impressed a last kiss upon the hand of the insensible Katharine, and then in a commanding tone he cried to the soldiers, 'now forward!' leading them off with a step as proud and as confident as if he were marching to battle and victory.

CHAPTER XII

The generalissimo of the converters, count Karl Hannibal von Dohna, with the governor, baron von Bibran, the Jesuit, Lamormaine, and some field officers, were sitting at a table, in the quarters of colonel von Goes. A large pile of ready prepared tickets, for quarters, were lying upon the table, among flasks and goblets, and the gloves and swords of the officers. A crucifix, kept upon the table for momentary use, seemed to look sorrowfully upon the horrors which were here perpetrated under its sanction. At the door stood colonel von Goes, to whom a deputation of the inhabitants of the suburbs were complaining with trembling humility, that his quarter-master had exempted each householder among them, for the sum of two dollars each, from having troops quartered in their houses, and now he had compelled them to receive two squadrons, who were allowed to oppress them with every species of cruelty.

'If the quarter-master has deceived you,' answered the colonel, 'he will not escape due punishment; but you must submit to the quartering until you return to the only true church; for on no other condition can you be relieved.'

The poor denizens departed with heavy hearts. 'Inquire into this villany,' said the colonel to a subaltern officer, 'and if you detect a rogue, let him be arrested and reported.'

The officer went in obedience to the command. The colonel seated himself with the others, drained a goblet, and striking his fist upon the table, exclaimed, 'a curse upon this whole expedition!'

'Jesus Maria!' cried Bibran and Lamormaine, crossing themselves, while Dohna earnestly inquired why he uttered such an imprecation.

'Because so much baseness, sir count,' fiercely answered Goes, 'mingles with the performance of our great and holy duty. Our people plainly show, that they are more anxious about the gold than the souls of the heretics. Every thief in the regiment will become a rich man in Schweidnitz. In the end it will become a disgrace to be called a Lichtensteiner, and I have a hundred times regretted, that in my pious zeal I opened a path for the entrance of these vagabonds into the poor city.'

'It could be wished,' interposed father Lamormaine, in a conciliatory manner, 'that the business had been undertaken in a less public and violent manner, and I have heretofore expressed the same opinion to the count. This open and public assault upon these heretics will serve as a warning to the others, and enable them to rally in their own defence. By rallying their forces they will learn their strength; their courage and obstinacy will increase, all who suffer for their erroneous belief will be considered martyrs, and in the end they will make many converts. We should have operated cautiously and quietly; commencing with them softly, we should have increased the pressure by slow degrees, and should have thus avoided every open scandal. A constant dropping will wear a stone, and I am confident that we could easily and quietly have converted all Silesia in the course of a year.'

'Yes, that is the way with you gentlemen with shaven crowns,' cried the count with a savage laugh. 'You step very softly by nature, but when you have an object to attain, you also bind *felt* upon the soles of your shoes. Not so with me. My motto is, 'bend or break,--and so far I have found it a very good one. I can boast of having accomplished more than the apostle Peter. He indeed, upon one occasion, converted three thousand souls by preaching a sermon: but I have many times converted a greater number in a day, and that too without preaching. One year for Silesia! Give me soldiers enough, and I will convert all Europe for you in a year, by my method.'

'What sort of a conversion would it be?' asked Lamormaine, shrugging his shoulders. At that moment Dohna's adjutant entered the room.

'The rich Heinze,' whispered he to his chief, 'will make a present to you of that costly writing table, if you will allow him the quiet enjoyment of his faith. You know the splendid article, the one for which the duke of Leignitz offered him four thousand dollars. It is below.

'I will be with him directly,' cried Dohna, and taking a blank license from the table, he hastened out.

Meantime a tumult out of doors had attracted the whole company to the windows. 'Do you know the cause of this disturbance?' asked Goes of the adjutant.

'A merchant's clerk has killed captain Hurka in his quarters,' answered the latter. 'The guard are bringing him here.'

'That Hurka must have learnt the art of tormenting from satan himself,' growled the colonel. 'What was the provocation?'

'They say,' answered the adjutant, 'that, in order to compel his hostess to procure a certificate of confession, the captain tore her infant from her breast, and threw it upon the floor.'

This announcement caused a universal and simultaneous shudder among those present, despite the triple mail of pride and intolerance which encased their hearts, and Lamormaine discontentedly remarked, 'that is the way to *make* heretics, not to convert them.'

'This is a case in which mercy, rather than severe justice, should prevail,' remarked the strong-believing Bibran. 'The captain's conduct was too horribly severe, and must lead to greater evils.'

'Let the murderer be led hither,' said Goes. 'I will examine him.'

The adjutant retired, and soon returned with Dorn in chains and surrounded by guards.

As Goes glanced towards him, he started back with fright, exclaiming, 'my God, what a terrible resemblance!'

Calm and collected, the young man stood there, with his eyes stedfastly fixed upon the colonel.

With, much effort the latter recovered his equanimity, and now asked, 'know you what sentence the laws pronounce upon the assassin of one of the emperor's officers?'

'I have committed no murder,' resolutely replied Dorn. 'I have only punished, in the presence of his soldiers, a villain who abused his power, and trod under foot the holiest laws of nature.'

'That voice, too!' said the colonel to himself, then turning to Dorn, 'self-avenging is not to be justified. Your act is treasonable, and no evasion can save your forfeited life.'

'Well, then, pronounce sentence upon your son!' cried Dorn, with a sorrow which he could no longer control.

'Son!' exclaimed all present with the utmost astonishment, and the horror-stricken Goes fell back into a chair, sighing, 'it is, indeed, my son!'

The son beheld his father with deep emotion, and his tears freely flowed at the sight of the old man's grief. At length, falling upon his knee, he stretched forth his hands and said, 'I am sensible that according to your laws my life is forfeited; therefore give me your blessing, and then quickly pronounce the sentence that shall bring peace to this troubled heart.'

'Oswald, Oswald!' cried Goes, 'what a terrible meeting, after ten years of separation! Wretched youth! why did you flee from your father's house?'

'The conflicting opinions which now lacerate Germany,' answered the youth, 'placed a dreadful gulf between you and me. The idea of constraining the consciences of men by means of the sword was revolting to me, and, unable to approve or participate in your acts, and shuddering at your sectarian zeal, I left you, that no unnatural contest might arise between father and son.'

'Where have you been until now?' asked the colonel with an anxiety which indicated that he feared to hear the worst.

'In the military service of Denmark,' answered Oswald, 'until two years ago I found here in Schweidnitz, in the seclusion of humble life, the peace and quiet which I sought.'

'In the Danish service!' murmured the colonel; 'fighting for heresy against the mother church!'

His grief overpowered him. At length he roused himself by a powerful effort from the whirlpool of conflicting feelings into which he had sunk. 'What could prompt you,' he asked his son in a tone of firmness and severity, 'to the senseless deed of murdering an imperial officer in a city under the control of his brethren in arms?'

'Eternal ignomy to the man,' cried Oswald, 'who would see an honorable woman, a tender mother, a fellow believer, outraged and insulted by a brutal villain, on account of her faith, and not strike down the monster, reckless of consequences, as did Peter when his Lord was assailed!'

'A fellow believer?' cried Goes with terror. 'Hast thou then become a heretic?'

'I hesitate not,' said the youth with modest resolution, 'to avow myself a believer in the pure faith of Zuinglius.'

'He cuts me to the heart,' groaned the colonel. Then, summoning resolution, he turned to Dorn and said, 'I hope you have now perceived and are ready to recant your errors. That is the only way to save your life.'

'Would you have me deny what I believe to be true, through a pusillanimous fear of death? Is it possible you can have so poor an opinion of your son?'

The rage of the proselyting chief, which had been hitherto with difficulty restrained, now broke through all bounds. He caught the crucifix from the table, unsheathed his sword, and holding them both before his son, exclaimed, 'better to be childless than have a heretic for a son! Choose instantly. Abjure your false belief, or die by my hands!'

'You gave me life, my father,' said Oswald; and you can also take it from me. I remain stedfast in the truth. Therefore end quickly with me, in God's name.'

'God of Abraham strengthen me! cried the father, looking wildly towards heaven and raising his weapon; but Bibran and Lamormaine caught his arm.

'God does not require a father to sacrifice his son,' said the governor.

'Would you give the heretics cause to curse our holy faith through your senseless fury?' cried the Jesuit to him, in a tone of reprehension.

'Take him to prison!' commanded Dohna, who had returned to the room. 'He may there consider until morning, whether he will or will not abjure his heresy.' Should he continue obstinate, I will then permit justice to take its course upon the murderer of my officer.'

'God grant thee his light and peace, my poor father! Then shall we again meet above!' cried Oswald with filial tenderness to the colonel, who, exhausted by excess of anger, stared wildly about him as if bereft of consciousness, and finally rushed from the room without speaking.

CHAPTER XIII

Overcome by sorrow for his father's anger, and racked with anxiety for the fate of his beloved Faith, whom he could protect no longer, Oswald sat in the criminal's apartment of the guard-house, looking listlessly through his grated window upon the snow-covered market-place. It was a cold still night, and the stars shone through the clear atmosphere with unusual brilliancy. The persecutors and the afflicted were finally at peace, and had forgotten their insolence and their sufferings in the embraces of sleep. The clocks of the church towers struck the midnight hour. The guard was aroused for the purpose of relieving the sentinels on post, and the rattling of arms resounded through the guard-house. The noise, however, soon subsiding, quiet again prevailed, and Oswald, to whom the confused and restless working of his mind had become almost insupportable, laid his weary head upon the table and tried to sleep. Just then the bolts were drawn and his door was softly opened. A corporal of the Lichtensteins, with a dark lantern, and accompanied by two soldiers, entered the prison. Releasing the prisoner from his chains, he commanded him, 'follow me to the count!'

'Am I already sentenced?' asked Oswald, with bitterness. 'Am I to be executed secretly, under the veil of night? It is a sad confession that your deeds will not bear the light of day!'

'Silence!' said the corporal, motioning him to follow.

'God help me!' cried Oswald, throwing his mantle over his shoulders and advancing.

The whole guard were snoring upon their benches, the officer was in his well warmed little room slumbering amidst his wine flasks, and even the sentinel without, leaned nodding upon his halberd. He was roused, however, by the approaching foot-steps, and presenting his halberd to the corporal he cried, 'who goes there?'

'A good friend!' boldly answered the corporal, whispering the countersign. 'We are commanded to bring the prisoner to the general.'

'Pass!' said the sentinel, shouldering his arms.

CHAPTER XIV

The four hastened forth together. A sharp wind whistled over the market, while a raven, scared by the wanderers, arose with loud croakings from its snowy bed and with its heavy flapping wings slowly moved away. The shivering youth wrapped his mantle more closely about him and followed the corporal without troubling himself respecting the soldiers; these last soon fell into the rear, and, dexterously turning into another street, disappeared.

'Here we are,' said the corporal, suddenly turning to Oswald. The latter, startled from his death-dream, looked wildly about him. He was standing among the graves in a parish churchyard.

'Is this indeed to be my last resting place?' he asked, throwing off his mantle. 'Only direct me where to kneel, and be sure you take good aim.'

'Kneel, indeed, you must, my worthy youngster,' cried the corporal, with joyful emotion, and thank God for your rescue, as soon as you are in safety; but with the death shot we have now nothing to do. You are free.'

'Free!' cried Oswald, now for the first time missing the two soldiers.

'Have you really forgotten your old friend Florian?' asked the corporal, throwing the light of the lantern upon his face, of which Oswald soon recognized the well known lineaments.

'Thou true friend!' cried Oswald, embracing the good old man with grateful affection. 'Thou, who once so carefully guarded the boy against the trifling dangers of youth, wouldst thou now save the life of the man! I dare not accept the freedom you offer me,' he thoughtfully added. 'According to martial law you forfeit your life by this act. Rather than expose you to such consequences, I would prefer to resume my chains.'

'Do not trouble yourself,' answered the corporal. 'The two soldiers who accompanied me are secretly Lutherans, and had previously determined to desert this night. Your father supposes I am already gone. I have my discharge in my pocket. Although I am a good catholic christian, I cannot bring myself to approve of his method of making people blessed, and prefer quitting the service before I have wholly unlearned to be a man. As soon as the gates open in the morning I shall leave this wretched city for my peaceful home. If you are willing to accompany me, I will provide you with other clothes and pass you off as my son.'

'No, my old friend,' said Oswald. 'I am bound to these walls by strong ties. They enclose what is dearest to me on earth; and I must remain here to watch over and protect, until I succeed in rescuing her, or fall in the attempt.'

'Of course you will act your pleasure,' said the corporal. 'Besides, they will not seek for you very earnestly, for captain Hurka is by no means dead.'

'How, Hurka living?' asked Oswald with mingled regret and joy.

'It is harder to root out weeds than wholesome plants,' said the old man. 'Your blow was right well intended, but did not penetrate very deeply, and the long swoon which they mistook for death was only stupefaction.'

'Ha, how furiously will the fiend rage again!' cried Oswald with anxiety and indignation.

'Make yourself easy upon that score!' said the old man consolingly. 'He is now disabled by his wound, and your father has caused a lecture to be read to him, that may well satisfy him for the present. Besides, the merchant Fessel has been released from his imprisonment, together with his children.'

'How stands it with his wife?' asked Oswald.

'Indeed, she is to be buried the day after tomorrow,' slowly answered the old man.

'Eternal God!' shrieked Oswald in the wildest sorrow. 'Vice saved and virtue in the grave, and shall we yet believe in thy providence?'

'Yes, my son, we must!' said the old man, reprovingly. 'We must believe in the Father's guiding hand, not merely in the sunshine before the gathered sheaves, but also in the tempest which scatters the harvest. Else have we not the true faith. Treasure up this sentiment, even though it comes from the lips of an unlettered catholic. It has been a friendly light to me upon life's weary road, and will continue to cheer me onward to the grave. Now farewell. The morning wind already blows across the graves, and I have yet many preparations to make for my journey. Farewell, and remember me kindly. Should I never see you again upon earth, God grant that we may hereafter meet where the true Shepherd shall gather all his lambs, even those who have here strayed from the flock, into one fold.'

He once more shook the youth most cordially by the hand, and then with hasty and vigorous strides left the church-yard.

CHAPTER XV

The day appointed for madam Fessel's interment was drawing to a close. A crowd of people had assembled in the parish church-yard, with weeping eyes and pallid faces, awaiting in gloomy silence the arrival of the funeral procession. Two grave-diggers stood leaning upon their spades beside the open grave.

The procession came. 'Now for God's sake summon resolution,' said a young Franciscan monk, whose face was almost wholly covered by his cowl, to an elderly rustic woman and a beautiful young peasant boy, whose eyes were almost blinded by their tears, pressing forward with them to a grassy hillock in the vicinity of the grave. A Lichtensteiner who had found himself in the crowd, surprised at the exclamation, placed himself near them and continued to watch their movements narrowly.

The mournful hymn of the choristers was now heard approaching. High waved the crucifix upon the church yard gate, shining silvery bright through the evening twilight, and the choristers in double ranks drew slowly toward the grave. After them came the Lutheran preachers, with their heads cast down. Next came the black coffin upon the shoulders of the bearers; upon its appearance the whole assembly broke into loud sobs, and notwithstanding all the efforts of the monk to restrain them, the peasant woman and young man upon the hillock wrung their hands with irrepressible sorrow. After the coffin, came the weeping clerks, apprentices, and household servants. Then followed the bereaved husband, pale and tearless. With each hand he led one of his little daughters, who again each led a brother. To them succeeded, a nursery maid, bearing the little Johannes with his blooming angel face, who smiled upon the crowd and by his happy unconsciousness stirred the hearts of the people even more than the sight of the father and sisters, who followed their best beloved to the grave with a full knowledge of their irreparable loss.

An immeasurable line of neighbors and friends closed the procession, whose tears and sighs, an ample testimony of the worth of the deceased, solemnized the burial instead of tolling bells and funereal music, which the rigor of the new church government denied to heretics.

The corpse had now reached the grave. The bearers sat it down and removed the lid of the coffin, and a loud lament filled the air at the sight of the martyr. The kiss of the angel of death had removed all traces of her late sufferings from her countenance. With softly closed eyes, and a heavenly smile upon her lips, she lay, as if awaiting that blessed morning whose aurora seemed already dawning upon her spiritual vision.

With outward composure the widower approached the coffin, clasped the folded hands of the pale corpse, murmured, 'Farewell, thou true one; soon shall we meet again,'--and silently retired.

The weeping children now rushed forward, but the clergyman, Beer, directed the servants to lead them back. He then stepped to the coffin, requested the audience to be silent, and with a loud voice addressed them as follows:

"Father forgive them, for they know not what they do!' These words of Christ, with which he prayed for his persecutors, were the last words I heard from the blessed being whose earthly remains we are now about to consign to the grave. My anger was inflamed by the atrocities which were daily committed in our city under the mantle of religion, and I prayed that the avenging fire of God's wrath might descend and consume our tormentors. This deceased saint checked my imprecation by calling to my mind the divine prayer of our holy Savior, and with a chastened and humble spirit I repeated after her: 'Father forgive them, for they know not what they do.'

'And so must you henceforth pray, my hearers. Of the men who now by divine permission pursue and persecute us, by far the greater number are acting not from inveterate cruelty but under the influence of a mistaken sense of religious duty, and desire to lead us back to that path which they deem the only safe one; and this desire is not censurable.

'But that they seek, by means of persecution and torture, to compel us to receive what they hold to be the true faith,--that they would bind the immortal spirit with earthly chains, when the word of God cannot be bound or confined,--therein lies their error. It therefore becomes us as christians to forgive them; 'they know not what they do.'

'Even that terrible man whose barbarity has destroyed this blessed martyr to our faith, knew not, as we charitably hope, what he did,--and therefore will we not curse him, but pray to God that he will purify his heart and enlighten his mind.

'Therefore let us patiently suffer the afflictions which the Lord may yet send us for our good, without hatred towards the instruments he may employ for that purpose, and thus seek to become worthy of the glorious martyrs to the pure Christianity of the first ages, and of this our blessed friend. Should He require us also to lay down our lives for our faith, so will we without anger or opposition bow our necks to the death-dealing axe, and die with the departing exclamation of our Savior, 'it is fulfilled!--Amen.''

He retired. The lid of the coffin was fastened down, and it was then lowered into the earth.

In accordance with a pious old custom, the husband and orphans each cast three handsful of earth into the grave, as a last farewell, and the bereaved man then retired, tearless as he had come, while the children found relief for their sorrow in audible weeping.

All the spectators now-pressed about the grave to pay the last honors to the dear departed, and from hundreds of hands fell the earth upon the coffin below. The young Franciscan also, by great exertion made a path for himself to the grave; having thrown in his handful of earth, he hastily caught hold of his companions, and exclaiming, 'now forward, the moments are precious!' led them away.

'Why should the moments be so precious to this monk?' mused the observant Lichtensteiner; and then, after a moment's reflection, he suddenly cried, 'the captain may be able to explain it!'--and ran from the church-yard.

CHAPTER XVI

In a low chamber in the little village of Friedland, eight days later, lay the aged Mrs. Rosen on the sick bed upon which the effects of her long confinement in the cellar, the extraordinary exertions consequent upon her sudden flight, and more than all, her sorrow for the loss of her beloved daughter, had thrown her. The owner of the house, a weaver's widow, who had formerly been a servant to her, and who had been indebted to her liberality for her comfortable establishment, stood at the head of her bed with a phial and spoon in her hand, and with a countenance expressive of the tenderest sympathy. Before the bed sat Oswald and the weeping Faith.

'Compose yourself, my daughter,' said the matron. 'I shall surely recover from this illness. Alas, one may suffer much before the thread of life will break! I feel much better to-day than I did yesterday, and I hope not to be the cause of anxiety much longer.'

'God grant it!' sobbed Faith, sinking upon her knees before the bed, and covering her dear mother's hand with her kisses and tears.

At that moment Jonas, the widow's son, entered the cottage with his hat and traveling staff, gave them a melancholy and silent greeting, and began to unpack his bundle.

'So soon returned from Schweidnitz?' asked Oswald. 'What is the state of affairs there?'

'Still very bad, sir,' answered Jonas. 'The soldiers abuse and oppress the people in a manner that might soften a heart of stone; and you may consider it fortunate that you are here.'

'Did you succeed in speaking to my brother-in-law, my good friend?' anxiously asked Faith.

'I saw him last evening, and told and gave him all. He keeps about with difficulty, to save his household from entire ruin. He gave me this letter and this bag of gold for you, and sends kind greetings to you all.'

Oswald took the letter, broke the seal and read:

'The persecution still rages, and I thank heaven that you are for the present in a place of safety. Immediately after the funeral of my dear

Katharine, the clergymen were all compelled to leave the city. In the course of the night my house underwent a strict search, and even the vault in which you were so long concealed did not escape. The captain has already nearly recovered, and left his bed to-day for the first time, to wait upon the colonel. The latter, as I understand, gave him a very unpleasant reception. They afterwards conferred together for two hours, with closed doors. What was there agreed upon God only knows; but when the captain returned, I was standing in front of my shop, and he greeted me in a manner so terribly courteous that it made me shudder. I have just heard that a squadron of dragoons have orders to be ready for a movement to-morrow morning at day-break; but their destination is kept secret. God be merciful to the poor people upon whom they may fall. I send you what I can spare, and beg that you will not again write or send any message to me until I make known to you that you can do so with safety. My guests keep a sharp watch upon me, and I am very anxious about your last letter, which I mislaid in consequence of one of the soldiers having interrupted me while reading it. I yet hope to find it again. God preserve you and me!'

A death-like stillness prevailed in the room at the conclusion of the reading, and no one ventured to express the renewed apprehensions which the letter had inspired.

'This is a discouraging letter,' at length observed Oswald, interrupting the general silence; 'and I begin to fear we are not entirely safe even here. Would that we had fled to Breslau, as I advised! The capital of the province, which is at the same time the seat of government of the principality, will surely be spared the longest.'

He was interrupted by a disturbance out of doors very unusual for that quiet and retired village. People were running to and fro and calling to each other in the Streets, and Oswald, alarmed, sprang for his sword which lay in the recess of the window.

'Go out and see what is the cause of this disturbance,' said he to Jonas, 'and bring us word as soon as possible.'

Jonas obeyed, and his mother observed, 'something very dreadful must have happened; for the people are running and screaming, as if a fire had broken out or an enemy were at the gates.'

'Protect us, Oswald,' begged Faith, leaning tremblingly upon the youth.

'While I live!' answered he, grasping his sword.

'Save yourselves--the converters are coming!' cried Jonas, rushing into the room.

'It must be a false alarm,' cried Oswald. 'You must be mistaken.'

'I was told so by a farmer who has just returned from Waldenburg. He was about to leave that city, when a squadron of the Lichtenstein dragoons entered it. They dismounted for breakfast, and he had it from the mouth of one of the soldiers that this village was their place of destination. Whereupon he immediately left the city and drove home as fast as possible to give the alarm.'

'Then we must have at least an hour's start of them,' said Oswald; and turning to madam Rosen, 'if you feel able to travel, I will immediately provide a conveyance to Bohemia.'

'No, my son,' said the matron, with a melancholy smile. 'For this time I must remain here and await the providence of God. I should only hinder you in your flight, and you would at last have only a corpse to convey across the border.'

'I stir not from your side!' sobbed the tender Faith, clasping her mother with anxious affection.

'That would be folly, my child,' said the mother, earnestly, 'and a very childish demonstration of your love. You and your betrothed are the objects of the search of our persecutors. They would have little desire to encumber themselves with me. I have wandered here as a peasant woman, and our hostess can give them to understand, that I am a yarn gatherer suddenly taken ill at her house. Your charms, and Oswald's stately figure render it impossible for you to be concealed in the same way, and therefore you must instantly forth.'

'Never!' cried Faith, wringing her hands.

'It is my will,' said the mother, with decision. 'Will you, my daughter, increase the sorrows of your sick mother by disobedience, and betray by your presence what otherwise may remain undiscovered? Would you see your lover fall before your eyes, unable to defend you against superior force?'

'I obey,' sighed Faith; and she hastened to pack a small bundle and put on her cloak.

'By the holy faith which we profess in common,' said the hostess, 'you leave your mother in good hands.'

'I am sure of that, and consequently depart with confidence,' said Oswald, leading the inconsolable maiden to her mother's bed-side.

With bright eyes the mother placed her daughter's hand in that of Oswald. 'Be ye one, here and hereafter!' cried she. 'That is my blessing upon your espousals; and now let me beg of you to go directly, without any leave-taking, for which I have not strength, and which will rob you of time, every moment of which is invaluable.'

Faith attempted to speak again, but her mother pointed towards the door, and Oswald led her forth.

CHAPTER XVII

Daylight had long since disappeared when Oswald and Faith alighted from their wagon at a solitary inn beyond the Bohemian boundary. 'Here you are for the present in safety,' said the conductor who had brought them from Friedland, knocking at the door. 'The people of the house are honest, and of our faith at heart. The vicinity is full of secret Hussites.'

'Who comes so late?' asked a little, dark-complexioned old woman, opening the door with her hand held before a flickering torch.

'A young wedded pair, mother Thekla,' answered the conductor, 'who are fleeing before the converters. Receive them kindly and take good care of them. God will reward you for it.'

'It is but our duty,' said the woman. 'Come in, poor creatures.'

'Farewell,' said the conductor to Oswald. 'I intend to return directly; for my wife and children may not be safely left without a protector among the reckless soldiery.'

'And, that you have brought me here--' said Oswald, forcing into his hand a couple of dollars over and above the fee agreed upon....

'I have already forgotten it,' said the conductor, laughing. 'Besides, when I get into the forest, I intend to load my wagon with wood, which I shall gaily drag into Friedland early in the morning, and nobody will think of asking me what freight I took thence. May God protect you!'

He mounted his wagon and drove rapidly away, while Oswald led his companion into the bar-room. To their great satisfaction it was tolerably empty. Only in one corner of the room snored three men and four large hounds on some straw, and at a table near the gray-headed host, with a goblet before him, sat a large strongly built man in the dress of a Bohemian peasant. Oswald observed the sabre which the guest bore, and the large knife in his girdle, with some suspicion; but the honest lineaments and saddened expression of his brown, haggard face, again inspired him with confidence. He courteously seated himself at the table and called for a glass of wine, while Faith was arranging with the hostess for a supper and accommodations for the night.

'You are in flight on account of your faith, as I hear, my dear sir?' asked the stranger in a voice of the deepest bass, and at the same time glancing at him mistrustfully with his wild, black eyes.

'The time and weather would have been badly chosen for a journey of pleasure,' peevishly answered Dorn.

'You must surely have come from Jauer, or Loewenberg, or Schweidnitz?' further asked the man; 'for they are very strenuously pushing the counter-reformation in those places just now. 'You are by far too curious!' cried Oswald, with displeasure. 'I do not willingly listen to such questions from strangers.'

'It is the business of my office to ask questions, my young gentleman,' thundered the stranger; 'for I am a captain of Bohemian provincial troops, and am stationed here upon the border to guard against the influx of Silesian heretics.'

While he said this, the four hounds sprang up and placed themselves growling before Oswald, and the three men half raised their bodies from the straw, their flashing eyes peering from their dark brown faces, and their well scoured muskets glistening in their hands. Oswald instantly arose and drew his sword.

'Put up your weapon!' the man now cried in an altered tone, seizing his goblet. 'I but wished to be certain of my man. Come, be again quietly seated, and do me justice in a fresh goblet. The Bohemian goose and Silesian swan!'

'Huss and Luther!' cried Oswald touching glasses and emptying his own with a lighter heart, while the hounds and soldiers again stretched themselves upon the straw.

'Do not be offended that I thought it necessary to prove you,' said the Bohemian; 'but the tricks and artifices of the papists are so manifold, that these precautions are rendered quite necessary. You might have been a spy of the Jesuits. Since we now understand each other, however, I may converse with you without reserve. You are not safe even here. For my old friend, our host, I will indeed be answerable; but the converters sometimes come over the border to us; especially when they deem that they have important game in view; and you appear to me as though you might be of some consequence. Therefore, if it be agreeable, I will conduct you and your little wife to a place, where you may dwell in peace behind the everlasting walls which the Lord himself has built for the defence of persecuted innocents.'

'There is no falsehood in that face!' answered Oswald; 'and I accept your offer with gratitude.'

'You will not indeed find our residence very elegant,' said the Bohemian; 'and that delicate female form may be wholly unaccustomed to such quarters; but necessity reconciles one to privations, and a very little suffices for our actual necessities.'

'Be not concerned on that account,' said Faith, who had now seated herself near Oswald. 'A safe shelter is all we wish.'

'Well, eat your supper,' said the Bohemian, 'and retire quickly to rest, that you may be ready to start by day-break in the morning. I have been long accustomed to watch through the night, and will guard you faithfully. With the rising sun we shall be among the rocks.'

CHAPTER XVIII

Wrapped in his cloak, Oswald was yet sweetly and soundly sleeping upon the floor, before the only bed in the house, in which his fair companion was slumbering. A knock was heard at the door, and the Bohemian cried, 'bestir yourself, sir. The morning breaks, and we must away!' The youth sprang upon his feet and awoke the maiden with a kiss. Soon ready to set out, they took a grateful leave of their worthy hosts and stepped to the door. Every object was obscured by a thick morning mist; and the sun, like a large red ball of fearful size, was just rising in the east.

'Let us wait a little, until the sun has dissipated the mist,' said the Bohemian, 'lest the lady should hurt her feet among the rocks.'

They stood a short time, waiting and shivering in the morning wind. Oswald had thrown his cloak over Faith, and held her closely clasped to keep her warm. The mist moved before them like a waving ocean, and apparently resolved itself into numerous dark clouds, which settled down upon the earth, and seemed to root themselves there. Meanwhile the sun had mounted higher, the waving of the ocean of mist increased, and suddenly there came a powerful gust of wind which rent and pressed down the immense cloud-curtain, when a scene as singular as it was magnificent, lay before Oswald's astonished eyes. The dark clouds that had appeared to sink down upon the earth, had changed to huge masses of gray rocks, which, rising up into the blue ether like countless palaces, churches and high towers, assumed the appearance of a gigantic city. Softly rounded snow-domes, crimsoned by the rays of the morning sun and glistening with thousands of diamonds, adorned the summits of these natural edifices, and the undying verdure of the pines and firs which arose here and there from the clefts of the rocks, gave a cheerful aspect to the view.

'Great is the Lord, when seen in his works!' cried the enraptured Oswald, withdrawing his mantle from Faith, to enable her to enjoy the spectacle.

Opening her large and beautiful eyes, she stood awhile as if blinded. 'How came this strange and wonderful city here?' asked she with astonishment 'Is it indeed a city?'

'Certainly,' answered the Bohemian, laughing. 'We call it the stone city, and divide it into city and suburbs. It is here, however, properly called the rocks of Aldersbach.'

'Are we to go in among those rocks?' anxiously asked Faith, clasping her Oswald more closely.

'There is no other way, my child,' answered the latter. 'Be not alarmed--you see that I am not disturbed, which I should be, if I anticipated any danger to you.'

'Ah, you iron-nerved men never anticipate danger until it is close at hand,' said the maiden; 'and then it is too late to avoid it.'

'Go on in advance, Lotek,' said the Bohemian to one of his companions. 'Beat the path a little where the snow lies too deep; announce to the worthy pastor that I bring him guests, and kindle a good fire in my quarters, that the lady may be rendered comfortable on her arrival.'

Lotek threw his musket upon his back, whistled to his wolf-dog, stepped off with long strides, and soon disappeared among the rocks.

'Now, if agreeable, we also will start,' said the Bohemian. 'The sun is tolerably high, and I would not willingly remain abroad, in open day.'

'Come, my child,' said Oswald, offering his arm to Faith, which she took with a sigh, and they briskly entered among the rocks. The procession was led by the Bohemian, closed by his armed companions, and flanked by the hounds.

'These masses are frightfully high,' said Faith, looking anxiously up at their summits.

'They appear so to you,' said the Bohemian, looking back. 'These, however, are but small affairs. We are now only in the suburbs. In the city you will see rocks worth talking about.'

'Heaven take pity on us!' sighed Faith, wandering on until she came to an open space. Here towered up, solitary and frightful, a single monstrous gray rock, formed like an inverted cone with its base stretching high up into the clouds and its apex imbedded in a lake of ice.

'Do not go so near, Oswald,' said Faith. 'This large rock must in the next moment tumble over.'

'Fear it not,' said the Bohemian. 'This is the Sugarloaf, which has been standing thus upon its head for thousands of years, and will surely retain its position long after we are in our graves.'

They were still advancing, when Faith, who was somewhat ashamed to exhibit her fears to the Bohemian, whispered to Oswald, 'only see that horrible gray giant's head projecting over us from between those high towers. I can plainly discern a monstrous, solemn looking face, surrounded by flowing gray locks.'

'That is the burgomaster,' said the laughing Bohemian, who well understood the whisper. 'So is this sport of nature called, and it is the most beautiful of any here. You need not fear him, for he is the only burgomaster on earth who never troubled any one.'

They continued to proceed farther and farther, until at length they were interrupted by a purling mountain stream. Beyond it, stood a broad mass of stone. The Bohemian leaped across the rivulet, rattling down a quantity of loose stones behind him, and with the humming operation of some wheel-work, the heavy stone moved slowly aside, and discovered a low, narrow opening.

'Do we enter there?' asked Faith in a tone so disconsolate as to call forth a hearty laugh from all the Bohemians. Even Oswald joined in the laugh, and, clasping the maiden in his arms, he sprung with her to the opposite bank. They all now stood within a narrow passage, the wheel-work again moved, the entrance closed, and they were enveloped in darkness.

'It is very dark here!' cried Faith.

'We shall soon come into the light,' said their leader, advancing. The others followed, and they thus proceeded in a narrow path, floored with yielding planks, and bounded by high perpendicular walls of dark gray stone, between which was seen the dark blue sky--so dark indeed, that they could almost distinguish the stars in broad day-light. The trickling water glistened upon the walls like silver threads upon a black velvet ground; and here and there little waterfalls, forming dazzling crystals with their congealing spray, bounded down the rocks and disappeared under the planks upon which they were walking.

'If we follow this path much longer,' protested Faith, 'I shall die of fear and anxiety.'

'For shame, my love!' answered Oswald. 'Will you, who spoke so boldly for me to the grim Wallenstein, lose your courage here in the bosom of harmonious nature, where we are especially and wholly in the hands of a protecting God?'

'We are at the end!' exclaimed the Bohemian, stepping out into the clear sunshine. The fugitives followed him, and found themselves in a narrow but pleasant valley, surrounded by high snow-covered rocks which cut off this quiet retreat from the rest of the world. A clear, silver fountain, which gushed from a cleft in the rocks, meandered through the vale, while among and upon the rocks, like eyries, were to be seen about ten huts, built of rough branches, and well covered with moss, to secure their inhabitants from the inclemencies of the weather. Men, women, and children, were moving in and about these simple dwellings as quietly and confidently as if they had resided there all their lives. The fire ordered by the Bohemian twirled its smoke up into the clear heavens, and there sat Lotek, assiduously turning a haunch of venison which was roasting before it. An old and venerable man with a long white beard, in a black clerical dress, and with a black cap surmounting his white hairs, came forth from one of the best of the huts to meet the new comers.

'Welcome, ye who have become outcasts and wanderers for the sake of your faith!' said he, with solemnity, as he extended to them the hand of friendship. 'Welcome to the Hussite's Rest. In my hut there is yet room for you. Come, eat of my bread and drink of my cup. By the grace of God you have here found an asylum which will conceal and protect you as long as may be necessary; for the destructive storm which now rages over the land, reaches not here.'

'Heartfelt thanks for your hospitable offer, reverend father,' said Oswald. 'Have you dwelt long among these rocks?'

'For the last five years,' answered the venerable pastor. 'After our emperor (who will one day have to answer for the deed before the judgment seat) destroyed the sacred edict which assured toleration, and burned its seal, there was no longer peace or safety for the poor Hussites in Bohemia. As he openly declared that 'he would have none but catholic subjects,' more than thirty thousand of our most respected families, embracing all ranks, wandered abroad to strengthen and enrich foreign countries by their wealth and industry. The poor cultivators of the soil could not avail themselves of the generous permission to emigrate with their property. They could not carry the soil with them, and being thus compelled to remain, they seized their arms and fell upon their persecutors. I myself, with the cross in my hand, led my parishioners against the enemy, and we struck boldly for our religion. Fresh armies were sent against us; the gallows and racks were encumbered with the corpses of our brethren, and we were compelled to yield; but it was impossible for us wholly to abandon our father-land, and we therefore threw ourselves into the caverns among these rocks, where a deep seclusion from the world is our only safety. Here we live quietly and peacefully upon the produce of our labor and the chase, which we dispose of in Bohemia and Silesia, and are much rejoiced whenever a victim of priestly rage wanders hither to claim our protection and hospitality.'

'We may now dismiss all anxiety,' said Oswald to Faith. 'We have at last reached a safe and well concealed haven.'

'That beauteous form inclines so confidingly and yet so modestly toward you, young man,' said the venerable pastor, 'that I should judge you were not yet man and wife, but only lovers. If you desire it, I will pronounce the blessing of the church over you. I am fully authorized to perform the ceremony, having received ordination from our right reverend bishop, who now wears the crown of martyrdom before the throne of the Lamb.'

'Have I your consent, my dearest?' asked Oswald, warmly pressing the maiden's hand. 'We already have your mother's blessing.'

'Not now, dear Oswald,' said Faith, with mingled sadness and resignation. 'I cannot consent to take that important step while yet so deeply impressed with sorrow for the fate of my dearest relatives. Our love must now wear the mourning dress in which it has been clad by these unhappy times. It would be almost wicked to put on the myrtle now; and the decisive *yes*, which should be spoken out of a joyful heart, would be stifled by my sobs and tears, under the present circumstances.'

'Your wish can alone decide the question,' said Oswald, tenderly, impressing a chaste kiss upon her forehead.

'Maiden, it is evident you have chosen a worthy partner,' said the pastor. 'And early has your betrothed learnt the lesson of self-denial, the hardest in this life to be acquired.'

Delighted to hear from such reverend lips the praise of one so dear to her, the maiden threw her arms about Oswald's neck and embraced him with love and joy.

CHAPTER XIX

'The morning is fine,' said Faith to Oswald after breakfast, as their venerable host seated himself with his bible upon his knee; 'and the valley here is so narrow and close that these huge rocks seem to press upon my heart. Let us therefore walk out a short distance beyond their confines.'

'Venture not too far, my children!' said the pastor, in a warning voice without raising his eyes from his book. 'My old body is a true and faithful weather-prophet, and tells me that we shall have a severe storm to-day. These storms rage much more furiously here than in the plains, and, when they come, every living creature finds it necessary to seek a shelter.'

'We will soon return,' promised Faith, skipping forth by Oswald's side.

'Mark well the place of entrance to our retreat,' said the Hussite, who opened the outer stone door for them; 'that you may be sure to find it again. The passages among the rocks are very similar, and if by mistake you enter a wrong one you may be compelled to wander about all day long.'

'Never fear! 'answered Oswald. 'It would illy become a soldier to be unable to remember any locality it might be necessary for him to find again. He then looked at the highest peaks in the vicinity, impressed their relative positions upon his memory, carefully examined the secret door, and thus prepared, they went forth into the clear fresh morning air and soon became engaged in a conversation of such interest as to render them entirely heedless of the lapse of time.

'I know not how it is,' said Faith, fanning her glowing face with her handkerchief; 'it is yet mid winter here, and I am so very warm.'

'It is incident to the summer of life,' said their former guide, who suddenly stood before them as they turned a corner; 'especially when the sun of love shines warmly. It is not probable you will have much further occasion to complain of the heat to-day, for a storm is approaching.'

'With the sky so clear? Impossible!' cried Faith.

'You know nothing of the tricks of the mountain-sprites,' said the Bohemian. 'One moment we have sunshine, the next thunder and lightning. That is the way with them. You will do well to return to the valley betimes.'

He passed on and was soon out of sight.

'We had better follow him,' said Oswald.

'Yet but one quarter of an hour,' begged Faith; 'and then we will return as fast as we can.'

'Who can deny you any thing,' said the youth; 'even when you solicit what should not be granted?'

They still continued to advance, until they came where the rocks were less compactly clustered, and glimpses of the plain, presenting brilliant winter landscapes, were occasionally obtained through the openings.

'Ah, how much pleasanter it is here than in the pent up valley!' cried Faith, clapping her hands with childish joy.

Oswald suddenly started and listened. 'Did you hear nothing?' he asked the maiden. 'It sounded like a distant trumpet.'

'Yes,' said Faith, after listening a moment; 'it must be the blast of a trumpet.'

'It may be our pursuers!' cried Oswald. 'Let us hasten back to our asylum.'

He now turned quickly about with Faith, and, rather bearing than leading her, hastened to retrace the path by which they had come. Before proceeding far on their return, they were met by a colder and sharper wind, and the snow which it blew from the summits of the rocks involved them in a white fleecy cloud.

'Alas, Oswald, I can no longer see,' complained Faith.

'It is but little better with me,' answered Oswald, groping after the path to the right, which he supposed to be the one he should take. Still sharper blew the wind as the storm rapidly approached, and the dark gray mountain-clouds lashed the immense rocks with their mighty wings, sending down their accumulated snows upon the heads of the poor wanderers. Still more wildly rushed and whistled and howled the winds among the rocks, in strangely horrible tones, and in the midst of the uproar they distinguished the sounds of distant rolling thunder and the flashes of lightning in the low dark clouds. In this struggle of the elements, all the summits and other landmarks which Oswald had noted to guide his returning steps, had completely disappeared, and at length he impatiently cried: 'I have lost the way. Why was I weak enough to yield to the wishes of a child!'

'Chide not, dear Oswald,' entreated Faith, submissively. 'I will willingly endure every hardship which is suffered with you.'

'That is what distresses me,' said Oswald. 'Were I alone, I should enjoy this storm instead of trembling at it; for nature appears to me most beautiful in anger, and I have already been compelled to expose this brow to many a wild tempest. My anxiety for you troubles me. If your health should be injured by this exposure I should be inconsolable, and have only my own thoughtlessness to blame for it.'

A brighter flash and louder report now put it beyond doubt that a terrible storm was at hand. The echoes thundered among the rocks, now nearer and now farther off, until they finally died away in indistinct murmurs.

'A thunderstorm in winter!' cried the trembling Faith. 'That is doubly horrible.'

'Who knows that this tempest may not bring a blessing; and certainly it cannot do much harm here among these old rocks,' said Oswald by way of consoling her, still continuing to advance at random.

'Thank heaven, I hear human voices!' exultingly shouted Faith: and like a doe she skipped towards an eminence with such speed that Oswald could scarcely follow her.

A multitude of people were approaching, sure enough. It was composed of colonel Goes, the detestable Hurka, and a troop of the Lichtenstein dragoons, who immediately aimed their arms at the fugitives.

'Stand!' cried Goes, amid the thunder of the storm, to his son, whom he instantly recognised. 'Stand, or I command the troops to fire.'

'Father, do no violence!' cried the despairing youth, throwing himself before the maiden, who had sunk upon her knees; 'God judges righteously and protects the innocent! Hear how he warns you with the voice of his thunder!'

The captain gave a loud and scornful laugh.

'Seize the rebel and his heretic bride,' shrieked the angry colonel. The captain, nothing loth, motioning his dragoons to follow him and confiding in his superior force, hastened forward, swinging his sword high above his head. The colonel accompanied him and the dragoons followed.

'Save me, my God, from the crime of parricide!' cried Oswald, advancing to meet his opponents.

At that moment came a blinding flash of lightning, accompanied by a deafening clap of thunder, and with it rushed down from the highest summit a monstrous mass of stone which caused the earth to tremble as if there had been an earthquake; a short, sharp cry was heard, and the pursuers and pursued were prostrated upon their faces.

CHAPTER XX

The first glance of Oswald's opening eyes, when consciousness returned, was directed in search of poor Faith. She lay near him in a deep swoon. Flying to her aid, he applied snow to her temples and warmed her lips with his kisses. At length she opened her eyes.

'You are yet alive, my Oswald!' cried she, with pious ecstasy, folding her hands as if giving thanks. 'The Lord has passed over us in the tempest; but he has remembered us in mercy!'

'Pious maiden,' said Goes, who stood behind them, leaning like a dying man upon a dragoon. 'Pious maiden, so mayest thou speak, out of the fulness of thy pure heart,--but the sinner must smite upon his breast and cry. The Lord is just, and in his wrath has executed a righteous judgment! Yet I may also give thanks for his mercy; for he has only punished the incorrigibly wicked, warning the deluded with the voice of his thunder, and leaving him yet a space for repentance and amendment. Forgive me, my son. I had unlearned to be a man and a father; but will again become one, even at this late hour of my life.'

'Your goodness restores me to new life, my father,' said Oswald, pressing the paternal hand to his lips. His thoughts then instantly recurred to the monster who had allured, his father there and stimulated him to the commission of crime; and, catching up his sword from the ground, his death-flashing glance sought the captain.

'He whom you seek is not far off,' said Goes, speaking low, so as not to attract the maiden's attention, lest she should be too much shocked. With a trembling hand he directed his son to the enormous rock which, still smoking with the fire of heaven, lay in the path. The youth shuddered as he turned his head and beheld a naked sword projecting from under the mass, in the grasp of a stiffened hand. The captain's plumed hat lay near, and the surrounding snow was reddened by a small rivulet of blood which came trickling forth.

'Behold the judgment of God, and implore his mercy for your repentant father,' said Goes, sinking into the arms of his son.

CHAPTER XXI

Three months later, Frau Rosen was sitting in the little cottage of the weaver's widow in Friedland, with an expression of soil serenity upon her still pale countenance. On either side of her sat Oswald and Faith, each holding one of her hands, and all rejoicing at her convalescence. The rattle of an approaching carriage was heard without, and directly four black horses, attached to the carriage of colonel Goes, trotted up to the cottage door. The merchant Fessel, yet thin and pale from his past illness and sorrows, descended from the carriage and entered the room.

As calamities suffered in common, only strengthen the bands by which good hearts are united, so the meeting of these friends evinced increased tenderness and affection; while the memory of the dear departed, which it called up, received the tribute of many tears.

'How stand matters in our good city of Schweidnitz? at length asked the matron.

'Badly enough, as yet,' answered Fessel; 'but not near so bad as when you left us. There seems, indeed, no prospect of an end to our oppressions. The Jesuits are constantly multiplying their encroachments and assumptions, and the royal judge whom the count has installed there commands that all shall become catholic communicants, and prohibits attendance upon the Lutheran churches out of town. These commands cannot be very effectively enforced, and the military executions have been discontinued ever since the departure of the tyrannical Dohna. Many of the troops also have been withdrawn, and but two squadrons now remain in the city. I must do the colonel the justice to say, moreover, that he has done every thing in his power to mitigate our sufferings, even at great hazard of injuring himself.'

'The Lord reward him for it,' said Frau Rosen, 'and allow it to balance the long account in that book where his sins are recorded.'

'I am here as his messenger,' continued Fessel; 'to conduct you all to the little inn near the rocks of Aldersbach, where he intends to hold a family festival.'

'There?' asked Oswald with surprise. 'That indicates some important, and certainly some joyful purpose.'

'He keeps his plans and objects very secret,' said Fessel. 'I have my conjectures; but can divulge nothing. That it is to be a great festival I know by the extent of the preparations. He has been there with a stone-cutter and gardener from Schweidnitz, since the day before yesterday; and he wishes you all to come in full dress to-day.'

Fessel, having returned to his carriage, soon came in again with two large packages, which he delivered to the lovers. Faith hastened to her mother with hers, that they might examine and comment upon its contents together.

Meanwhile, Oswald opened his package and found therein a splendid Danish officer's uniform with all its usual appendages. 'The time for these gilded ornaments has long since passed with me,' he observed with a feeling of dissatisfaction; 'and I do not deem it proper to wear the costume of a station which I intend never again to occupy.'

'He anticipated the objection,' said Fessel; 'and requests me to beg of you to wear it only this day, for his sake, notwithstanding your own disinclination.'

'Ah, Oswald, look!' exclaimed the happy Faith, holding out her present for his examination. 'See this beautiful white silken dress and this splendid diamond ornament!'

'It is very beautiful,' said Oswald, giving it a careless glance; 'but is there no myrtle-wreath with the dress?'

'I have already sought it in vain,' answered Faith, with a slight blush.

'Alas!' sighed Oswald, 'then the most acceptable present is wanting. My dearest hope for to-day is at once annihilated.'

'Murmur not against your father, my dear brother-in-law,' begged Fessel. 'I will be answerable that he means well with you and our little Faith.'

'It is well!' said Oswald, taking his package under his arm and retiring to dress; 'but he ought not to have forgotten the myrtle-wreath!'

CHAPTER XXII

Panting and foaming, the four black steeds drew up before the little inn at Aldersbach, which was now gaily decorated with evergreens. The happy old colonel stood in the door, ready to receive them. Oswald assisted Faith, and Fessel his mother-in-law, to alight. Goes advanced to the latter and clasped her hand. 'You have lost much through us,' he sorrowfully said, 'can you forgive?'

'Should I else deserve to be called a christian?' answered the matron.

'May God reward your kindness!' said the colonel, leading her into the house, in the largest room of which several protestant officers of the imperial army were assembled. Oswald then entered with Faith, in all her youthful beauty, which was much heightened by her rich dress.

'Ha, what a charming maiden!' exclaimed Goes. 'Yes, my son, her appearance would excuse thy choice, if indeed it needed an excuse.'

'I cannot share any part of the satisfaction which seems to be so general,' said Oswald with forced gaiety, 'as it is impossible for me to feel comfortable in a dress which is unsuited to my station and calling.'

'It is exactly suited to your station,' said the colonel with solemnity, handing a folded paper to him. It was a major's commission in the Danish service.

'This is wholly contrary to my wish,' exclaimed Oswald with surprise, as he perceived the nature of the document. 'I have laid down the sword forever!'

'That cannot be done with safety at present in any part of Europe, my dear Oswald,' said Goes. 'In these rough times a man must bear the sword, if he would not be compelled to bow his neck under it; nor is there any prospect that it will soon be otherwise. You have repeatedly shown, that you will never be able to reconcile yourself to the humble and submissive condition of a burgher. Whenever occasion has offered, you have unhesitatingly drawn that sword with which you have professedly wished to have nothing more to do. I most heartily rejoice at it, because of the evidence it affords that my blood flows in your veins; but at the same time it proves your unfitness for the counter and yard-stick. You must again serve,--it is required both for your honor and mine. To serve the emperor would be against your conscience. I have therefore sought out a service which, as matters now stand, cannot be objectionable to either of us. A permanent peace has been concluded between the emperor and the king of Denmark. Your new situation will lead you from Silesia to the land where your own faith, which is persecuted here, is openly and triumphantly professed. You will be spared the grief of being compelled to witness innumerable evils which you can have no power to remedy. All these considerations were well weighed by me before I applied in your name for the honorable appointment which you surely will not now reject.'

'You are right,' cried Oswald. 'You see farther than I do, and I gratefully receive the commission from your paternal hands.'

'My application alone would not have met with such ready success,' continued Goes. 'For that, you have to thank one whose friendship and patronage you literally conquered at Dessau,--the duke of Friedland. He wrote himself to Copenhagen in your behalf; and the mediator who brought about the treaty of Lubeck could hardly be refused so small a request by the king of Denmark.'

'Honor to the lion!' jocosely exclaimed Frau Rosen. 'Those large wild beasts generally have some generosity about them.'

'All is in readiness!' said the old Hussite host, entering the room and throwing open the doors.

'Give your arm to Faith, my son, and follow this man,' said Goes. The lovers looked at each other with some surprise, and obeyed the command. After them came the matron, supported by Goes and Fessel. The officers followed.

The procession entered directly among the rocks, and at length, magnificently gilded by the evening sun, the eventful mass of stone which had been detached and overthrown by the lightning, shone upon them with a far different and more friendly aspect than when it had last met their view. It was hung around with evergreens and adorned with flowery garlands; and upon the most conspicuous part of it a medallion had been cut out, with these words engraved upon it: '*The lightning of heaven here punished and warned.*' Underneath was cut out the day of the month and the year. In front of the huge mass stood an altar, built of the fragments which were shivered from it when it fell. The old pastor of Huss's Rest waited at the altar, in his clerical robes and with opened book. On each side of him stood Fessel's children, holding wreaths of flowers.

'What can all this mean?' whispered Faith to Oswald, in sweet confusion, while the colonel placed the missing myrtle wreath upon her blond locks.

'Unite this pair in marriage, reverend father,' cried the colonel, with gushing tears, leading the lovers to the altar.

CHAPTER XXIII

Mild toleration has spread its dove-like wings over the states of Austria for many long years since the period above referred to,--the colony of Huss's Rest is no longer to be found among the rocks of Aldersbach,--and the silver rivulet again meanders in silent solitude through the concealed valley. The huge rock hurled down by the lightning's stroke yet lies, a lasting monument, in the middle of the road, and the medallion may yet be recognised. Time has effaced the inscription, and the guide who now conducts the curious visitor knows only a legend of an English gentleman, who atoned for his desire to view a thunderstorm among the rocks by being very nearly crushed by the fall of this rifted fragment. In memory of his imminent danger, and in gratitude for his almost miraculous preservation, he is said to have caused the medallion to be carved in the rock. Of the punishment of the reprobate captain and the deep repentance of the colonel of the converters, they have long since forgotten the tradition; and FANCY may therefore be allowed to erect her light and airy castle upon the granite foundation of history; to picture forth to those now living the savage contests for opinion, of former times,--and to warn them against the evils of an exclusive and intolerant spirit, into which we are in constant danger of relapsing.

THE SORCERESS

BY

C. F. VAN DER VELDE

CHAPTER I

The first rays of the morning sun were brilliantly reflected by the polished arms of Ryno and Idallan, as they rode gaily forth in search of adventures. It was not their first similar excursion. As usual with errant knights, they had struck down many a dragon, vanquished many a giant, and rescued many a damsel from the clutches of wicked magicians. Delicate arms had clasped their knees in gratitude, tender bosoms had feverishly beat against their iron breastplates, ruby lips had pledged them in golden cups of the juice of the Syracusan grape, and yet their hearts remained cold and impenetrable as the pure steel of their armor. The delightful consciousness of freedom, strength, and youthful spirits, spoke in their every movement. Stately and beautiful they passed on their way, their sharp lances resting quietly upon their right stirrups, their swords peacefully clinking in their scabbards, and their hands carelessly holding their highly ornamented bridle reins.

Suddenly they heard female voices uttering distressing cries for help. The steeds snorted and pricked up their ears; the knights involuntarily drew a tighter rein, seized their lances, and applied the spur; and thus they darted forward with perfect indifference whether this new adventure should be crowned with wounds or kisses, blows or treasures, a martyr's chains, or an hymeneal altar.

Their panting chargers soon bore them to a forest filled with oaks of a thousand years, whence had proceeded those outcries, which were now subsiding to sobs so low as to be almost lost to the ear. At length a green meadow opened upon them through the wood, and there, enclosed by a circle of Moors, stood two powerless maidens of angelic beauty, bound to a tree. An old, meagre, yellow monster, in the rich dress of the east, appeared to be feasting himself with gazing upon their charms. He had just drawn a dagger from his girdle and was about to approach one of the maidens, when Ryno and Idallan burst upon them from the thicket with the suddenness of the lightning's flash, and the fury of the storm. Knight-errant like, without asking any questions, they nailed six of the Moors to the nearest oaks with their lances, and then, (as if Vulcan had sent his cyclops to the work,) their blows fell like hail upon the astonished Moors.

Courage, strength, knowledge of the use of arms, and the consciousness of a good cause, enabled them quickly to overpower their venal opponents. Those, who were not killed by the sword or trampled down by the horses, threw away their weapons and fled. Only the horrid looking yellow old man kept his ground, and he was busily employed in drawing strange characters in the air with a black wand. 'You lose your pains!' cried Idallan, laughing. 'You must know, sir wizard, that our arms, tempered by the fairy Diamanta, fear no magic charm, and that only superior natural power can prevail against them.'

'If you wish a proof of it,' interposed Ryno, springing from his horse, 'I am here ready for the trial, and you may call back your flying Moors to arm you.'

Without answer, but with a glance that disclosed the hell within, the sorcerer strode with uplifted dagger, towards his poor bound victim; but Ryno's ready weapon interrupted him in full career. With rifted head the fiend sank to the earth, which immediately opened and swallowed his hideous form; while a blue smoke, accompanied by fearful sounds, gnashing of the teeth and scornful laughter, issued from the spot where he had disappeared.

The knights hastened to the damsels, and by the aid of their bloody swords quickly severed the bands by which they were confined. Water brought from a neighboring spring soon restored the fainting sufferers to consciousness, and with the first glances of their large blue eyes arose a new sun upon their deliverers. The charming girls cast a shuddering glance upon the field of slaughter, kneeled before the knights with their arms folded in thanksgiving, timidly murmured to them some words in an unknown language, and, after a short internal struggle, rushed into their preservers' arms. An ardent kiss burned upon the lips of each of the enraptured heroes; but before they could recover from their delightful surprise, the maidens had escaped from their embraces. One bound of their little feet lifted them into the air,--a zephyr expanded their dresses into sails,--and with glances of ineffable sweetness they rose high over the gigantic trees, and swept beyond the vision of their astonished beholders.

CHAPTER II

'By my knightly oath, it is not fair,' said Ryno, after a long pause, 'to leave us standing here alone.'

'It is ungrateful,' murmured Idallan.

Ryno.--Say not that; for had all my heart's blood flowed upon this spot, the kiss impressed upon my lips would have been a sufficient reward.

Idallan.--I am wounded in the arm.

Ryno.--And I in the heart, which is far more dangerous.

Idallan.--What is now to be done?

Ryno.--Resume our travels. The heavenly forms moved towards the west, and happily no direction can be the wrong one for us.

Idallan sighed, and they proceeded towards their horses.

'Hold! what do I see?' cried Ryno.

'Where?' asked Idallan.

'A white veil, the earthly covering which the fairies left behind them when they mounted into the air.'

The two knights rushed towards the veil, and both caught hold of it at the same moment. 'It belonged to the damsel saved by me, and is therefore mine!' exclaimed Idallan.

Ryno.--I saw it first.

Idallan.--My blood flowed in the strife by which we have obtained it!

Ryno.--It is mine, I will not yield it up.

Idallan.--Nor I, but with my life.

Both held the veil fast, and it was in imminent danger of being torn in pieces.

'Hold!' said Ryno. 'Why should we senselessly destroy that which, uninjured, would make one of us happy. Let us calmly and peacefully determine our respective claims by an appeal to argument and reason.'

'I never will resign my claim,' scornfully exclaimed Idallan. 'If you persist in yours, the sword must decide.'

Ryno.--You are my brother in arms, and wounded; I will not fight with you!

Idallan.--Has the struggle with the Moors already exhausted your stock of courage?

Ryno.--Idallan! Even this shall not provoke me!

Idallan in a rage seized the veil, which Ryno reluctantly released, to save it from destruction. He hung it upon a high branch, and placed himself before it with his sword drawn. 'The veil is mine, if you are too cowardly to contend for it.' The noble Ryno half drew his sword, but, recollecting himself, immediately returned it to its sheath, and was about to mount his horse.

'Do you slight me?' roared Idallan, running after him sword in hand. Ryno was compelled to turn and draw, and a furious battle commenced over the dead bodies of the Moors. The attack and defence were conducted on both sides with equal courage and skill, so that neither obtained any advantage over the other. Sparks flew at every encounter of their weapons, the frightened birds flew screaming from the place, and the timid deer fled to the protection of the remotest thickets.

CHAPTER III

Under a natural arch of primeval granite, in the most secluded recess of a wild and savage mountain, was situated the deeply indented cave of the sorceress, Hiorba. The cavern was filled with sieves and cauldrons, mummies and bundles of herbs, hieroglyphics and mirrors, crystal globes and crocodiles, in mystical confusion. Two torches, held by skeleton hands, lighted the whole. In a circle of strange characters and human bones, lay the aged and despairing Hiorba, her face to the ground, frantically tearing the last remains of her silver hair with her withered hands. Two large black cats were caressingly and soothingly purring about her. Suddenly she appeared to be shaken as by an electric shock. She arose with flashing eyes, stretched out her magic wand towards the largest of the mirrors, and murmured some words of unknown meaning. Strange confused images appeared upon the clear crystal. As she anxiously watched the figures her interest seemed to increase every moment, and every moment her joy became more plainly visible, until at length she gave a cry of ecstatic delight as Aliande and Daura, her charming foster-daughters, rushed breathlessly into the cave.

'Here we are, good mother,' cried Daura, embracing her with ardor.

'Escaped from death, from shame, and from the terrible Rasalkol!' cried Aliande, pressing the old woman's hand to her lips with filial love. 'Saved by the noblest, bravest and handsomest youths....'

'Silence, children!' said the sorceress, interrupting them. 'My true mirror has already told me all, and more perhaps than you will be willing to confess.'

Blushing and confused, the maidens cast their sparkling eyes upon the ground.

'Quickly, ah too quickly, has love for your deliverers found its way to your young hearts. Faithfully until now have I guarded you against this dangerous passion; but the moment in which the traitor Rasalkol succeeded in abducting you from this protecting cavern, my power over you ceased. The reprobate's hellish plan of destroying both you and me has indeed failed; but you may yet one day wish that you had bled under his dagger;-

-for the sorrows of unrequited love cut more keenly into weak woman's heart than a thousand daggers.'

'You do not know our knights,' interposed Aliande in a scarcely audible murmur.

'I know them to be men. As the wolf resembles the hyena, and both of these the jackal, so also do the whole profligate sex resemble each other,--differing only in their outward appearance and capacity for seizing their prey. The inexperienced eyes of the harmless doe are easily fascinated by the beautiful stripes of the blood-thirsty tiger!'

Tears trickled down the maidens' cheeks, at this reproof.

'I love you my children,' continued Hiorba in a tenderer tone. 'You are the grand-children of my good niece, whom I buried on my hundredth birth day. Willingly would I have rendered you happy, which you can only be in an unmarried state; but you are in love, and all my warnings are spoken to the winds. For once, however, yield to a mother's anxiety: Let me *prove* the men of your choice.'

'Has not their battle with Rasalkol and his Moors already proved them sufficiently?' asked Aliande.

'Their knightly courage,--but not their hearts.'

'If all men were proved in advance,' answered Daura, with a faint smile, 'who would come unscathed from the furnace?'

'Your questions contain a significant denial of my request,' answered Hiorba. 'Since you have seen these strangers I have no longer any influence over your hearts. Consider well my last warning.'

She again raised her wand to the mirror and the field of battle again presented itself. Aliande saw the fluttering veil, and the furious contention of the knights.

'For God's sake, Hiorba,' shrieked the maidens; 'help, protect save!'

'See you those rough and savage men?' said Hiorba; 'They do not know which has the best right to the flimsy web, and yet each knight is ready to murder his brother-in-arms for its possession. You have here a specimen of what men call honor; and believe me, as their feet now recklessly trample upon the delicate wood-flower in their deadly struggle, so will the tyranny of their strength, their pride, and their sensuality, trample upon all your tenderest feelings and finally break your hearts.'

'Why waste so many words,' complained the maidens; 'save, good mother, separate the frantic knights.'

Shaking her head in token of disapprobation, Hiorba reluctantly took her wand and opened a cage which hung from the arch above; a bird of paradise came chirping thence, and perched confidingly upon her shoulder.

'Go, bring me the veil, Immo!' said Hiorba; 'and lead hither the contending knights, also.'

With her wand she softly touched the bird between its wings, and, sweetly warbling, it shot off like an arrow from the bow.

CHAPTER IV

Ryno and Idallan still continued their insane struggle. Their helmets and scarfs were hacked to pieces, and hung in fragments about their shoulders. The green sward was already dyed crimson from their many wounds, when the thrilling song of a bird, fuller and sweeter than the voluptuous tones of the nightingale, filled the neighboring air. Through the soothing influence of those tones, softer feelings were awakened in the breasts of the combatants. An armistice was tacitly concluded; and with suspended breath they listened to the heavenly music, until they at length perceived a beautiful winged songster fluttering about the branch upon which the veil was hanging. Softer and more soul-thrilling were the seductive tones poured from its little throat, and Ryno hazarded the remark:

'How foolish to be hacking each other's bones for a thing of so little consequence!'

'You are right!' said Idallan, putting up his sword and extending his hand to his brother-in-arms. A clear-ringing song of triumph resounded from the beak of the wonderful bird as their hands met with the grasp of reconciliation, while the little mediator seized the veil in its purple claws, and moved slowly and gracefully toward the west, still continuing its enticing music. 'It calls us, brother, shall we not follow?' asked Ryno.

'Yes, let us pursue the veil!' cried Idallan: 'this beauteous banner leads us to more delightful conquests!'

They resumed their saddles and hastened to follow their mysterious guide, keeping their eyes immovably fixed upon the bright and waving emblem, which remained constantly visible in the distance.

CHAPTER V

The gray-haired Hiorba was standing with her blooming daughters upon the ruins of an ancient castle. 'You will not listen to my warnings,' she sadly and affectionately remarked. 'You scorn to consecrate your virgin purity to the gods, as I have done, and receive rare knowledge, great power, and almost an earthly immortality, in return. The ardent wishes of youth kindle only for sensual enjoyments, which are ever mingled with sorrow and of short duration. Your desires shall be gratified. You shall possess whatever can bless mortal maidens: wealth, splendor, honors, and the husbands of your choice. The rest must depend upon the gods.'

'Why so earnest and solemn, good mother?' said Aliande.

'Your present situation, your inconsiderate choice for a whole life, the reflection that your days will be embittered and abridged by unappreciated and betrayed love, all contribute to make me sad. An equal affliction threatens both of you, for it is not in my power to call back spirits from the blooming fields of Walhalla to furnish husbands for you. It is done! I hear the distant song of Immo, and hasten to prepare your future abodes.'

Drawing a circle which included herself and the maidens, Hiorba then pronounced the mysterious words of conjuration. Subterranean thunder was heard, the earth heaved, gleams of lightning escaped through the cleft rocks, and a thick smoke almost destroyed the power of respiration. In an instant they became fearfully conscious that they were no longer alone among the ruins. Innumerable demons surrounded Hiorba's magic circle, respectfully awaiting her commands.

'Spirits of the Earth!' cried the antiquated virgin with great dignity, 'my foster-daughters, Aliande and Daura, require of me a dowry. Spirits of the east and west! I command you to convert these ruins into a splendid castle for the residence of Aliande. Spirits of the north and south! Prepare upon yonder hill a similar abode for my Daura. To the work! In nine times nine twinklings of the eye must all be completed.'

A motion of her wand, and half of the demons disappeared. The other half cleaved the earth for the purpose of bringing forth the granite, marble, gold, iron and other materials required for the edifice. The lightning played and the thunder rolled incessantly, earthquakes followed each other in quick succession, the winds howled, and the subterranean waters rushed and roared most fearfully. All nature appeared to lie in convulsions, as if it were a wicked invasion of her rights that immortal hands should perform the work of mortals. Powerless and insensible lay Aliande and Daura within the circle. Terrible flames burst from the crevices of the earth, giving fearful tokens of the subterranean labors of the gnomes. Hiorba stood amid the general uproar, calmly directing the raging elements, which never for a moment disturbed so much as one of the silver hairs of her head.

CHAPTER VI

The nine times nine moments had expired; the subterranean flames were extinguished, and the bright sun shone upon a magnificent palace encompassed by high walls, while its rays were brilliantly reflected by the metal roof. The gilded summits of its seven towers flashed in the sunlight like the seven stars. Hiorba viewed the labor of her mysterious agents with satisfaction, and then awoke the damsels with a touch of her wand. They looked around with astonishment upon the new world in which they found themselves. They had fallen asleep among ruins, upon damp moss overgrown with thorns and nettles, and now awoke upon soft couches of velvet and gold, in the balcony of a splendid edifice. The building was of granite, faced with marble, uniting the strength of the Gothic with the lightness and beauty of the Grecian style. Masterpieces of Grecian sculpture adorned every nook, step, and landing-place,--while the magnificent pleasure-garden, with all its fountains, cascades, lakes, temples, shaded walks, islands and obelisks, extended down the mountain slope. It was some time before they were convinced that it was not all a dream.

The damsels embraced their kind foster-mother, while tears of affection and gratitude eloquently spoke their thanks. 'Enough,' said Hiorba, withdrawing herself from their embraces; 'you know not, as yet, whether I deserve your thanks. That will be discovered hereafter, when the roses and thorns of this life shall have been weighed and balanced by the immortal gods. I must be brief, for already do I hear the approaching steeds of Ryno and Idallan, and I cannot look upon the men who are about to pluck, and perhaps to crush and destroy, the two sweetest roses of my garden. I now take my leave. I shall always act a mother's part by you,--but, only three times is it allowed me to become visible to the wives of Ryno and Idallan; at the moments of their greatest happiness, of their deepest misery, and of their untimely deaths. Preserve the same purity of soul which I have so carefully nurtured, so that in your last sad hour I may kiss the dews of death from your foreheads, and conduct your liberated spirits to the elysian fields of Walhalla.'

A soft and heavenly light overspread Hiorba's countenance, the wrinkles of age disappeared, and golden locks surrounded her clear forehead like a halo. Azure and purple wings unfolded from her shoulders, a robe of light enveloped her tall, majestic form, and on an amber cloud she floated away from the sisters, who watched her disappearance with speechless awe.

The tuneful Immo now fluttered through the castle gate with Aliande's veil. The draw-bridge fell, and the two knights, who had closely followed her, leaped from their horses, bounded up the steps, and threw themselves at the feet of the maidens; whilst Immo, perched upon the highest castle tower, sweetly warbled forth the bridal song.

CHAPTER VII

A crystal lamp, suspended from the arched ceiling of a lofty chamber, shed a soft moonlight over the silken tapestry of the bridal bed where Ryno was slumbering upon the bosom of the happy Aliande. The beauteous bride was watching the peaceful slumber of her beloved partner with mingled and undefinable feelings of joy and sorrow, when she suddenly heard a rustling of the drapery, and immediately the well known form of the sorceress stood before her.

'You are happy, Aliande?' she asked.

'Unspeakably!' murmured Aliande, hiding her blushing cheek in the bosom of her faithful foster-mother.

'Does your heart suggest no wish yet ungratified?'

'Only one!' timidly answered the lovely bride.

'Yet one?' rejoined the astonished Hiorba. 'Thus it is with poor mortals. Upon the highest pinnacle of earthly happiness they are still tormented by insatiable aspirations. Confide your secret wish to me, my daughter.'

'During the bridal supper, as my husband was giving a rapid sketch of his knightly adventures, and painting the charms of the various damsels he had saved, in glowing colors, I began to fear that I--perhaps soon--might be no longer the *only* object of his love.'

'Already jealous, Aliande, on this your bridal night!....'

'Death, rather than a rival!'

'What is your wish of me?' asked Hiorba.

'To relieve me from the torture of uncertainty, I desire a faithful monitor which shall inform me when Ryno kneels before strange altars, that I may win back the idol of my heart with redoubled love, or,--learn to despise and scorn the inconstant.'

'An unfriendly star rules over both you and me,' said Hiorba in a desponding tone. 'I am convinced that the fulfilment of this wish will make you most miserable, and yet I am constrained by a power greater than my own to grant it.'

She stamped upon the floor, and immediately two hideous gnomes appeared with a time-piece made of the most costly materials, curiously wrought into the form of a temple of Venus.

'Take this production of magic art,' said Hiorba, 'but conceal it carefully from your husband, lest in the exasperation of conscious guilt he should destroy his innocent accuser. This clock will always stand still, this bell will always remain silent, and this mirror will reflect only your own features, so long as Ryno remains true to his vows; but should he ever yield to the common vice of his sex, voluptuous melodies will issue from the temple, the index will indicate the time, and the crystal mirror will reflect the image of the favored rival.'

Aliande was about to express her gratitude, but Hiorba interrupted her. 'Thank me not,--for with this present you receive enduring sorrow and late repentance. Soon shall I greet you a second time, but then it will be in tears.' She spoke, and disappeared.

CHAPTER VIII

Transporting herself to the splendid seven-towered palace of the other sister, the sorceress entered Daura's chamber and awoke her from her sweet dreams of happiness with a kiss. Then came the same questions, and the same protestations of unspeakable happiness; yet the quiet and contented Daura, also, seemed to have *one* wish concealed in the secret recesses of her bosom. After Hiorba's long and tender entreaties for her confidence, she finally said: 'through repeated and pressing inquiries of both Ryno and Idallan, I have learned of the exhibition of savage rage by my husband in the bloody contest for the lost veil, which Ryno would have resigned for the sake of peace and friendship, refusing to fight until he was compelled to do so in his own defence. I fear that Idallan's violence, which did not spare even his beloved brother-in-arms, will also rend my heart and prepare many sad days and tearful nights for me. Oh that I were in possession of a charm which, like David's harp, would allay the demon of anger! What then could be wanting to my happiness?'

'Immo!' cried Hiorba, with a complacent smile, opening the window. In came the delicate bird, bearing about its neck a radiant diamond chain to which a small ivory flute was attached. 'Take this flute, my gentle Daura,' said the sorceress; 'pass this chain about your neck, and let your faithful mother's gift remain always upon your bosom. When Idallan's wild passions begin to kindle, when his inconsiderate bursts of anger threaten to wound the peace of my gentle daughter, then will the soothing tones of this instrument soften his rage and shed balm upon his mind.'

With glad surprise Daura extended her fair hand for the talisman, and Hiorba vanished.

CHAPTER IX

A year had passed from the stream of time into the ocean of eternity since the marriage of the two sisters, when Hiorba arose out of the rocks in the oak forest between the two palaces. The proud edifices yet shone in all their original splendor, and their majestic walls cast long shadows over the vale below; but the rock upon which the sorceress was standing had changed its appearance. Instead of being bare, as formerly, it was now shaded by tall cedars, lofty pines, and trembling poplars, and encircled with blooming rose-hedges, A gilded dome, supported by nine Corinthian pillars of alabaster, adorned the summit. The sorceress inquisitively examined the temple, and with surprise and pleasure encountered her own statue crowned with fresh cypress and faded roses. Tears of joyful emotion filled Hiorba's eyes, and her first impulse was to fly immediately to her foster-daughters, that she might, invisible to them, impress a kiss of gratitude upon their unconscious foreheads; but while hesitating which of the happy brides she should first visit, she discerned two female forms approaching from opposite directions. Discovering that they were her two daughters, she wrapped herself in impenetrable clouds, that she might be a secret witness of their interview. Their appearance gave her no pleasure. Their pale cheeks were not lighted by the sun of matrimonial peace,--their lingering steps and downcast eyes spoke not of happiness,--and with fear and sorrow Hiorba leaned against the altar which supported her statue. At length the sisters reached the place and rushed sobbing into each other's arms.

'My sufferings have reached their utmost limit!' exclaimed Aliande.

'My last hope is annihilated!' sighed Daura.

'How ineffably miserable,' said Aliande, 'has our good mother's last gift made me! With almost every change of the moon does the warning voice of my magic clock rend my poor betrayed heart. My fatal mirror is constantly reflecting new faces which seldom indicate delicate feminine charms, never mental elevation. All my tears have hitherto been able to obtain but empty promises of amendment from the faithless one; and my just reproaches only exasperate him. To-day I see the hated features of my last waiting maid, the light and impudent Rosa! No, I will bear these mortifications, these repeated insults, no longer!'

'Ah, how much more miserable am I, good sister!' sobbed Daura. 'It was but the intoxication of the senses which led Idallan to my arms; and in addition to my other sorrows I now feel that he has never, never loved me. The first week of our honey-moon had scarcely passed when he found himself annoyed by the gentle tones of my flute, which, against his will, moderated the severity of his fierce disposition. In a confiding moment, after he had successfully feigned the tenderest affection, he succeeded in drawing from me the secret of the maternal gift. With pleasant jests and agreeable trifling he unwound the chain from my neck; but no sooner was the delicate instrument in his hands, than his brow became clouded, his eyes flashed with an unnatural fire, and with a voice of thunder he denounced me as a vile sorceress who had disgraced his knightly bed. Then with furious rage he dashed the flute to the earth. Yet once more were heard its soft and tranquilizing tones. Too late! Idallan's foot was already raised, and trampling it in his anger, he annihilated its sweet melody forever. What, what have I not suffered since that unhappy hour!....'

'His heart is depraved--forget him!' cried Hiorba, stepping visibly between the sisters, who threw themselves at her feet in glad surprise.

'You both decided too rashly!' continued the weeping foster-mother. 'I warned you in vain. In vain did I entreat permission to prove your lovers. The evil is done,--and requires help, not reproaches. Your case, Aliande, may possibly be remedied; yours, poor Daura--never! That you may not doubt the truth of my words, I will now commence the trial of both husbands, and wo to him who shall prove base!'

She concluded with a voice of thunder, and disappeared. The unhappy sisters silently embraced each other, and then slowly returned to their splendid prisons.

CHAPTER X

Idallan was restlessly tossing upon his solitary bed on the first anniversary of his marriage night, whilst the repudiated and suffering Daura rested in a distant chamber, steeping her pillow with her tears.

Idallan's heart was radically bad, as might be inferred from his conduct in the contest for the veil. Savage and boisterous passions tarnished the splendor of the many knightly virtues which adorned his nature; and his real character appeared, when fortune, from her cornucopia, suddenly poured the full stream of love, wealth and splendor upon him. This unexpected and overabundant fulfilment of all his wildest hopes, gave the finishing touch to his temperament. The beauteous woman, whom unreflecting love had conducted to his arms, he valued merely as the slave of his rough and savage will. The princely treasures which Hiorba's generosity had heaped in his coffers, had only excited his thirst for gold. Hundreds of families who had sought the protection of his castle, and converted the surrounding forest into fruitful fields, were happy to be considered his subjects, and thus ministered to his love of power and dominion. Schemes of ambition disturbed his brain. He already in imagination saw himself a prince, perhaps of the whole earth, with Ryno his vassal, and an emperor's daughter for his wife; but he looked upon his gentle and faithful Daura as the greatest obstacle in the way of his success. His undisguised scorn and contempt had taught her to weep the rash choice made during the brief intoxication of love. There lay Idallan, disturbed by dreams which naturally took the tone of his daily thoughts and the color of the black soul whence they emanated. A glimmering light suddenly disturbed his uneasy sleep. Idallan leaped wildly from his bed, and before him stood the monster Rasalkol, surrounded by a pale sulphurous light, and horribly disfigured by the wound which Ryno gave him in the oak forest.

'Your first matrimonial year is ended!' said the fearful phantom in a sepulchral tone, 'and thank the Gods! you are unhappy. Your great soul must feel the pressure of the chains which bind you forever to a lowly bride. Daura suffices not for a man of noble ambition, and fate has destined you for greater things. Three crowns are waiting to grace your brow, when you shall have rendered yourself worthy of them.'

'Messenger of Heaven!' cried Idallan in ecstasies.

'You must know,' continued the spectre, 'that since the day when you and Ryno attacked me with such inconsiderate zeal, I have been condemned through Hiorba's cruelty, to wander about among the subterranean caves of this mountain, until some firm and courageous adventurer deliver me from the power of that ugly witch. The brave man who shall accomplish this, I will raise to the first throne in the world, give him the daughter of the most powerful ruler for a wife, and lay my inexhaustible treasures open to him.'

'O that it may be my destiny to end your sorrows, wise magician!' said Idallan, sighing.

'You alone can do it, brave and noble knight,' answered Rasalkol. 'You alone have the means in your hands, to destroy Hiorba, deliver me, and procure unspeakable happiness for yourself; but he who would serve Rasalkol must not fear to shed blood!'

'Give me but wealth and power, and I will slay millions for you.'

'Take this withered twig,' said the phantom, handing him a wand. 'Bear it to the chamber where Daura sleeps, strike your dagger to her heart in such a manner that the warm blood shall sprinkle the wand. The twig will acquire new life; leaves, buds and flowers will instantly put forth, it will take root in the earth and bear a magnificent fruit, containing within itself the seeds of death. Divide the fruit and send it in the name of Daura to Ryno and Aliande. As soon as you hear that they are dead, bring their bodies here and lay them by the corpse of your wife. Then tear out their hearts and burn them with the wood of the tree. When the fire shall have destroyed the last fibre, Hiorba will expire with dreadful torments. I shall then be free and eternally grateful.'

'I am yours!' cried Idallan, cautiously proceeding to the sleeping chamber of the unhappy Daura, with the magic wand in one hand and his dagger in the other. A mysterious light preceded the monster's steps. Softly opening the door, the angelic form lay before him, wrapped in peaceful slumber. The sweet smile of innocence played upon her pale lips. In a tone of melancholy tenderness which would have softened a tiger, she exclaimed in her sleep, 'lovest thou me no longer, Idallan?' Yet did Idallan, with a malicious scowl, raise his arm to strike. At that instant a flash of lightning hurled the dagger from his hand, and, instead of Rasalkol, the sorceress Hiorba stood before him. Her piercing glance seemed almost annihilating, and the trembling culprit cast his eyes upon the earth, as if imploring it to open and swallow him.

'Daughter, your tender husband would become your murderer!' said Hiorba. 'Thus is your hasty choice rewarded.' Then turning to Idallan: 'the soul's deepest grief, the eternal loss of her heart's peace, punishes your unhappy wife for her disregard of the maternal advice; but what can be a sufficient punishment for you?'

Idallan was silent.

'Your obdurate heart was steeled against your wife, your faithful brother-in-arms, and against me, to whose kindness you were indebted for the foundation of your fortunes. Ambition and shameful avarice have incited you to the blackest crimes! Be your punishment proportioned to your deeds! Therefore up, demons! drag this condemned one to Hecla's ever flaming gulf! There let soul and body suffer the pain of the dreadful sulphur bath, until the mortal part has become changed to gold. For a thousand years may the sordid dross remain, until by millions of accidents it becomes transformed into a circle, and presses a crowned and joyless head. When the crown thus formed sparkles with gems, awaken in the miserable metal its gnawing consciousness, and, so long as the diadem endures, torture the soul with the perception of treasures and honors never to be enjoyed!'

Having spoken thus, Hiorba waved her fearful wand. Two horrible demons appeared, and, with a laugh, which extorted a howl of anguish from the criminal, forced him away.

CHAPTER XI

The inconstant Ryno had one day been belated while engaged in the chase, which had become his favorite occupation since the destruction of his matrimonial peace. He had pursued a wounded doe into a thicket out of which he was unable to find his way. The evening air blew chill, the stars shone faintly through the nebulous atmosphere, and the moonless night was spreading its brown mantle over the earth. A deep silence pervaded the forest, broken only by the hootings of the owl, and the howlings of the wolf. Ryno dismounted to grope for the devious path. He wandered on in this manner for the space of a quarter of an hour, leading his horse by the bridle-rein, when suddenly he heard a flourish of drums and trumpets. Looking up, he was astonished to find himself at no great distance from a magnificent and brilliantly illuminated castle. Pleased and surprised, for in all his hunting excursions he had never encountered it before, he threw himself upon his horse and hastened toward its gates. Trumpets and comets rang a merry peal, the drawbridge descended, the gate flew open, and he soon found himself in the inner court, surrounded by a band of richly clad and golden locked pages. They seized his bridle, relieved him of his hunting-spear, bow and quiver,--one of them respectfully held his stirrup, while another, on bended knee, bade him welcome.

'Do you know me?' asked Ryno with astonishment.

'Who does not know the knightly Ryno, so renowned for his personal beauty, and indomitable courage!' humbly answered the courtly page. 'Will you please to follow me to the banqueting hall? You are expected there with affectionate impatience by count Arno, the lord of the castle, and Rosamunda his charming daughter.'

Readily yielding to this welcome invitation, he left his horse to the attendants, and followed the smooth-tongued flatterer into the castle. A marble vestibule, supported by a colonade of porphyry, led him to a broad alabaster stair-case, which was surmounted by a gilded and richly ornamented balustrade. Twelve servants in dresses of white silk, embroidered with gold, preceded him with torches to light his steps. The folding doors of the banqueting room flew open. A richly covered table, glittering with golden vessels and surrounded by knights and ladies, stood in the middle of the hall, and a splendid chandelier poured a flood of light from above. Uncertain whether he could trust his senses, Ryno entered, and the most delightful music from the balcony of the hall greeted his arrival. The knights and dames rose respectfully from their seats, while a venerable old man in a knightly costume, with a delicate female whose beauty was too dazzling for mortal pen to describe, advanced to meet him. Touching a full goblet with her rosy lips, the female thus addressed him: 'With this cup, Rosamunda, the daughter of the house, greets the brave Ryno, in the name of the lord of the castle.'

Already intoxicated by what he saw, Ryno drained the golden cup, impressed a glowing kiss upon Rosamunda's delicate fingers, shook the proffered hand of the old knight, who led him to the upper end of the table and seated him by Rosamunda's side. Familiar conversation, jests and laughter, the delightful music, the exhilarating cup, and, more than all these, the proximity of the blooming maiden, so warmed his blood and confused his mind, that the question never occurred to him how the castle came to be there, and its inhabitants to know him. He soon became engaged in a tender conversation with Rosamunda, and but too soon did they comprehend each other's glances. The table was now cleared, and the dance began. Drunk with pleasure, Ryno floated through the assembly with Rosamunda, pressing her divine form to his beating heart, and amid the tumult and giddiness of the waltz robbing her of a first kiss, which was warmly returned. When the dance was ended, the company sought the refreshing coolness of the gardens. The lovers soon found themselves in a solitary grotto, where, sunk in Ryno's embrace, Rosamunda murmured that she would be his forever, and that she doubted not of her father's consent to their union.

This brought the inconstant Ryno to his senses. With much embarrassment he stammered:

'By my knightly oath and duty, I love you beyond measure, charming girl, but I cannot become your husband, for--I am already another's.'

Tears flowed in torrents from Rosamunda's eyes, upon this declaration. With the most violent sorrow she reproached him for having stormed her heart and destroyed its peace, while bound by earlier ties. She declared that she could not live without him, and at last implored him to dissolve his first marriage, that he might become her's alone.

Ryno anxiously endeavored to effect a retreat. 'Aliande is my lawful wife,' said he, in a tone of decision: 'and never, never will I repudiate her.'

New reproaches, new tears, and new solicitations followed. Ardent kisses burned upon his lips, the softest arms twined about his neck, and the most voluptuous bosom beat against his throbbing heart. He was almost subdued; but he summoned resolution and, gently repulsing her, said: 'Leave me, charming maiden,--my integrity must soon wither under your warm embrace, and with a consciousness of my baseness, I should then stand before you as a faithless husband, a seducer of innocence, and a dishonored knight. Pardon my frankness. Your personal charms and yielding disposition captivate my senses, which have too often led me astray. You desire marriage. That must not, cannot be! I am weak and giddy; but no severity of torment shall make me a faithless villain! My wife is good; I am indebted to her for all my earthly prosperity and happiness. She has already suffered too much through my inconstancy,--and rather should this hand wither than I would repudiate Aliande for the purpose of pledging it to another; even were that other the divine Rosamunda.'

Once more she threw her arms around him in a last effort to subdue his heart;--and while he was vainly striving to escape from her embrace, the grotto was suddenly illuminated by torches, and the lord of the castle stood before him surrounded by knights and servants, and foaming with rage.

'What do I see!' thundered he: 'What shame and disgrace are visited upon my gray hairs! Rosamunda in this solitary grotto under the mantle of night, in the arms of a youthful stranger! My house is forever degraded and my lineage dishonored!'

'Your daughter is innocent and inviolate,' answered Ryno; 'and her lips will inform you, that no unworthy knight now stands before you.'

'You are in error, my good father,' cried Rosamunda, embracing his knees with anguish; 'Ryno is already married!'

'Married!' growled the old man, repulsing his daughter with a violence that caused her to sink to the earth in a swoon: 'Married! Then is my daughter's dishonor beyond remedy! That word decides your fate, Ryno! and you shall feel how the abuser of the laws of hospitality is punished in Arno's castle. Seize him, slaves! bind the wretch in fetters!'

Ryno's hand rushed to his side, but having thrown off his sword for the dance, he found no weapon there. He struggled manfully against the rabble host however, until he was finally overcome, cast upon the ground, bound, and thrown into a deep dungeon beneath the castle.

He lay upon mouldering straw, confined with clanking chains which were made fast to the wall. A dim lamp lighted the place clearly enough to show all its horrors. 'This is undeserved!' cried Ryno, as his eye wandered about his new residence and finally rested upon the heavy iron door. 'How many times have heavenly enjoyments rewarded my faithlessness to my Aliande; and now that I, for the first time, have conducted myself as became a virtuous knight, I sigh in these chains. If dame fortune will persist in such blindness and stupidity, I shall take care how I trust her hereafter!'

The prisoner had lost himself in sad rumination, the name of Aliande now and then escaping from his laboring bosom with many a sigh. At length a lively contention arose outside his prison door. A female voice was heard in earnest solicitation, and a manly one opposing; finally he heard the clinking of gold, and the bolts were withdrawn.

In the most seductive night dress, with streaming hair, tearful eyes and pale cheeks, which increased her beauty a thousand fold, Rosamunda tottered into the prison. With a trembling and mournful voice she said to him, 'you have rejected me when you were yet free to choose; but I come not now to speak of myself, of my love, or of the grief inflicted by your rejection. Your welfare alone has induced me to seek you once more. Your life, which is dearer to me than my own,--dearer even than my eternal happiness,-- stands upon a cast.'

'I am sorry that such a momentary hallucination should be followed by such serious consequences,' said Ryno.

'The lioness robbed of her young, is a lamb in comparison with my father when the honor of his family is concerned. You have only the cruel choice between my hand and a miserable death.'

'That is a hard alternative!' said Ryno with a shudder.

'Reflect that you are forever lost to Aliande. If your wife loves like Rosamunda, she would rather yield you to another's arms than deliver you up to a horrible death.'

'No artful sophistry, or seductive blandishments, can change my resolution. Your father must cite me before a court of honor, if he be an honorable knight. There will I answer his charge, and give him all the satisfaction he has a right to claim. If he do not that, if he be determined to destroy a chained and defenceless man in a secret dungeon, he is a despicable assassin.'

'Ryno!' cried Rosamunda, again clasping him with wild self-abandonment. Gently releasing himself from her embrace he bore her as far as his chains would permit, and called the sentinels. Upon their entrance he committed the weeping maiden to their care and commanded them to conduct her to her father.

'A night of torment!' sighed Ryno, throwing himself back upon his straw: 'but I have one consolation amid all my sorrows. By my death I shall seal that fidelity which I have heretofore but ill kept, and expiate the tears which my inconstancy has cost Aliande,--thus becoming purified and prepared for the joys of Walhalla. The gods bless and protect my wife and children!'

Again were the bolts withdrawn, and, in a mourning dress, the lord of the castle entered.

'You may thank a feeling of compassion that I condescend once more to parley with you!' said the old man with a painful suppression of his rage.

'I desire not your compassion.'

'You have violated the laws of hospitality and seduced my only child.'

'That is not true!'

'Knights and serfs were witnesses of my shame, which blood alone can efface. Were your previous marriage dissolved, however, and Rosamunda your wife, I might, perhaps, forgive you.'

'That can never be.'

'Rosamunda's person is fair, and yet fairer is her guileless heart. She is of the noblest lineage. Immense treasures lie in the caves of this castle, and my lands extend twenty days' journey towards the north. Take your life from my daughter's hand!'

'Place everlasting torments in one scale, and an imperial crown in the other, I repudiate my wife at no price.'

'Will Aliande be less inconsolable as a widow than divorced?'

'Waste not your breath!'

'By the eternal gods! I warn you for the last time. These prison walls see you Rosamunda's husband, or echo the death-sigh forced from you by the rack!'

Ryno tore one of the golden locks from his head and handed it to his persecutor. 'If one spark of humanity yet slumbers in your bosom you will send this lock to my poor wife, with the message--That I die faithful to her, and that I wish her to train up my son as a good and virtuous knight.--Now let your executioners come on, I am ready.'

'Then, by Woden!' roared the foaming parent, 'you never behold the rising of another sun!'

He struck a bell, and twelve armed men with closed visors and drawn swords, slowly and silently entered. One of them detached Ryno's chains from the wall. Again the bell sounded, and at the other end of the prison the heavy doors of the torture vault flew open with a horrible clang. The cave-like room was hung with black and lighted with torches. Every instrument which the cruelty of man has invented for the torment of his fellow man, brightly polished and arranged with frightful regularity, met the glance of the unfortunate prisoner. Large pincers were glowing in a chafing dish, and in the centre of the room stood the dreadful rack with its fearful and mysterious equipments. Three hideous ruffians, with naked arms, in blood-red caps and doublets, stood waiting beside it. On the right was an open and empty coffin.

'For the last time, choose!' cried the incensed tyrant.

'Death!' said Ryno, calmly, and sighing the name of Aliande, he advanced toward the rack with a firm step. A beam of light suddenly illuminated the dungeon. The torture-chamber, the guards, the rack, the executioners, had all vanished,--and Ryno found himself again in a magnificent room whose azure star-besprinkled dome was supported by rose-crowned pillars. With a friendly smile the sorceress Hiorba approached him; and, as on the first day of his marriage, with the glow of newly awakened love, sank the happy Aliande upon his breast, thanking him for his unshaken fidelity to his early vows.

'You have sustained the trial!' said Hiorba, 'and thereby expiated many a former folly, which Aliande must now forget. Love has returned, confidence is born anew, and I shall leave the again united pair with unshaken hope. The unhappy Daura will accompany me. Possibly she may learn forgetfulness in my quiet and peaceful retreat, which she ought never to hare left. Farewell, my children. Forget not the true watchwords of hymen--LOVE AND FIDELITY! Ryno, remain the same Ryno you were in the grotto and in Arno's dungeon. Aliande, never forget that, not tears and reproaches, but kindness and affection only, can reclaim an erring husband.'

She disappeared in a cloud of incense, and the reunited lovers sealed their mutual promise to obey her sage instructions, with a kiss.

Faithfully was that promise kept. Even when Aliande's head had become silvered with age she alone was the happiness of Ryno, as he was hers; and it was many years before the venerable matron, surrounded by her grandchildren, was surprised by her friend Hiorba, who came in a robe of light to kiss her expiring breath from her pale lips.

THE ANABAPTIST

A TALE OF THE FIRST HALF OF THE SIXTEENTH CENTURY

BY

C. F. VAN DER VELDE

CHAPTER I

It was on a fine morning in February of the year 1534, that the journeyman armorer, Alf Kippenbrock, proceeded from Coesfeld toward the free imperial city of Munster. Already had he left Baumberg and Stestendorp behind--Saint Lambert's tower stretched high its gigantic head at the edge of the distant horizon,--and the fruitful plain, in which venerable old Munster is situated, gradually spread itself out before the wanderer with its other towers and churches peeping from the broad level,--while the bright silver of the distant and beautiful river Aa glistened in the rays of the morning sun.

Alf stopped at a stone cross which stood by the road side,--and while a deeper red suffused his blooming cheeks, and his pious eyes sparkled with enthusiasm at the sight of the ancient episcopal seat, he took off his hat and swung it toward the city for joy.

'God bless thee, dear native city!' he rapturously exclaimed; 'it is long since we parted--and I now look in vain for my good old parents, who, seven years ago, accompanied me as far as this cross. Nevertheless thou appearest kind and friendly, and ready to offer me a hearty welcome. Ah, nothing is dearer to man than his native home; thank God I have again found mine, and in it that true and genuine faith in which I hope to live, and, one day, happily die.'

He then replaced his hat and walked briskly in the direction of St. Lambert's tower. At that moment the morning breeze brought suddenly the sound of the many voiced bells to the youth's ear, while an immense cloud of vapor rolled up in the well known region of St. Mauritius's cloisters. 'Holy God! some terrible misfortune has happened!' exclaimed Alf, redoubling his pace. At the same time he saw an immense multitude of people running toward him from the city. The nearer they approached the more distinctly he discerned the motly combination of the crowd that came gushing forth on foot, on horseback and in carriages. It had the appearance of a formal national migration. Judges and clergymen, patricians and plebeians, the old and the infirm, women and children, indiscriminately mingled with various kinds of property apparently collected in the haste incidental to a sudden conflagration, packed up and borne along with them, successively and rapidly passed the wanderer. The men in a state of great excitement conversing eagerly with each other, the women weeping, and the children crying, they moved on in a seemingly endless procession.

Alf, transfixed with surprise and astonishment, and resting on his walking staff with his heavy knapsack on his hack, stood gazing upon the passing multitude. All had finally passed except one old burgher who toiled singly on after the crowd, panting for breath. Alf stopped him in the way and said, 'by your leave father, what means this general flight? Is Munster beset by hostile armies?'

'Alas, worse than that,' answered the graybeard, wiping his eyes, 'the anabaptists have become masters of the city this fearful night, and are driving before them all who do not belong to their sect, sword in hand.'

'God be praised!' cried Alf with wild enthusiasm, 'the true faith is triumphant!'

The burgher cast upon the youngster an angry and scornful look. 'Folly may be forgiven to rash, inexperienced and imprudent youth,' said he, 'yet you may nevertheless be compelled to answer to the Lord for this horrible praise of his name.'

He then turned his back upon the youth and strode on after the procession. Alf no longer felt the weight of his knapsack, but sprang forward toward Munster with joyful leaps. He soon, however, encountered a new mass of fugitives, among whom he could not easily penetrate--and the dust raised by people, cattle, horses and carriages, becoming insufferable, Alf retreated into a solitary inn by the way side, until the tumult had passed away.

As he laid down his knapsack in the tap room and called for a cup of wine, the door opened and in tottered a pale thin man in a long black clerical robe. He was followed by a light dashing fellow with the countenance of a satyr, who carried his bundle for him.

'I can go no further,' groaned the pale man, sinking down upon the nearest seat.

'Now, doctor, you are for the present indeed in safety,' said his attendant to him, depositing the bundle upon the stove-bench. 'Permit me to take a refreshing draught, and then to bid you farewell.'

'Thou dost not wish, then, to go to the good Hessenland, my son?' asked the doctor, sorrowfully.

'No,' answered the youth, 'but do not consider me unkind. I return to Munster. New governors will require new clothes, because much of the dignity of office consists in the dress. My needle will not be permitted to remain idle there, and I shall make great profits. Moreover the doctrine of liberty and equality was plain to me from the beginning; and if the good people would not come so easily to blows, nothing could be said against it.'

'I thought you held fast to the ancient faith,' said the doctor complainingly, 'since you sustained me so truly.'

'No,' laughingly replied the hare-brained youth. 'I held to you while you benefitted me; and on that account I could not reconcile it to myself to desert you in your hour of need. Now you are in safety; and I must return to the only place where fellows like myself are held in some degree of estimation; in any other I might remain all my life a wandering ragamuffin.'

'One deception less,' sighed the doctor sinking into gloomy meditation, when the host entered with a mug of wine for Alf. When he perceived the doctor the mug fell, and, clasping his hands over his head, he cried: 'Holy God! are you also driven away, reverend sir?'

'The true shepherds must first be driven away,' said the doctor with a melancholy smile, 'when the wolf desires undisturbedly to break into the unfortunate fold. Nevertheless I may congratulate myself that I held out until the last moment, and only yielded to open violence.'

'How was that possible in so short a time, doctor?' asked the host. 'The adherents of the Augsburg confession were certainly very powerful as yet, in the city, as the papists also were.'

'The terrible Matthias,' replied the doctor, 'had sent circulars through the neighborhood and collected all the anabaptists at Munster. Consequently, all the low rabble, who had nothing at home to lose, rushed into the poor city, and last night, taking possession of the arsenal and town house, they set fire to the cloisters of Mauritius. They ran, as if possessed, howling through the streets with naked swords, crying, 'Repent and be baptised!' and 'Depart ye Godless!' Neither condition, age, nor sex availed; delicate women, the sick and dying, were all mercilessly thrust out at the gates of their native city unless they would profess the heretical, heathenish worship. The choice between death, flight, and apostacy, only remained, even to me; and as I thought it better to be useful through the preaching of the word to honest christians than through martyrdom in the paws of such raging brutes, I shook the dust from my feet and escaped,--and God must judge.'

'I am very sorry for you,' cried Alf, much agitated: 'because you have such a venerable appearance, and doubtless think yourself truly faithful, though you wander in darkness. Nevertheless, it is a culpable stubbornness in you Lutherans, to struggle so violently against the new doctrines, which have the right and the holy scriptures so clearly on their side. Has not our Lord and Savior expressly commanded his Apostles--'Go ye into all the world and teach all people and baptize them?' So therefore, the teaching must precede the baptism, according to Christ's own words. How dare you, then, presume to baptize new born children who can know nothing of God?'

'What, another anabaptist!' grumbled the host, with a discontented glance at the speaker; and the worthy doctor directed his eyes, full of heartfelt sorrow, upon the youth, and sighed--'Another lamb gone astray from the flock, whom I cannot lead back to the protecting fold. This it is, that makes me sad.'

'You have not answered my question,' said Alf, with the triumph of the controversialist.

'Of what advantage is it to show the way to the blind, who will not see it?' cried the doctor: 'I could answer you, that Christ's apostles could only baptize adults, because those only came over to christianity at first; but that, at a later period, the burning zeal of the great Augustine placed near the heart of the christian fathers the duty of consecrating their children to Christ through the holy baptism into the covenant, and thereby to deliver them from the original sin and impart to them the redemption through Christ, before peradventure they should be snatched away in their tender youth by a premature death. Would to God that this schism was the only one that your companions in your mistaken faith defend with such terrible obstinacy and fierceness. You have yet other dogmas which you advance, sufficient to convert our earth, God's beautiful temple, into a den of murderers. Your community of goods, your equality of rank, your struggle against secular authority, lead directly to lawless confusion, robbery, murder, and unhappy revolution.'

'Even the best opinions may be misconstrued,' replied Alf, angrily. 'The gospel looks upon all men as equal. The distinctions made among them by birth, rank, and wealth, are contrary to its spirit. Christians who possess the doctrines of God as precepts, and take his spirit for their guide, need no power that destroys religious liberty without authority. They are able to govern themselves by the word of God, and the Holy Spirit will always guide them, that they stumble not in the paths in which they are led by their faith.'

'Unhappy, infatuated youth!' cried the doctor, with a majestic prophetic look and tone. 'Go now into the unfortunate city, and behold how the anabaptist spirit has conducted your companions to robbery, incendiarism and murder, in the smoking ruins of the cloister, and in the bleeding bodies which strew the highways! If this horrible spectacle be not enough to move your heart, think of the words which in this sad hour I address to you in the name of that God whom your proceedings profane. These crimes will be but the beginning of your afflictions. Your equality will yet be to you but equality of misery--your community of goods will bring you to beggary. Instead of the magistracy which you now drive away, miscreants will rise up from the midst of you, and with bloody hands rend your own entrails, until the wrath of a long suffering God finally awakes, until the avenger appears, and you all perish in one common ruin.'

'There come horsemen galloping,' cried the doctor's attendant, who was standing at the window with his cup; 'and, if I see rightly, they bear our lord bishop's colors. It might be well for me to go back to the city.'

'The bishop's riders!' sighed the doctor. 'It often happens that the avenger only lingers near; but this time the Lord in his anger has given him wings.'

'The bishop's riders!' cried the host, anxiously: 'May God be merciful to us. Those fellows make no distinctions, but shear both Lutherans and anabaptists over one comb.'

Alf's eyes flashed fire at this; he drew from his portmanteau a large, two edged dirk-knife, screwed it upon his walking stick, and placed himself in a defensive attitude.

Meanwhile the horsemen had stalked into the inn.

'Here is a whole band of anabaptists collected together,' cried the officer. 'Halters from the horses! we will bind them together in couples.'

'I am the doctor of theology, Theodore Fabricius,' cried the reverend gentleman, with all the dignity of his station; 'driven from Munster by the anabaptists, and am under the special protection of his grace the landgrave of Hesse.'

'Why should we trouble ourselves much about the heretics,' exclaimed the serjeant. 'Don't trifle and spend your time in unnecessary discourse;

submit without resistance!' cried another, seizing the poor doctor by the collar.

Then sprang forward Alf, and struck aside the strong hand of the horseman. 'Back!' cried he, holding his dirk-spear before him, 'I will stab the first who touches the old man.'

'That is brave!' cried the host, exultingly; and, armed with a small hatchet, he stationed himself at Alf's side.

'Young man, why do you interfere?' cried the horseman, recoiling. 'Out broadswords!' shouted the officer, and the broad blades were already flashing, when a new trampling of horses drew all eyes to the window, and in an instant a fresh band of horsemen crowded into the room.

'God be praised!' cried Fabricius, with folded hands; 'those are the colors of my lord, the landgrave.'

'What mischief are you episcopalians carrying on here?' angrily asked the captain of the new comers.

'We surely shall not answer to a Hessian concerning that, while standing upon our lord bishop's own ground,' blustered the serjeant. 'With greater right may I ask how you could yourself venture upon our territory with weapons and arms, without escort?'

'Madman!' cried the captain, 'is that the way you speak to your allies? We are sent by our lord to help yours against the rebellious anabaptists. At present I am commanded to the defence of the evangelical preachers, who are compelled to flee from Munster, and I will not permit you to abuse them.'

'If you expect that I shall believe every thing you say upon your mere assertion,' sneeringly answered the bishop's serjeant-major, 'you are for once mistaken. The heretic priest is my prisoner.'

'Contemptible slave of a priest!' thundered the captain, 'when the word of a knight is doubted, he has no other voucher than his good sword;' and drawing forth his blade, he called to his followers, 'strike flat, comrades.'

As if all the furriers of Munster had collected together in the tavern to beat their skins, so clattered the Hessian blades upon the broad backs of the episcopalians in mighty chorus. In a moment the room was cleared, and the Hessians were sitting behind their full jugs, making themselves merry over their easy and bloodless victory.

'Where do you desire to be conducted, reverend doctor?' asked the captain courteously.

'I intend to go direct to Cassel,' answered Fabricius, 'to give an account of my mission to the landgrave. If you will give me a file of horsemen as far as Paderborn, I shall reach my destination without difficulty.'

'With your permission, Mr. Captain,' said the landlord, 'I will myself convey my confessor as far as Paderborn in my little wagon.'

'It is well!' answered the captain, casting a glance upon Alf, who had unscrewed the knife from his staff and was preparing to proceed on his way.

'Who art thou?' he asked in a severe tone.

'An honest journeyman armorer,' answered Alf, boldly, 'who am returning to Munster in search of employment.'

'To Munster?' angrily repeated the captain: 'to that heated furnace where the frantic mob are preparing misery for the country?--and now,-- directly? Dost thou belong to them?'

'Shame to him who denies his faith through fear of men,' cried Alf; 'yes, I am an anabaptist.'

'Munster needs no armorer now,' said the captain, with decision; 'sharp weapons are not good for children and drunken men: they injure themselves and others with them. Thou goest with us back to the head quarters at Walbeck.'

'Never!' exclaimed Alf, in wrath, drawing his knife.

'Pardon his imprudence,' entreated Fabricius, stepping between them. 'His spirit is diseased and heavily weighed down; but his heart is better than his mistaken faith. He has hazarded his life in my defence against the episcopalians, regardless of the difference of our creeds. Let him go in freedom.'

'You know not what you ask, doctor,' said the captain, displeased. 'Ought I to permit the rebels to strengthen themselves by the acquisition of such a stout fellow?'

'There are already, alas! a plenty of wicked men,' said Fabricius, 'ferociously raging in the unhappy city. It seems to me it is to be wished, that there should be some good souls among them, who might mitigate many an evil, and prevent many a crime. The whole conduct of this youth convinces me, that his erroneous opinions will not hold out against the misdeeds he will witness, and against the voice of truth in his own heart; and then may even he become a fit instrument in God's cause. Let him go, by my desire.'

'Go then,' impatiently cried the captain, returning to the drinking table.

'God reward thee,' said Alf, with deep feeling, and pressing the hand of Fabricius to his bosom; 'thou hast saved me from murder.'

'The Lord enlighten thee!' said Fabricius, laying his hands upon the youth's head for a farewell blessing, 'so that we may one day joyfully meet again.'

'Yon say that with great confidence, sir,' cried Alf, perplexedly, 'as if the error were certainly upon *our* side. I firmly believe it to be upon *yours*. For God's sake, then, which of us two is right in these dreadful contentions?'

'If that doubt itself do not already tell thee, my son,' said Fabricius, in a friendly manner, 'only submit the new belief to the touchstone of thy reason and thy honest heart--bring it to the test of the holy scriptures,--seek the truth with diligence and thou shalt find it.'

'No, no!' cried Alf, in the wild conflict of his soul. 'The holy spirit, that spoke by our prophets, cannot err. Satan himself must have whispered the wicked doubt to me: I reject and cast it from me, as, according to God's commandment, I ought the eye that offends me. I am, here, yet within the confines of anti-christ, and his power darkens my vision. Wherefore, forward to the realm of light! Up, toward the holy Zion!'

As if beside himself, the enthusiast strode out of the house, the worthy Fabricius with saddened looks, watching his retreating form.

Alf was already advancing toward the city with vigorous strides, when he heard some one calling behind, and the nimble tailor came running after him. 'Take me with you, compatriot,' begged he: 'I have taken my leave of the worthy doctor, and would willingly return to the city in good company.'

'Where were you during the first part of the fight?' asked Alf of him.

'Behind the stove, dear compatriot,' laughingly confessed the tailor; 'and when it began between the Hessians and the episcopalians, I crawled under the stove, lest perhaps both parties might take me for an enemy, and I thus receive a double portion of blows.'

'For shame,' said Alf, scornfully.

'What is there in that to be ashamed of?' babbled the tailor. 'Let each honor his profession. An armorer, with legs and arms to his body, as you have, by the grace of God, must hammer upon his enemies as he would upon old iron--it is his duty; but a poor little tailor, like me, has the privilege of running away from such affairs of honor; and I should little grace my fraternity by exhibiting an ill-timed valor in old quarrels.'

'Under such circumstances,' said Alf, 'I cannot understand how your cowardice can suffer you to return to Munster, which just now is very tempestuous and clanging with arms.'

'Why, not a hair of my head can be injured!' triumphantly answered the tailor. 'I am the old boon companion of the second of the prophets who are now very powerful in the government of the city, and they cannot fail me. When once the old order of affairs shall be wholly overturned, I may be clothed with a station of high honor in the new government. For a generalship in the field my stars have certainly not directly designed me; but a chancellorship or treasurership I may fill as well as another.'

'For that must God in his anger have created you,' cried Alf, with indignant laughter.

'Because I am a tailor?' asked the chancellor-in-expectancy, angrily. 'How blind does the pride of your hands make you, friend armorer! Does every thing depend upon strong bones in this world? What was Johannes Bockhold of Leyden, our great prophet, more than a tailor? What does he now appear, and to what will he not hereafter attain! The days and nights have not yet all passed. He has a head for twenty; and when we loitered about together as comedians, while business in our line was dull, then did he play the parts of emperors and kings, and played and ranted in such a manner as to compel respect from all. Give him the world and he will govern it in fine style.'

'A man who plays the buffoon for bread, selected to carry on the work of the spirit in my native city!' sighed Alf, losing himself in sad reflections until they arrived at the closed gates.

Here all was crowded with the busy activity of the burghers. The city walls were repaired and raised,--the ditches were deepened and furnished with palisades,--new bulwarks and towers arose on high,--hammer and trowel, shovel and pickaxe, were in constant motion,--and the dirt carts creaked incessantly. Aged and distinguished men worked unweariedly, like day-laborers; women and children assisted; and the pleasure and satisfaction, with which every thing was accomplished, rendered it very apparent that the most ardent enthusiasm was the soul of this body.

'Do you not perceive,' cried the tailor, gaily slapping Alf's shoulder, 'that the bishop will be compelled to break many a tooth upon our walls before he will be able to eat us up?'

'What does that denote?' asked Alf, disregarding the boast, and pointing to two large stone slabs covered with letters which were hanging upon the gates.

'Those are the commands of our second Moses, of our great Matthias,' replied the tailor, reverently. 'He has caused them to be cut in stone and to be hung thus on all the gates of the city, to keep the people in the fear of God, so that every man may conduct according to them.'

At that moment a confused drumming alarm rattled in the city, and a desolate thrilling cry of the raging populace answered the warlike call; an icy chill diffused itself through every member of Alf's body, as it seemed to him as if the people were roaring for blood.

'The prophets are calling the people together,' said the tailor, dragging Alf forward. 'Come, we must hear what they have to say to us; we belong to the mass, and can give our opinions upon public affairs whenever it may seem good to us.'

They hastened toward the market, where the human tide, as if agitated by the wildest storms, waved to and fro, thundering and roaring.

The thickest crowd was about St. Lambert's church, and the mass, armed with clubs and spears and muskets, seemed here to form a large circle, from the centre of which a single commanding voice occasionally rose above the general bustle of the crowd.

Alf swung himself up to the corner stone of a house near the market, held fast to the iron supporters of a pitch-pan, and looked towards the centre of the circle.

'What do you see,' cried the tailor to him above.

'A stout man,' answered Alf, 'clad in a coarse woolen capote. I can scarcely see his face through his disheveled hair and bushy beard. He poises a stout spear over a vigorous burgher who is kneeling before him.'

'That is our great Matthias,' exclaimed the tailor.

A fresh multitude at that instant came up and pulled Alf down from his corner stone. The tailor held on with all his might to prevent being borne away by the crowd, and grumbled, 'it is very wrong that one should be hindered by the crowd from seeing what the people do in their sovereign judicial capacity.'

'Thank God! I find one acquaintance here at least!' exclaimed a pale girl, tremblingly seizing the hand of the tailor. 'If you have the heart of a man, my good fellow, help us out of this great difficulty. You have much influence with Johannes Bockhold, the prophet; beg of him, therefore, mercy for my poor uncle!'

'For your uncle, mademoiselle Clara?' inquired he with astonishment. 'What has happened to the worthy master Trutlinger?'

'Trutlinger, Hubert Trutlinger, the armorer?' exclaimed Alf, in great agitation; 'my good old master? What has happened to him?'

'Alas, they have dragged him before the tribunal of the people!' complained the weeping girl; 'he is said to have spoken evil of the prophets.'

'That is a bad case,' said the tailor, 'and in such an unpleasant predicament there is not much to be hoped from any interference.'

'But you must attempt that possibility,' said Alf, 'of serving the upright man and this loving child.'

There fell a shot in the midst of the circle, which was directly followed by a horrible cry from the thousand voiced multitude. 'God! what was that?' exclaimed the girl, aghast. 'I fear my intercession comes too late,' said the tailor dubiously. At that moment the circle opened and the doomed one was brought forth, borne in mournful silence upon the halberds of several burghers. The blood was streaming from a spear wound in his side, and from a reeking shot wound in his breast; yet the unhappy man was not dead, but breathed, although with infinite pain, and had his eyes directed imploringly toward heaven. 'Not even to be able to die,' groaned he. 'Thou punishest heavily my foolishness, O God!'

'Be satisfied unhappy man,' exclaimed the terrible prophet, who had followed him. 'Heaven has revealed to me that the hour of thy death has not yet come. God has determined to show thee mercy. Convey him to his dwelling,' said he to the bearers, 'so that he may be taken care of by his own family. The Lord desires not the death of sinners, but that they should be converted and live.'

'Bear me forward quickly,' begged the dying man to those who were carrying him. 'These bible-sayings cut me to the heart,--for, out of his mouth, they sound to me like a blaspheming of God.'

They bore him toward his house. Alf tremblingly followed the poor Clara, whose eyes were streaming with countless tears, and who on the way vainly sought to check with her handkerchief the flow of blood from the gushing wounds.

At the door of Trutlinger's house the sad train was received by a beauteous maiden. Around her noble, blooming face, floated in profusion the rich curls of her dark locks. The fire of her black eyes, increased by enthusiasm, pierced deep into the heart. Her high forehead, her finely arched nose, her slender and majestic figure, imparted to her whole appearance something queenlike, which even her burgher garb, (in consequence of the strictness of the new belief deprived of every ornament) could not counteract. When she perceived the situation of her unhappy uncle, she wrung her white hands, tears burst from her eyes, which in the bitterness of her grief were raised to heaven, and embellished by her sorrow she stood, a weeping Madonna. The meek, unassuming Clara became wholly eclipsed by her noble figure, at which Alf stood gazing with true devotion. 'For God's sake, what has happened to you, dear uncle?' cried she, accompanying the bearers, who conveyed the sufferer into the nearest lower room and there laid him upon a bed.

'He has practised continual mocking of the holy mission of our prophets,' answered one of the bearers, 'and the prophet Matthias has judged him before the congregation.'

'God be merciful to his poor soul!' murmured the departing populace, and Alf was left alone with the maidens and the dying man.

'How came your senses so entirely to desert you, my poor uncle, as to permit you to fall into so heavy a sin?' moaned the beauteous girl, who was bandaging his wounds with the quiet sorrowful Clara.

'Be silent, simpleton!' angrily replied the old man with his remaining strength. 'My senses have indeed deserted me; but only with the lying spirit of the wicked wretches whom in my madness I held for God's prophets. With my gushing blood departs the delusion which perhaps has cost me my salvation, and I perceive with horror that my poor native city, led astray by crafty imposters, is on the way to ruin for time and eternity.'

'Gracious heavens! he already repeats his offences,' sobbed the gentle maiden. 'We are not alone, uncle,' Clara reminded him in a voice of gentle entreaty.

Trutlinger, raising his weary eyes toward the youth, remained fixedly considering him for a long time; and, as if he finally recollected him, a smile dawned upon his face, which his sufferings chased away. 'If I see rightly,' said he faintly, 'that is a good old acquaintance, before whom no precaution or constraint is necessary. Do I mistake, comrade? Are you not my former faithful apprentice, Alf Kippenbrock?'

'I am the same, my worthy master,' said Alf, approaching and taking his hand, while his tears flowed more mildly.

'This is the finger of God!' exclaimed Trutlinger, and a feeble light relumed his eyes. 'These girls are orphans--their last protector goes to the grave in me. The thought that I must leave their inexperienced youth behind me without protection in this den of murderers, renders my death most afflicting. You were always a good and capable man, Kippenbrock. Promise, then, to your dying master, with the hand and word of a man, that you will shelter and protect these poor children according to the best of your ability.'

Alf cast a friendly glance upon the protegés confided to him. The dark-haired young maiden gleamed upon him with a burning glance, while Clara timidly cast her blue eyes upon the ground. The heart of the youth swelled. He quickly pressed Trutlinger's cold hand and cried, 'I promise it.'

'God reward thee!' faintly uttered the hoary man, his head sank hack and his lacerated breast labored with the death-struggle. Yet once more he suddenly opened his eyes. All radiant were they raised toward heaven. 'Yes,' cried he aloud and joyfully,--'yes, thou hast forgiven the son of earth his errors! I see thy brightness!'--and he was no more.

'Lord, deal not with him in judgment!' prayed the enthusiastic young woman, with pious zeal.

'My second father!' cried Clara, mildly weeping, and, bending down over the dead body, she softly kissed his pale lips.

'No,' cried Alf, with angry grief, 'this sentence was not pronounced and executed in accordance with thy will, Spirit of Mercy!'

CHAPTER II

The next morning Alf stepped into the apartment of his kinsman, Gerhard Kippenbrock, to salute him. The good old man, a worthy butcher by calling, had by the overthrow of all established customs been made second burgomaster of the imperial free city of Munster, without clearly knowing how that precise result had been attained. He advanced to meet the new comer, uncommonly magnificent in his black official dress, with the lace collar and golden chain of honor, and introduced him to a large, raw-boned, meagre man, in a similar dress, who sat at the table staring on vacancy with half-extinguished eyes, in which the flashes of a quiet insanity were occasionally playing.

'Thou hast here the best opportunity to recommend thyself to the favor of our first burgomaster, of brother Bernd Knipperdolling,' said the elder Kippenbrock to the youth. Alf bowed himself low before the singular man, whose appearance affected him disagreeably, and stammered some expressions of respect.

Knipperdolling cast upon him a searching glance, and then said in a hollow and monotonous voice, 'a well formed vessel for the spirit!--thy kinsman, my brother? He may become a bailiff of the city of Zion.'

'God preserve me, revered sir burgomaster!' protested Alf. 'I by no means understand all that the office requires, and should disgrace my undeserved promotion.'

'Whoever hath the spirit,' said Knipperdolling, decisively, 'needs no earthly wisdom.'

'I have taken upon myself a holy duty!' exclaimed the youth with anxiety, shuddering at the burthen of the proffered dignity. 'I have promised to the unfortunate Trutlinger on his death-bed, to take upon myself the care of his two nieces, whom he left unprotected. I shall have plenty to do,--for six journeymen are employed in the workshop of the orphans, and much work is ordered.'

'Let him have his will,' entreated the elder Kippenbrock of his colleague. 'I have known him from his youth up; his head is not equal to the governing of lands and people, but he is a capable armorer, whom we much need in these times when our all rests upon the points of our swords.'

'Have you already been baptised?' asked Knipperdolling.

'Your faith became mine at Amsterdam,' answered Alf, but I have postponed being baptised until I could receive that holy ordinance here, in my native city.'

'Our orator, brother Rothman, will prepare you for it,' said Knipperdolling.

'I hope this brother has already laid a good ground,' said a man in a black ministerial robe, with a cunning, bold, peaked face. 'I shall hold a great baptizing one of these days at the river Aa, and shall expect to see the catechumen previously at my house.'

'We will be his witnesses on that holy occasion,' said Knipperdolling, with a gracious nod of his head, 'I and my colleague Kippenbrock.'

The candidate for baptism stammered his thanks for the unexpected honor, when the door of the room was thrown open with violence, and a young man of Alf's age strode fiercely in. His countenance might have been considered handsome, had it not been for the deathlike paleness and distortion which disfigured it. His large and restlessly rolling eyes-- his dishevelled, bristling hair--his loose coarse garments, which scarcely covered the nakedness of his body--all these gave to his figure a frightful appearance; and Alf was thereby reminded, with a secret shudder, of the altar-piece of a church, where he had seen the adversary represented as tempting our Savior in the wilderness. All present rose reverently at his entrance, and, with their hands crossed upon their breasts, bowed low before the youth.

'Thus speaks the spirit by the mouth of your prophets,' cried he with singular gestures. 'Make outcry in all the streets of Zion, that every one bring all his wealth in gold, silver and jewels, and lay it at the feet of the great prophet, Matthias. There must no longer be rich or poor in the community which the Lord has chosen for himself. Let all belong to all!'

'So mote it be,' cried the hearers, and a gentle sigh from the rich butcher accompanied the response.

'A true christian needs no erudition,' continued he prophet. 'The internal word is of more value than the outward. All books written with the insolent wisdom of men are fruitless and unprofitable, if the doctrines they contain are already proved in the holy scriptures,-- ungodly, if they are opposed to them. Wherefore you must bring all books, except the bible, out of Zion, and collect them at the market before St. Lambert's church, and cause them to be consumed by fire, a burnt offering to the Lord.'

'So mote it be!' again submissively repeated all mouths.

'Whoever sins against one of these commands, roared the prophet, with wild flashing eyes, 'shall die the death!'

'Amen!' said the trembling chorus, and the prophet stalked haughtily out of the door.

'Who was that!' Alf timidly asked his kinsman. 'Johannes Bockhold, our second prophet,' answered he, dejectedly, 'the right hand of the great Matthias.'

'All the books!' sighed the orator Rothman.

'All the gold and silver!' sighed the worthy Kippenbrock, after him, involuntarily raising his hand to his head, as if for the purpose of scratching it, but recollecting in season that this movement was rather unseemly for a new burgomaster, he quickly let it fall again.

'The Lord wills it, and his servants must be obedient,' said Knipperdolling to Kippenbrock. 'Let the commands of the prophet be proclaimed, my brother. I have yet much to do with recording the estates of the exiles, which have become forfeit to the community!'

He departed, and Rothman followed him. 'All the gold and silver!' repeated the elder Kippenbrock sorrowfully, yet once more, and he went after them.

'God forgive me if this feeling be a sin,' cried Alf, when he saw himself alone; 'but these prophets appear horrible to me, and I shall never be able to reconcile my heart to them.'

CHAPTER III

Some days passed away; daring which Alf, without troubling himself much about the disturbances of the city, labored unweariedly in the workshop of the deceased Trutlinger, which in these times gave him an immense deal to do. He was animated by the idea of working and accumulating for the beauteous dark-haired Eliza; and although he could not gain any decided token of favor from the haughty girl, the friendly glances, which she now and then bestowed upon him, were sufficient to keep the flame of love always brightly burning at his heart; and the poor Clara, whose eyes ventured towards him when she thought herself unobserved, became wholly overlooked, as usually happens to the modest violet in the neighborhood of the queenly rose.

One day the wild rattling of the drums called all who could bear arms to the market place. Obedient to the call, Alf equipped himself and his journeymen from the military stock of his workshop, and they were all standing in polished casques and coats of mail, well armed with swords and halberds, when Trutlinger's two nieces entered the shop.

'You are going forth to battle, Kippenbrock!' said Eliza, pressing his hand for the first time with the kindest affability,--whilst Clara remained silently and sadly standing at a distance.

'And with a right good will, dear maiden,' answered Alf, tenderly, 'if your kind wishes accompany the new warrior upon his first expedition.'

'You go to the field of battle for the Word!' exclaimed Eliza with enthusiasm; 'the Holy Spirit is with you and you must conquer.'

'Be careful of your life!' whispered the timorous Clara, scarcely audible, and Alf hastened forth with his companions.

The place of rendezvous, before St. Lambert's church, was already crowded by the people of Munster, collected in compliance with various commands from their prophets. Here, a great fire which was consuming the doomed books of the city, blazed to the heavens,--there, stood two of Munster's deacons for the reception of the jewels of the citizens; two female diviners, well acquainted with the jewels of the city, had the oversight of the business, and accused every one who endeavored to keep back any thing.

Many a pearl, from beauteous eyes, silently bedewed the costly trinkets which were compulsorily brought as offerings to the spirit.

Meantime the military power of the anabaptists had assembled at the rendezvous, and now appeared Matthias in his dark hair-cloth robe. In his hand he held the spear still clotted with the unhappy Trutlinger's blood, and his mouth was foaming with rage.

At his nod the armed men closed in a circle around him.

'That true son of anti-christ,' roared he, 'that reprobate priest of Baal, who once tyrannically ruled over the free burghers of this city, the bishop, with his mercenary troops, comes against you. He has already stretched his camp all about the city; and if we give him time to perfect his entrenchments, the cowards, who dare not meet us man to man, may conquer us at last through hunger. Wherefore thus speaks the spirit: 'Arise, Matthias, gird on thy sword, take with thee five hundred men from out the congregation, go forth and destroy the ungodly whom I have this day given into thy hand.' Arise, then, my brethren! Whoever is truly devoted to our holy cause, whoever is determined never again to bend his neck under the iron yoke, which we have just thrown off, let him step forth from the congregation; the Lord has chosen him for his champion, and the host of the enemy shall be scattered before his arm like chaff before the wind. Amen.'

During this speech Alf was suffering a severe mental conflict. Too readily would he once have measured himself with the episcopalians, whom in his fanaticism he fiercely hated; and nevertheless he had a decided aversion to the prophet under whom he must fight. He was finally decided by the hope of the reception which he should meet with from the fair Eliza, returning home a conqueror; and, as the amen of the prophet was heard, he stepped forth into the centre of the circle. His journeymen and all those who were armorers by trade followed him. To these were joined the other workers in iron, from connection in business. The butchers attached themselves to the nephew of their chief; and, this example being actively imitated, the number of five hundred volunteers was soon more than complete and ready for the field.

'Thou wast the first to step forth,' said Matthias to Alf; 'therefore be thou the first in the army, after me, and lead it on as my general.'

The orator Rothman then embraced the youth, saying: 'Thou shouldst surely this day be taken up into our band through the holy baptism--but now, proceed to the greater business to which the Lord hath called thee;-- and shouldst thou even fall in the field in the cause of God, so wilt thou win the baptism of blood, which is still more efficacious for the remission of sin, according to the doctrines of the oldest church.'

'Come holy spirit, O Lord God!' sang Matthias, the whole multitude joining him in chorus; and brandishing his spear, singing with a louder voice, with uncovered head, and without protective armor, the prophet led to the gates. Alf followed him with the singing host. No sooner had they left the last outworks behind them, than they were met by a portion of the enemy's forces, who were making an attempt to win the city by surprise. The episcopalians were not a little startled when they perceived so stout a band, which, in consequence of the shining mail of the armorers in the front ranks, seemed to them extremely well accoutred.

'Now ask we the Holy Spirit!' exclaimed Matthias, commencing anew the harsh chant, in which his troops joyfully joined. The prophet plunged, singing, spear in hand, into the enemy's ranks. Near him fought Alf, who, more than true to the duty he had undertaken, made of his armor a shield for the protection of the defenceless body of the prophet. The troops, all singing, followed them with the impetuosity of fanaticism. The episcopalian mercenaries, frightened by the furious assault, (and not, like their opponents, inspired with a contempt for death,) made a feeble resistance, soon gave ground, and finally fled with winged feet back to their camp.

'The Spirit has heard us, brethren!' cried Matthias. 'Let us now startle the crimson, seven headed animal, whose name is full of blasphemy, from his den. Let us hurl down the great Babylon from its golden saddle,--that they both may fall into the fiery lake which burns with brimstone. On, on, on!' and, commencing the death song that, under the command of Munzer and Metzler, had before inflamed the unfortunate German peasants to the most furious war of extermination, the prophet pursued the flying episcopalians. 'On, on, on!' he roared incessantly, his spear dripping with the blood of the cowards who gave themselves up to slaughter rather than fight. 'On, on, on!' song the troops, who followed him in quick step, and the victors soon stood before the fortified camp, behind which the armed episcopalians were crowded.

'Yield or die! 'cried Alf, in whom the battle had kindled the warrior's enthusiasm,--and, rushing, to the barrier, he surmounted all obstacles, and stood upon the wall, where his halberd became like the scythe of the angel of death to the besieged. Incited, unceasingly, by Matthias, the crowd followed him as the defenders were driven back, and the anabaptists penetrated deep into their camp, until they reached the place where the banner of the church waved over a richly decorated tent.

'That is the hold of anti-christ!' cried Matthias, rushing into the tent, while Alf drove the enemy wholly out of the camp. As he returned from the pursuit, he heard a mournful cry in the bishop's tent. Pushing in, he saw the prophet pitilessly raging among the defenceless domestics of the runaway bishop. Many dead bodies were already stretched upon the ground, and two beautiful pages were kneeling with closed eyes, before the monster, about to receive the death blow.

Alf forcibly seized the uplifted spear. 'Thou hast appointed me to be the leader of the forces, brother Matthias,' said he, earnestly, 'and I dare not allow that thou shouldst give my troops an evil example by the murder of these defenceless boys, whom we had better take prisoners and keep as hostages, preparing their souls for heaven through our holy baptism. Besides, we have not a moment to lose. The flying men have carried the alarm to the other camp, and new multitudes will soon be thronging here to oppose us. Let us therefore return to Munster while we can convey the booty there in safety.'

'Thou art right, brother!' cried the prophet, subdued by the boldness and decision of the youth. 'Thou understandest the business of war. We will forth. Let our people be called together. This young dragon's-brood, however, we will take with us, and thou shalt be answerable for them with thy head. I will baptise them myself to-morrow morning before all the people.'

The drums called the plundering anabaptists together. The host retreated to the city, laden with rich booty, and the bishop's troops, who had hastened to the assistance of the assailed quarter of the encampment, came just in time to see the rejoicing anabaptists reentering the gates of Munster.

CHAPTER IV

A countless multitude exultingly met the returning victors. The prophet Johannes Bockhold at their head, in white festival garments, with green branches of fir in their hands, the maidens of the city sang to them in loud, joyful hosannas. It pleased the gallant, good humored Alf uncommonly well to receive praise from such beautiful lips. As he reflected, however, that this song of praise was intended as much for Matthias as for himself, there came over Alf a silent vexation, instead of the pleasure of flattered vanity, and he strode on gloomily in front of his troops. The army halted upon the market place, and the booty, being common property, was secured in St. Lambert's church; the two pages were given over to the orator Rothman, preparatory to their baptism; the soldiers having been praised and dismissed, and the evening having already approached, Alf with his surviving journeymen, half their number having fallen either in the first battle or in the storming of the camp, proceeded toward Trutlinger's house.

As he approached the house door, which was surmounted by a triumphal arch covered with pine boughs, he was met by the bewitching smiles of the beautiful Eliza, who was still clad in her white festival garments.

'Welcome from battle and victory, brave soldier of the Spirit!' cried she; and, casting aside all maidenly bashfulness and constraint, she spread wide her arms toward the youth.

'Dear maiden!' stammered he, most agreeably surprised by this second and dearest triumph. He pressed the charming girl to his mailed bosom, when, notwithstanding his unaccommodating helmet, they sought and found each other's lips, and united them with the double glow of fanaticism and sensuality, which both in their blindness mistook for the fire of pure love.

At that moment out stepped from the parlor door a little, withered, yellow man, whose tattered garments were covered by a ragged black mantle. With friendly simpers he squinted out of his little, gray, malicious eyes upon the pair, and then, stretching his meager, death-like hand towards Alf, cried with a hoarse howl, 'Thee have I this day seen in my dreams, brother, contending and conquering in God's cause, and lo! my eyes have verified it, and the Lord has achieved great things through thee, his servant.

Wherefore be glad, because God has chosen thee for yet greater things, and through thee shall his name become glorified in Zion!'

The little hobgoblin with ridiculous pomposity then strode out of the house. Alf looked after him with his hand over his forehead, and said, 'sometimes, though in my native city, it appears to me as if I were in a residence of madmen, where all the fools go at large. Who was that strange man?'

'John Tuiskoshirer,' answered Eliza, reprovingly, 'an impoverished goldsmith; but a great man since the spirit has come upon him. Often, already, has he edified the public by his elevated discourses and divine prophecies; and, next to our great Matthias and Johannes, he is now the first prophet in Munster.'

'Good God! what a multitude of prophets,' sighed Alf; and by this time Eliza had led him into the room.

Behind a table illuminated with wax tapers and decorated as for a festival, sat the fair Clara. Her loose golden locks flowed down over her white gala dress. Her right arm supported her pale, sad face, and bright tears were falling from her eyes upon her white bosom.

'Do you not bid me welcome, lovely little Clara?' Alf kindly asked of the sorrowing girl. 'Do you celebrate our victory with such bitter tears?'

Clara lifted up her eyes toward the youth with gentle sorrow. 'Be not angry with me for it, dear Alf,' she begged in a soft, subdued tone; 'every drop of blood shed in this unhappy war of opinion, falls envenomed upon my heart. Never shall I lose the remembrance of my poor uncle. He also was butchered for the new faith, of which I do not yet rightly understand whether it is the genuine worship of God, or a hellish sacrifice.'

'Leave the foolish girl!' cried Eliza, handing a goblet to Alf. 'Her spirit is not yet born again to the light. She still lies bound in the chains of darkness. She is not able to offer every feeling joyfully upon the altar of the holy God.'

'May He preserve me from such joy!' sighed Clara, almost inaudibly; and Eliza with a quick warm pressure of the hand drew the youth upon a seat near herself. His fellow soldiers seated themselves opposite the beautiful couple, and the ceremonies of the repast began. With the pleasing narration of the conquering warriors and the sweeter praises of the fair Eliza, the generous Rhenish of old Trutlinger glided swiftly and deliciously down, and gradually extinguished in Alf all thoughts of the movements in Munster, which his right worthy head and heart had from time to time obtruded upon him. Deeper glowed the flush upon the blooming faces of the youth and maiden; constantly brisker and more radiantly moved their eyes; with constantly increasing warmth were their kisses given and received. The journeymen, rejected by the grieving Clara, could only keep to the goblet, until, overcome by Bacchus, they staggered one after the other to their places of rest. Alf and Eliza remained quietly sitting at table, as much occupied with each other as if there had been nobody else in the world. Leaning sadly upon her arm, Clara looked through her tears upon the happy pair. Now and then a half suppressed sigh stole from her bosom, and she then placed her hand upon her heart as if she felt a sudden pain there. Already had the second hour after midnight struck upon St. Lambert's tower. Finally Clara rose from her seat, took one of the low-burnt tapers from the table, and remarked with assumed tranquillity, 'it is late, and I am now going to bed,--wilt thou not go with me, sister?'

No answer came, and the poor maiden sorrowfully retired to her own sleeping room.

CHAPTER V

Early in the morning Clara was awakened by a disturbance in the street and came from her chamber, when she saw the couple still there. She hastily disappeared with an exclamation of alarm and grief.

'That must have been my sister!' cried Eliza, starting up with terror, her dark locks breaking loose from the band which had confined them.

'Be not alarmed my beloved,' said Alf with sweetly soothing tones. 'Immediately after my baptism brother Rothman shall bless our union, and our weakness will meet with mild judgment from the spirit of mercy which rules over the new Zion.'

'I will so explain the matter to that foolish girl,' cried Eliza, eagerly--'that she may not again offend me by her cold insufferable silence, her customary weapon when we occasionally disagree. She may censure and envy, but she shall respect me even in my aberration.'

She hastened to her chamber, while Alf prepared to go about his daily pursuits in the workshop. He was met at the door by his fellow wanderer the tailor.

'What have I prophesied?' asked the latter, unceremoniously seating himself at the table which remained as it had been prepared the previous evening. 'What have I prophesied?' he asked again, helping himself to a large slice of the gammon of bacon which he found opposite him upon the table. Then, pouring out a goblet of wine from the bottle and swallowing it, he a third time asked, 'what have I prophesied?'

'The devil only knows!' cried Alf, impatiently. 'There are so many prophecies in Munster that my head has already become wholly confused by them.'

'I have foretold,' said the tailor, with pathos, 'that my beloved friend and brother, the prophet Johannes Bockhold, would one day become a great man in the world. You would not believe it, because in the pride of your big fist, you could not be brought to entertain a good opinion of a tailor. And now a tailor has become your master and sovereign; lord over your life and death.'

'You have got into your cups early,' growled Alf, 'and now being drunk, you make me lose the precious morning hours with your miserable fables.'

'What I say is true,' muttered the tailor through his stuffed cheeks; 'and it is you who are mad and foolish. Only hear how cleverly every thing has been brought about. This morning by day-break, while you were indolently sleeping, the prophet Matthias called all the people to the market. He there declared to them that he would go forth with a handful of people, like Gideon, and slay the host of the ungodly. He called and took with him to the bishop's camp, only thirty men. I know not whether he had not asked of the Spirit aright, or whether the Spirit did not answer him rightly: to be brief, a slaughter did indeed follow,--not of the host of the ungodly, but of the good Gideon and his thirty men; not a man of them escaped. As I afterwards went to the market place, a mournful wailing sounded in my ears. The people were beside themselves, to think that they had lost their ruler in so shameful a manner; and here and there some fools maintained, that the great Matthias must have misinterpreted the Spirit in this affair. Then the still greater Johannes Bockhold stepped forward, and spoke to the multitude. God! what words did this man use to calm, console, and elevate the people! He had known the death of Matthias beforehand. He had seen in the spirit that that great prophet must fall, a second Maccabeus, fighting for the people. Thence we directly perceived that all was in order, that it could by no means be otherwise, and we were content. Then, upon the market-place, we called the preacher of consolation to be our chief ruler,--and he already commands in such a way that it is a pleasure to see him,--he has a wilder and more lordly manner than his predecessor Matthias. His maxim is--that the high shall be brought down, and the lowly shall be exalted. Consequently we shall destroy the churches and make them level with the earth,--because they are the highest buildings in the city. It will be a little tedious, and we also need stout arms for the defence of the walls; we shall, therefore, for the present only plunder the churches a little, until we have leisure for their complete demolition.'

'The churches also to be destroyed!' sighed Alf, 'must that also be? it is most horrible!'

Meanwhile a wild popular tumult arose out of doors. Both hastened to the window. A great multitude of the populace ran by, shouting incoherently. They were followed by a naked man, who came leaping forward as if impelled by a demon, and who, with foaming mouth and strange bodily contortions, incessantly bawled, 'the King of Zion comes!' Thus vociferating, he passed rapidly by. 'The King of Zion comes!' cried the mob who followed him; and Alf, disgusted with such indecent madness, withdrew from the window.

'Who was that madman?' asked he of the tailor, after a moment's pause.

'Did you not know him?' asked the tailor in return. 'That was our highest prophet, Johannes Bockhold himself. The spirit has come over him. I must follow and see what further he will do.'

He went; and Alf, in fearful dubitation said to himself, 'by such a chief is Munster to be governed! It will not and it cannot come to good.'

CHAPTER VI

This last specimen of fanatical rage had made such a decided impression upon the good Alf, that he no longer felt any special desire for that baptism which was to complete his spiritual union with the great prophet; and as, notwithstanding his adherence to the new doctrines, he began to feel a secret loathing of the unceasing exhortations, revelations and prophecies, by means of which the people were kept in such a constant ferment, he devoted himself to assiduous labor for arming the defences of the city, and under this excuse withdrew himself from the public meetings of the populace which were daily drummed together.

For a time his attention was entirely absorbed by his workshop and his Eliza, whose wild tenderness steeped his youthful senses in a sea of pleasure, such as he had never before dreamed of. Clara in her quiet, patient way, observed the happiness of the lovers, who placed no restraint upon themselves on her account; and the only discoverable effect it produced on her was, that she became every day paler and more fragile.

This was perceived by the kind-hearted Alf, and as he happened to find the good child on one occasion alone in her sitting room, engaged at her distaff, he seated himself beside her in a familiar manner and, pressing her hand, asked her, 'what ails thee, my good sister?'

'Ah! call me not so, Kippenbrock,' said Clara, sorrowfully; and gently withdrew her hand.

'Wherefore not?' cried Alf, surprised. 'May I not call thee sister, as thy brother in the faith, and as the future husband of the dear Eliza?'

The maiden raised her tearful eyes to Him on high. 'You pierce my wounded heart,' said she, 'but you do not know the pain you inflict, and therefore do I right willingly forgive you.'

'Again I do not understand you,' said Alf. 'I see you always sorrowful, and I can endure it no longer. I feel myself so happy with your sister, that I desire to render all about me as happy as myself. Therefore confide in me, good maiden, and take my word for it, I will do everything in my power to mitigate your sorrow.'

'*I confide in you!* in *you!*' cried Clara, rising and attempting to retire.

The stout youth held her fast in his arms. 'No,' said he, 'beloved Clara, I will not let you go until you have opened your heart to me. By the holy God, mine is well disposed toward you.'

At that moment the door opened, and the detestable Tuiskoshirer, closely wrapped in his tattered mantle, walked in.

'My God!' shrieked Clara, as she caught a glimpse of him, and violently disengaging herself from Alf's arms, she sprang out of the room.

With a smirk upon his lips, which he seemed to have borrowed from a monkey, the little man followed her with his eyes until she disappeared--then, stepping solemnly in front of Alf, called to him in a hoarse, howling voice, 'art thou willing to become king of Zion, brother?'

'I king of Zion?' asked Alf in return, with the greatest astonishment. 'How can such a thing be?'

'I ask thee,' howled Tuiskoshirer, 'if thou wilt be king over the new Zion, formerly under the anti-christ, called Munster?'

'I rule over this same Munster as its chief magistrate?' cried Alf, laughing. 'That is a wonderful proposition, and besides, it appears to me as if we were not the men to accomplish it.'

'Short sighted man!' growled Tuiskoshirer, 'knowest thou not that the first shall be last and the last shall be first? We are all clay in the hands of the Potter. The Spirit has just seated himself near the board in order to make a king. To that eminence will I raise thee up; for thou art a brave warrior, and moreover a handsome youth, and wilt administer the government with power and mildness, for the welfare of all.'

'Ah! do not propose such pranks to me,' said Alf. 'You have others more suitable for that office than I; and besides, Johannes Bockhold would make a powerful opposition to my mounting the throne.'

'Johannes Bockhold,' answered Tuiskoshirer, 'is a feather in the breath of my mouth. He has indeed thought of announcing himself as the new king of this city, yet shall have only served you, if you will but accept the sceptre. I have seen through the prophet's character; he has much madness, yet little courage, and we need a consummate man upon this iron throne.'

'Are you wholly in earnest in making these propositions?' asked Alf. 'Then I must indeed answer in earnest. I do not feel myself fit to govern a nation and people, nor to take upon myself an office for which I have not been prepared,--from which may God mercifully preserve me!'

'Fool!' cried Tuiskoshirer; 'ruling is as light and easy as it is pleasant.'

'Yet heavy and severe is the reckoning above for bad government,' replied Alf. 'No, seek thee another king.'

Tuiskoshirer then flung open his tattered mantle, and drew from under its folds a magnificent regal crown, ingeniously formed of fine gold, and splendidly radiant with diamonds, rubies, emeralds and sapphires, and, as he turned and waved it here and there in the sunlight, the golden and colored sparkles played so gaily about the room, that Alf was compelled to turn away his blinded eyes.

'In this crown is placed all my earthly wealth,' said Tuiskoshirer, pathetically. 'Ingeniously have I made it, during the stillness of the night, as an offering for the Spirit, that he therewith might crown the new king of Zion. Thee have I selected therefor, from among a thousand. Do you but consent, and I will set this emblem of royalty upon your head, and with God's help I will maintain it there.'

The youth looked at the beautiful crown for a moment, and its golden lustre seemed to awaken his ambition; but his better self soon conquered. 'Leave me, tempter!' cried he with vehemence, and forcibly replacing the bauble under the prophet's mantle, he dexterously pushed him out through the door.

'You will repent of this,' howled the little man as he disappeared.

CHAPTER VII

'The duodecemvir, Dilbek, would speak with you,' announced an apprentice to the industrious Alf an hour afterwards. Surprised at the visit of a person whose name and office were alike unknown to him, he repaired to the parlor, where, in respectable black judicial robes, his comical fool's face peeping above a colossal white ruff, and his diminutive form attached to a long thrusting sword, strutted before him the aerial tailor.

'Knowing that you would feel an interest in my happiness, my good fellow,' (snarled and lisped the new duodecemvir, in an incredibly gentlemanlike manner,) 'I could not forbear informing you in person of the good fortune which has come to me through the mercy of the Spirit.'

'What means this masquerade?' cried Alf, peevishly. 'Take off that fool's jacket again; it does not become you, upon my word.'

'Have respect, my friend,' said Dilbek, earnestly. 'Every official dress confers honor upon its wearer, and this it has become my duty to wear, as one of the twelve judges over Israel.'

'You? you become a judge?' laughed Alf. 'Go and seek some other fool to believe you.'

'You are and always will be an unbelieving Thomas,' cried Dilbek angrily; 'and doubt every thing that you cannot feel with your hands. I repeat to you that I have even now come from the market, where the people have established the new tribunal.'

'And the mayor and aldermen, who governed until now?' asked Alf.

'Unseated, all unseated!' answered the tailor, who stalked about the room examining himself. 'Your kinsman again slays his cattle and his swine with his own hands; and the good Knipperdolling, a learned man, and therefore not able to turn his hand to any thing useful, has become the official hangman, with which the poor man will still be able to procure a livelihood.'

'Good God!' exclaimed Alf, 'who has done this?'

'This wise transformation of our government proceeds from our chief prophet,' answered the tailor-judge. 'Since he, moved by the Spirit, ran through the streets in the condition of holy nature, he had not spoken a word, but made himself understood by writing; he was compelled to remain mute three days. When that time had elapsed he declared the new commands of the Spirit. Yesterday the honorable counsellors obediently laid down their offices, and today I have been installed with my lordly colleagues.'

'God preserve my reason!' cried Alf. 'By these mad movements and continual changes, I incur the danger of losing it.'

'Only be patient,' said the tailor mysteriously. 'Better things will come. I have already heard various whispers. Our prophet is not the man to stop half way. Think of what I told you when we were traveling to Munster; it is not yet the end of time! I must now leave you, as we judges are invited to a feast by the chief prophet. He marries, this day, the beautiful widow of his predecessor, the great Matthias. Farewell! I shall always remain friendly to you, and should I hereafter rise yet higher on the scale of honor, you will always find in me a patron and protector.'

After one or two failures, the duodecemvir finally succeeded in passing himself and his new sword through the room door.

'Surely!' cried Alf impatiently, 'if this tailor-spirit is to set such vagabonds upon the judgment-seat of my native city, I may soon repent that I refused the crown. It would at least have given me the power to hinder many acts of madness.'

CHAPTER VIII

Some time afterwards, Alf was sitting arm in arm with his Eliza in the family sitting-room, while Clara was spinning near the window, and moistening the thread with her bitter tears. Suddenly the door flew open, and in clattered a stout young trooper, who extended his hand to Alf, joyously exclaiming, 'God bless you, my dear school fellow! Do you not know me?'

'Hanslein of the long street!' cried Alf, embracing the friend of his youth. 'Welcome to Munster!'

'Hanslein of the long street?' asked the beautiful Eliza, with surprise and displeasure. 'How is this? were you not an episcopalian?'

'Certainly,' answered Hanslein, 'with body and soul, until the day before yesterday. On that day I got into a quarrel with my serjeant while drinking with him, and laid my blade over his head in a way that he will not easily forget. Life is as dear to me as to any other man, and therefore I made my way out of the bishop's camp, rode over to yours, and now let your orator but once more wash my head, and I am prepared to contend bravely with my old brethren in arms.'

'When the chief prophet holds you worthy of being received into our community!' sharply observed Eliza, who was highly offended at the frivolous conversation of the renegade.

'The worthy tailor has already received me with open arms,' answered Hanslein. 'I have become captain of the seventh company, and am quartered with the burgomaster-hangman Knipperdolling, where we have wine and women in abundance.'

Eliza rose up indignant, and silently motioned to Clara to follow her. The latter obeyed, and the two friends were left alone.

'A pair of pretty maidens!' said Hanslein, looking admiringly after them; 'and you are indeed a lucky dog, to be a favorite with both.'

'I am the promised bridegroom of the eldest,' answered Alf, 'and know my duty.'

'An anabaptist, and so affectedly coy?' laughed the hair-brained fellow. 'You court them both at the same time, I'll be sworn; and should any one attack you on that account, you need only refer to the example of our chief prophet.'

'It cannot be possible!' exclaimed Alf with abhorrence.

At this moment Clara stepped into the room, placed before Alf a pitcher of wine and two goblets, and then again retired.

Hanslein observed her attentively, and said as she went out, 'deny no longer, you rogue, that both the maidens are yours. I found you in the arms of one of them, and the long, tender glance which the other just now threw upon you, confesses enough.'

'I tell you that you are mistaken!' cried Alf impatiently, filling the cups to the brim; 'leave your joking, and join me in drinking success to our good cause.'

'With all my heart!' said Hanslein, striking his glass against Alf's, and then pouring down the wine; 'although I am not yet quite clear as to exactly where the good cause is to be found, here, or in the camp of our old master. To return once more to my former theme, you render life needlessly unpleasant both to yourself and to the poor damsels. You would do much better to marry them both.'

'You are out of your senses!' exclaimed Alf, angrily. 'How can I sin against the commandments of God?'

'First point out to me one passage in the bible which prohibits polygamy,' said Hanslein; 'and what is not prohibited is allowed! The old beards, the patriarchs, always indulged themselves in that way. To be sure, when the wives come directly in each other's way, it may be a little stormy in the house, as father Abraham learned long ago to his sorrow; but, after all, you are the man to seize and hold the reins of government firmly, and to interfere decidedly, if your wives should show a disposition to kick out of the traces.'

Alf could not refrain from laughing at the chatterer, and finally said, 'I know not how you came by the conceit of advocating double marriages, but to a poacher like you, I should suppose it would be pleasanter to beat up game in the preserves of others.'

'There will remain enough for me on both sides of the hedge,' said Hanslein; 'and a handsome young man like you must be the first to follow any new fashion, especially so pleasant a one as this.'

'The chief prophet might disapprove of the new fashion,' said Alf; 'even according to our old laws, there is a heavy penalty against polygamy.'

'The chief prophet!' laughed Hanslein. 'The doctrine which I have just now been preaching to you came from his own mouth. How else could I have conversed so learnedly upon the subject?'

'The chief prophet!' cried Alf in amazement.

'Just so,' answered Hanslein. 'When he saw that I recognized him, he beckoned me to approach, and presented a purse of ducats to me, giving me at the same time an excellent lecture upon the duty of every christian to take more than one wife; it is a prerogative, said he, which God reserves for his holy children; and he intimated his determination to explain the matter to the community, and moreover that he would himself take fifteen wives, on account of the good example which he was bound to set the people.'

'This can never prosper!' thought Alf, shaking his head.

'What can be impossible to the godly tailor?' exclaimed Hanslein, swallowing the last glass. 'Farewell brother! I must now to the parade, and relieve the early morning watch. When I am at liberty, if you should indeed conclude to marry both of the damsels, then I ask it as a particular favor that I may be invited to the marriage feast.'

He bustled forth; but Alf remained sitting in a melancholy reverie. 'Even polygamy is now encouraged!' sighed he. 'Every good old moral custom is broken! How must it end?'

CHAPTER IX

At the new gate, where the river Aa empties itself into the Ems, Alf had his watch as the chosen captain of the armorers. It was already deep night--he lay upon his field bed, and the images of Eliza and Clara were floating confusedly before his half closed eyes. Suddenly he heard the burgher sentinel hail some one, and immediately afterwards Hanslein stepped into the officers' quarters, wrapped in a mantle.

'What brings you here so late, brother?' asked Alf, springing up in astonishment.

'Mischief, my brother,' whispered Hanslein. 'I come in the name of the chief prophet. First of all, get your men quickly and quietly under arms, and let their guns be carefully loaded; double all the guards, and let strong patrols be sent out. The city is in danger from without and within!'

Alf proceeded silently to the large guard room, to execute the command; then, returning to his friend, he eagerly asked him the cause of the alarm.

'Polygamy,' answered Hanslein, of which we examined the pleasant bearings the day before yesterday has now turned out confoundedly serious. Early this morning while you were upon guard, the prophet Johannes Bockhold caused the populace to be drummed together and laid the hazardous question before them. An old burgher, who might already have had domestic trouble enough at home, coldly gave his opinion that the adoption of such a course would be warring against the bible and against all christendom. Thereupon Johannes, who cannot bear much contradiction, became furious, caused the old man to be seized on the spot, and made, by the aid of friend Knipperdolling, a head shorter. Such a mode of stating the counter argument was too sudden and too violent for the people. They laid their heads together here and there, and a number of malcontents determined, at a secret meeting, to give up the city to the episcopalians this night. But lord Johannes, who has a very fine nose, got wind of them in time. He has taken his measures yet more secretly than his foes, and Knipperdolling will do a fine business early in the morning.'

'Never-ending slaughters!' murmured Alf, sorrowfully. 'What we have gained is hardly an equivalent for the blood spilled in its attainment.'

'The tree of spiritual freedom,' said Hanslein ironically, shrugging his shoulders, 'must be properly watered, if you would have it grow and thrive.'

Meanwhile, the patrols having returned to the guard room, Hanslein went out to meet them. 'All right!' was the word from all sides. Only the detachment who had been scouring the out works, thought that they had heard a suspicious rustling of arms in the distance.

'And you went no nearer to see what was going on?' interrupted Alf: 'Then I must take a turn myself, and see what mischief is brewing. Forward!'

He and Hanslein carefully led the patrol through the little side-door out over the bridges. 'Stand here silently,' commanded Alf,--'I will go softly forward with the captain. As soon as you hear any noise, move quickly towards it.'

Alf and Hanslein now proceeded stealthily forward, constantly further and further, behind the angles of the outworks, carefully bending close to them. Suddenly they heard at a distance the clattering of spurs which rapidly approached.

'Let us conceal ourselves behind the palisades,' whispered Hanslein to Alf. They had hardly concealed themselves when the rattling of the spurred heels approached. The obscure forms of two men became visible in the darkness. They passed by the concealed friends and then stopped.

'That is the place,' said a deep bass voice. 'Give the sign, serjeant.' The other figure then raised his hand to his mouth, and repeated three times a clear-sounding tone imitating a bird-call.

'Now upon them!' cried Alf, springing from behind the palisades, seizing the first figure by the right arm with the strength of a bear, and placing his sword at his breast. At the same moment Hanslein dealt a powerful blow upon the second figure. 'Jesus Maria!' cried the latter, and instantly disappeared in the darkness.

'Coward! 'growled the other; but Alf mastered him. 'No noise, nor any attempt at resistance, or I shall be compelled to strike you down. You must follow us into the city.'

'Thus to end!' groaned the prisoner--and at that moment the first rays of the rising moon beamed over the edge of the horizon and threw their light upon the captive. He was a stately old cavalier, with a chain of honor over his shining silver harness, and a most venerable countenance, from which even his unhappy accident had not been able to drive the impress of determined spirit and courage.

Alf was troubled by his steady gaze, which excited emotions of respect and esteem. He looked inquiringly at Hanslein, who returned a similar glance, and both remained standing by their prisoner, as if by tacit agreement.

'Shall we deliver this noble form to the terrible Johannes?' at last asked Alf of his fellow soldier.

'It would certainly make me very unhappy to see this head fall under the axe of the executioner,' murmured Hanslein.

'You think and feel as I do, brother,' cried Alf, joyfully. 'Therefore pursue your way in peace, sir colonel, or whatever else you may chance to be. We will have no part in the shedding of your blood!'

'Shall I have to thank anabaptists for my life and liberty?' asked the knight, half indignant and half astonished.

'Accept it, however,' said Alf, 'and with it the proof that the people of Munster are not all such monsters as you may have believed until now. If this friendly service appears to you to be thankworthy, you can repay it with like clemency when one of our brethren falls into your hands.'

'That will I, comrade, by my word,' answered the knight, much affected. 'To prove that my feelings are equally good toward you, I invite you to follow me into our camp. People of your stamp are not in their right place in that den of wild beasts, who sooner or later must come to an ignominious end.'

'Spare your words,' answered Alf. 'We hold fast to our faith.'

'And have divers cogent reasons besides,' said Hanslein, (grasping his neck in a manner not to be misunderstood,) 'to decline the honor of visiting the lord bishop.'

'Our men approach,' said Alf, looking toward the city. 'Depart, sir knight, before it is too late.'

'God teach you the right path, poor erring wanderers,' said the knight, compassionately, as he hastened away.

Scolding as he went, Alf approached his troops. 'Were you not ordered to advance upon the first alarm?' growled he. 'Heard you not when I gave the word for the onset? Had you been there, as it was your duty to have been, we should have taken an episcopalian field officer. He has escaped to his followers, and we must hasten back to the city, lest we be finally cut off and taken prisoners.'

The honest Munsterers exculpated themselves in the best way they could, entreating that their oversight might not be made known to the grim prophet; and with drooping heads followed the two friends back into the city.

CHAPTER X

An alarm, as if the world were sinking, was now raised in Munster. The bells rung, the drums beat, and the armed masses ran together, filling the air with their wild shouts. Alf and Hanslein mounted the wall over the gate and looked down upon the city, in the streets of which torches were every where blazing. From the market before St. Lambert's church the light of an immense fire arose to the heavens, and the sounds of a horrible shouting and screaming as from many thousands came thence over the city.

'This is a dreadful night,' said Alf, leaning sadly upon his sword.

'If I should say,' observed Hanslein, 'that the appearance of the city was particularly pleasing to me, I should tell a falsehood. Were it not for my unlucky affair with the serjeant, I would have gone to the episcopalian camp with the field officer, in God's name.'

Finally, a certain degree of order seemed to prevail in the chaos about the market place, although like every thing there, it was of a horrible nature. To a short, ferocious yell of the populace succeeded a profound and terrible pause--then cracked a volley of musketry, and then again another pause--and so alternately screams, pauses and reports of fire-arms, until Hanslein had counted twenty volleys.

'What can that musketry mean?' asked Alf in an undertone, with some misgivings as to the nature of the proceedings.

'Master Johannes may just now be undertaking to sift his flock,' said Hanslein.

'Must it then be,' exclaimed Alf with bitter grief, 'that by every revolution, although intended to promote the welfare of the whole people, men must be placed at the head who have no hearts in their bodies, and who rule by destroying the lives of their brethren!'

'It appears so, answered Hanslein; 'Whoever is placed at the head by popular commotions, must himself be a bold demagogue who has no property, character or conscience to lose. To leap over every obstacle and ward off every danger by the destruction of a dozen or two of his fellow men, is nothing at all to him. People like you, my brother, would make right good leaders, for which nothing is really requisite but vigor, honesty and sound sense; but honest people draw back from such opportunities from a want of self confidence, and thereby give the devils free scope to do evil, which is very wrong!'

Alf, reminded by this conversation of Tuiskoshirer's rejected crown, and of old Fabricius's prophecy, at last sorrowfully exclaimed, 'in an unhappy hour came I home, to my native city!' and proceeded to join the guard.

CHAPTER XI

The next morning, when Alf's guard was relieved, he marched his men by the market place. Horrible was the sight which there awaited him. The square before St. Lambert's church was converted into an immense slaughter yard, and filled with human flesh. A great number of unfortunates were bound to stakes and shot through; a part of whom had bled out their lives, and a part were still writhing and twisting in the agonies of the death struggle. Others lay upon the bloody pavement, some hacked to pieces with the sword and some beheaded, The ranting Knipperdolling in his robes of office, his face flushed, with naked and blood-sprinkled arms, was continually and unweariedly swinging his broad executioner's sword over victims, who, either voluntarily or forced by armed men, were kneeling before him.

'Left wheel!' commanded Alf, averting his eyes; and he led his men through side-streets and by-ways to the company's parade ground.

As the men were separating, and Alf proceeding to his own quarters, he was met by poor Clara, who came to him, her eyes red with weeping, and with despair depicted on her countenance.

'Will you grant me a private conversation?' said she; 'it concerns my life--and though you may deem that of little consequence, still your heart is too good not to feel a sympathy for an unfortunate being, whose last hope is in your protection.'

'In God's name, what is going forward?' asked Alf, alarmed, leading the maiden into the garden adjoining the house. 'Speak, dear Clara, and open your heart to me. My blood for thee!'

'The chief prophet and the twelve judges,' answered Clara, 'have published a mandate, by which a plurality of wives is not only allowed but commanded. Not to avail one's self of this spiritual license, is deemed a crime. Spies search all houses and drag forth the marriageable maidens; who are compelled to marry instantly. I hoped to find a defence of my maiden honor in my insignificance; but the hideous Tuiskoshirer has selected me for his third wife. Rather than consummate my ruin by giving my hand to that disgusting madman, I would jump into the river Aa, and there find an end to my life and my afflictions.'

'With God's help,' cried Alf, 'you shall neither jump into the river, Clara, nor into Tuiskoshirer's arms; in which indeed you might find worse repose. Is the old wizard mad, that he lifts his eyes to so pretty a maiden?'

'There is but one way left for my deliverance,' said Clara. 'You are too many my sister, dear brother-in-law--wherefore I beg of you to bestow upon me, out of compassion, the name of one of your wives, that it may protect me from the impudence of his hateful assaults. Understand me rightly,' added she, earnestly;' I ask to be one of your wives in *name only*. This relation shall give neither to you nor me new duties nor new rights--and when the fate of this unhappy city once changes, then shall we two in no respect be bound to each other.'

'Such an apparent marriage only, will be but little pleasant to either party,' replied Alf. 'Should you not rather find in Munster some young handsome fellow, with whom you may be married in a proper and orderly manner, according to the commandments of God?'

'God preserve me from men!' cried Clara, a deep crimson suddenly suffusing her pale cheeks. 'After what I have here witnessed they have all become my detestation. Even you I select only upon irresistible compulsion, and because the connection can be so arranged that I may be called by your name without belonging to you.'

'This courtship is certainly not particularly polite, my little Clara,' said Alf; 'but before you leap into the water with me, it is necessary that I should say yes. I wish I could have first explained the matter properly to your sister--I know not whether the imperious damsel will be so willing to accommodate herself to the new decree of the twelve judges.'

'The life of her sister is at stake,' cried Clara, in deep agony, 'who will most willingly remain a maiden after, as before, and renounce every right to even a friendly look from her husband.'

'It will be a strange marriage,' mustered Alf, rubbing his hands in much perplexity; 'nevertheless let us trust in God. It would be well, if these times produced nothing more wonderful in old Munster.'

'There comes the monster! Protect me, Kippenbrock!' shrieked Clara, hiding her face in Alf's bosom.

Alf looked up and saw Eliza conducting Tuiskoshirer into the garden. After him pressed a ragged and armed multitude.

'Whatever you may do, my brother,' howled the prophet, 'I yet cannot desert you. Our names must stand near each other in the book of the Spirit.

You have contemptuously rejected the alliance which I proposed to you out of the goodness of my heart; nevertheless, to-day I propose a new band which shall bind us both in brotherhood. I ask for the sister of your betrothed, dear brother-in-law, and desire to take her home with me as my christian wife.'

'I regret, my brother,' said Alf, encircling Clara with his arms, 'that you come too late. In obedience to the new law, I have asked the maiden to become my second wife, and have obtained her consent.'

'Indeed!' escaped from the proud Eliza, while she bit her lips and darted a not altogether sisterly glance at the poor Clara.

'Heigh!' stammered Tuiskoshirer, in a tone of mingled fear and anger.

'Your courtship take precedence of that of the great prophet Tuiskoshirer!' cried one of the ragged bridal train, springing towards Clara, seizing her by the arm and endeavoring forcibly to drag her to her detested suitor. Alf instantly seized him by the body and with a powerful swing threw him over the garden fence. 'Who else will interfere?' cried he, lustily, making after the multitude, who in great trepidation were seeking the door.

'An insolent reply was all that I wanted,' snarled Tuiskoshirer, as he followed his retreating rabble.

'Sister and sister-in-law at the same time?' asked Eliza in a tone of bitterness, pointing towards Clara. 'I might at least have been previously informed of it,' said she, leaving the garden in a rage.

'Necessity knows no law, dear Eliza,' pleaded Alf, following her.

'It is a heavy duty which I have taken upon me,' said Clara to herself, 'to preserve the appearance of coldness toward the man whom I love better than all the world beside; but God will help me.'

CHAPTER XII

In the course of the next week Alf had sufficiently softened Eliza's anger: she had with a heavy heart learned to share her beloved husband's name with her unloved sister, and Alf now went to his worthy kinsman, the former burgomaster Kippenbrock, to invite him to the marriage feast. He found the good man a perfect contrast to his terrible ex-colleague; in the short brown butcher's jacket and white apron, with his sleeves rolled up, he was standing in his shop, making sausages;--his full, red, contented face covered with glistening drops of perspiration, a proof that he pursued his occupation with right good will.

'I am rejoiced, good kinsman, that you have so easily submitted to the loss of political greatness.'

'Yes, kinsman,' answered Gerhard familiarly, laying down his sausage-knife, 'to thee I may say it; thou wilt keep clean lips, and so it will remain in the family--when I was compelled to lay down the burgomastership and take off the chain of honor, I might as well have been knocked on the head with an axe, like one of my own fat oxen, and I bore my deposition not at all submissively; but as I reflected more upon the subject, I came to consider it less an evil, and now all is well with me. There was much vexation about the office also, and I oftentimes felt that I was not adapted to it. When a man once undertakes to perform duties, which his education has not prepared him for, he always continues unsuitable for the place, and often inadvertently does great injustice to the people. It was truly a fortunate circumstance, however, that my learned colleague Knipperdolling had sufficient acuteness to keep us out of difficulty, else I should have been compelled to abandon my office on the first day. Now, comparatively, I live in heaven, slaughtering my oxen and my swine, which I understand thoroughly--my sausages are always the best in Munster--and it is wholly a different thing when one is quite at home in his employment. Mark me, if the chief prophet should at any time offer me an office, so true as my name is Gerhard Kippenbrock, I would say NO, and would stick to my hatchet and chopping-block!'

Alf praised his noble renunciation of office, and then formally brought forward his invitation.

'I wish you much happiness!' cried Gerhard, heartily shaking his kinsman's hand. 'That all the preparations of the meat kind for the marriage and festival are to be my care, is already understood; and I may, moreover, take some care for the new housekeeping.'

Alf wished to protest against such great generosity; but he answered,--'I, an old housekeeper, must understand these things better than a young chicken like you,--I know what one housewife has cost me, and you take two at once. There are the rich trencher-caps, the bodices, the cloth and silk doublets and robes, and the furred cloak, and shoes and stockings, and the golden ornaments, and the bed and other white linen, all in double proportion--and, God preserve us, finally the baby-clothes and the cradle also. You will be compelled to wield your hammer merrily in the workshop, and will be too much occupied to be able to make the necessary preparations, and your old butcher kinsman will stand you in good stead.

To strike out one half of this formidable list, Alf related to him how he had come by his second bride.

'Heigh! surely! let us see!' exclaimed Gerhard: 'the child's conduct pleases me very much. To be sure it is a singular circumstance, and the prophet might make various objections to it if it were made known to him; but I rejoice heartily that it has afforded you an opportunity to obtain the maiden; who, I honestly confess to you, was the one of the two sisters whom I always wished you might have. She has an angel's heart. Eliza is not bad; but she has an imperious domineering spirit, and will often warm your head for you; particularly if the little Clara should in time excite an interest in your heart.'

Alf's asseverations, that he could be in no danger of so great an evil, were drowned by the noise and cries of an immense multitude of people who crowded the streets on their return from the market place.

'There has been another public day,' grumbled Gerhard, looking through the window; 'and so it goes on continually. They crowd to the public meetings and make much noise with their debates; but nothing is effected for the general good, and meanwhile the bishop is constantly diminishing the limits within which he has enclosed us; so that we shall soon be unable to go outside the city walls. I am heartily tired of the whole business. So long as my oxen hold out, and I can drive them to our pasture, so long will I look on; but when that ends, God will forgive my sins if I become an episcopalian as well as others.'

'Hush, kinsman!' cried Alf, who that moment caught a glimpse of the duodecemvir Dilbek, passing by the street window.

Gerhard clapped his hands upon his mouth as the tailor danced into the shop and embraced the stout butcher with friendly warmth.

'I greet thee dear brother and colleague!' cried he in ecstasy.

'Colleague?' murmured Gerhard, turning himself again to his sausage table. 'We are not so far.'

'What did I say,' cried Dilbek, slapping Alf upon the shoulder: 'what did I say to you on our way towards Munster?'

'Your conversation has not so much weight with me as to cause me to mark or remember it,' answered Alf, peevishly.

'I said,' declaimed Dilbek, 'give to our prophet, our great Johannes, the world, and he would govern it in fine style. Now, the commencement is made. Johannes the First, has this day become king over Zion, otherwise called Munster.'

'King!' cried Alf and Gerhard in a breath.

'King,' repeated Dilbek. 'And he has obtained the honor in his usually sly way. Early this morning he caused us, the twelve judges, to be called to his house. 'Thus saith the Lord,' declared he to us; 'Even as I aforetime have taken Saul and after him David, from tending their sheep, and made them kings over my people, so set I Johannes Bockhold, my prophet, to be king over Zion.'

'King!' sighed Alf inaudibly, and once again thought with bitter repentance of Tuiskoshirer's crown.

'Honestly to confess it,' pursued the chattering Dilbek, 'this declaration was not much to our taste, as it lessened our official authority, and we had much to urge against it; but there we struck the wrong chord. 'Ye short sighted men!' cried the prophet; 'must I not take this office upon myself against my will? Rather would I drive horses and oxen, did I not feel myself irresistibly drawn by the hand of God. Therefore down, instantly;--resign your offices and do homage to your king.'

'The man has a methodical madness in depriving people of offices and honors,' growled Gerhard, vexed by his reminiscences.

'Still we were not satisfied,' continued Dilbek; 'and as we knew of no other expedient, we referred the whole matter to the people. That, however, did not help us. While Johannes labored with us, that withered old fox, Tuiskoshirer, wrought upon the people; and as we judges in a body accompanied the prophet to the market-place, the little man came to meet us there with a large naked sword, which he presented to Johannes, saying in a howling voice, 'In the name of God I give to thee, Johannes, the kingly dignity: govern thy people well! Long live the king of Zion! shouted the multitude with one voice, while we judges were standing and looking as though the butter had fallen from our bread. His kingly majesty, however, permitted mercy to prevail over right, and advanced a part of us to high honors; graciously remembering his old fellow laborers in God's kingdom. Knipperdolling is raised from the office of executioner to be governor of the city, Varend Rothman is the royal orator, I am lord steward, four of the twelve judges have been made royal counsellors, and in you, sir Gerhard, have I the honor and pleasure of greeting the royal treasurer.'

'No jokes!' blustered the butcher, whilst his full-moon face, lighted up by joy, once more exhibited a glistening crimson.

'I should be ashamed of myself,' said Dilbek, 'to jest in an unseemly manner with one of the high officers of the kingdom of Zion.'

'These incessant changes and innovations are almost enough to turn one's brain,' said Gerhard, while Alf was pouring water upon his hands with which he carefully washed his face and arms.

At the same time Dilbek continued: 'I bring to the lord treasurer the invitation of his majesty to repair immediately to the royal palace, to receive further commands.'

'My black dress suit, Susanna!' cried Gerhard, looking into the sitting room; 'my mantle, my plumed cap, my golden chain and sword!'

'Is your name nevertheless still called Kippenbrock?' asked Alf, significantly, by way of reminding his fickle kinsman, of his former protestations.

'Hold your tongue!' cried the new treasurer, as with inconceivable celerity (notwithstanding his corpulency) he encased himself in the official robes which his wife with joyful surprise had brought him.

'If it be agreeable to you, my lord steward,' said Gerhard to Dilbek, 'I will now accompany you to the king's majesty.'

'I commend myself to you, lady treasurer,' said Dilbek with a profound bow to the butcher's wife, and the two lords of the new kingdom departed.

'Now is Munster indeed wholly mad,' said Alf, 'and my worthy kinsman with the rest. If I were only so myself, I should feel better than I now do in my clear moments.'

CHAPTER XIII

About mid-day some time afterwards, Alf came from his workshop to the parlor. The dinner already smoked upon the table; but his two elected brides were standing at the window eagerly examining some pieces of money which Tuiskoshirer was showing to them. Alf approached the group.

'The gold and silver money which the new king has caused to be coined,' said Tuiskoshirer in a friendly and honied tone, laying a couple of pieces in his hand. Alf read on the reverse:

'The Word has become flesh and dwells amongst us. Whosoever is not born of water and of the Spirit cannot enter into the kingdom of God. One king over us, one God, one Faith, one Baptism. At Munster, 1534.'

'That is God's government, may it soon extend over the whole world!' sighed Tuiskoshirer, most religiously rolling up his eyes.

'Under these kings we shall soon arrive at the pinnacle of prosperity!' exclaimed Eliza, turning over the money in Alf's hand. On the other side, the wild inspired face of the prophet, in his kingly dress, boldly cut and well resembling the original, presented itself to the eyes of the beholder.

Alf looked upon the wild and passionate eyes of the presentment, which seemed almost to roll in the masterly impression, and, mentally recurring to the pitiless human butchery with which the prophet had commenced the exercise of power, shudderingly cast the money upon the table.

Eliza hastily took up the largest piece to gaze once more upon the crowned figure. 'Yes,' she finally exclaimed, forgetting herself, 'that is a king for the whole world or none.'

'What is the matter with you, Eliza?' asked Alf, with surprise. 'You have never before spoken of the prophet with such partiality.'

'Crowns make beautiful!' whispered Tuiskoshirer, with a malicious laugh, and at that instant lord steward Dilbek rushed into the room.

'To the windows, children, if you wish to see something very particularly magnificent. The king is making his first tour through the city on horseback, and will immediately pass this way.'

'The king?' asked Eliza with joyful surprise, a deeper and more beautiful crimson suffusing her face as she hastened out of the room.

'What can all this mean?' sighed Alf, looking a moment after her, and then stepping to the window.

Nearer and nearer sounded the cry, 'Hail king of Zion!' from the dense multitude who preceded the royal procession through the streets.

'Now give attention,--here comes the procession,' cried Dilbek. Already were heard the snorting and neighing of the first of the king's horses. At the head of the procession came four pages, in costly gold-embroidered velvet garments; a naked sword with a golden hilt, Tuiskoshirer's crown upon an open bible, the golden globe (emblem of imperial power), and two crossed swords, borne by lords and gentlemen, followed.

'That beautiful, light-haired boy who bears the great sword, is the bishop's own son,' whispered Dilbek to Alf, who recognized in the two foremost pages the victims he had torn from the tiger claws of the ferocious Matthias.

'Poor youths,' said he, 'hardly may I rejoice that I saved your miserable lives, since this compulsory servile duty rendered to your father's deadly enemy, must destroy the Spirit; which is a far greater evil than the destruction of the body.'

Now came, snorting and prancing, the dapple-grey charger that bore the king. The fair youth, who found himself quite at home in his high station, presented in his princely attire a truly majestic appearance. High white ostrich feathers waved over the jeweled ornaments of his purple cap. Through the slashed folds of his gold-embroidered over-dress appeared the under garment of purple velvet, trimmed with gold lace. The ermine mantle which floated down upon the golden saddle cloth of the noble steed, completed the beautiful *tout-ensemble*, and Alf himself, notwithstanding his inward dislike of the prophet, could hardly conceal his admiration.

'Is it not true, that dress makes the man?' triumphantly whispered the lord steward to him. 'All this is the work of my ingenious needle. For three nights I have not been in bed,--in which time I directed the execution of all the difficult portions of the work. Now, God be praised! every thing has prospered with me, and I want to see, who will recognize the mass-dress out of which I have put it all together.'

Meanwhile the king had passed by. Behind him came governor Knipperdolling and treasurer Kippenbrock, superbly mounted. Twelve yeomen of the guard, clothed in the royal livery, ash-color and green, upon princely horses with golden saddles, brought up the rear. The procession now halted a moment. Alf leaned farther out of the window to see what had occurred. He just then perceived that the king was bowing with indescribable grace to the fair Eliza, who, to see the better, had stationed herself before the house door. In sweet confusion the graceful girl returned the royal greeting, and, as the prince finally rode on after the bearers of the regalia, looked long and earnestly after him.

'This is a sudden and wonderful change!' exclaimed Alf, angrily. 'I see well that I must celebrate my nuptials to-morrow; if, indeed they are ever to be celebrated.'

'Hadst thou accepted my offer, brother,' said Tuiskoshirer, in a tone of friendly reproach, 'thou wouldst have spared thyself this, and who knows how many more afflictions.'

Followed by Dilbek, he went forth. Alf remained, in a pensive mood, thoughtlessly playing with the coins which had been left upon the table. 'Yes, truly,' murmured he at length, with bitterness, 'he who dares to coin money is held in higher consideration than he who is obliged to receive it in the way of business.'

The gentle Clara then approached him. 'Do not be angry with my sister,' said she, entreatingly, in her kind way. 'Her heart is good in the main, and she will soon repent of an error into which she has been led by her vanity and pride.'

'Good hearted child!' exclaimed Alf, affected by the faithful intercession of the rejected one; 'why has not that ungrateful girl thy heart and soul, or thou her beautiful exterior? Then nothing would have been wanting to my happiness!' He went out; and Clara retired to her chamber, where she secretly and bitterly wept over the well intended but deeply wounding eulogium of the beloved youth.

CHAPTER XIV

The next morning Alf returned from a visit to the royal orator Rothman, with whom, to make an end at once of all apprehensions, he had arranged that his baptism and his marriage with both of the sisters should take place that afternoon. As he approached Trutlinger's house he was not a little astonished to find some of the yeomen of the guard, in the green and ash-colored livery, before the house door, holding some saddle horses. A milk white palfrey with costly trimmings and a purple gold-embroidered covering, particularly attracted his attention. Anxious to learn what it all meant, he walked into the parlor, where he encountered Tuiskoshirer and the lord steward Dilbek, in their court dresses.

'Hail, hail! prosperity has befallen thee, my brother!' cried the little prophet, ardently embracing him. 'Even as Abraham was accounted worthy of being commanded to offer to the Lord the most beloved object which he possessed upon earth, so likewise art thou also elected and favored among thousands; not merely to present, but really and truly to offer up, thy heart upon the altar of duty to thy king and lord.'

'Madness seems to catch early in the morning,' sighed Alf peevishly, 'and I cannot understand a word of all this. Both of you being gentlemen, you have nothing to neglect, and have leisure to spend the day as you please. I, however, am a handicraftsman, who must labor for my livelihood; therefore tell me in short plain words what you want of me, so that I may give you a proper answer and then go to my workshop.'

'Thy answer, my good fellow, is of very little consequence,' replied Tuiskoshirer with a malicious laugh. 'We await our answer from the worthy maiden Eliza, to whom we are sent by our all-merciful king to request her to become his third wife and queen of Zion.'

'My God!' stammered Alf, becoming deathly pale and leaning against the wall for support.

'It cannot be helped now, my friend,' whispered the lord steward to him; 'therefore submit with a good grace to what must at any rate happen; so that you may hereafter be able to claim a recompense for your ready acquiescence.'

'Has Eliza already consented?' asked Alf, with tremulous lips.

'She has retired to her chamber,' answered Tuiskoshirer, 'to take counsel of the Spirit. As soon as she comes forth we shall all be enlightened as to her decision.'

'No, no!' cried Alf, wringing his hands, 'nature and love have bound us too closely; she cannot leave me.'

Meanwhile the chamber door flew open and the beautiful Eliza appeared. At the first glance she was not recognized by Alf. A dress embroidered with silver and fastened with a jewelled girdle, rustled about her slender and fascinating figure; her bosom and arms sparkled with the richest gems, and from her dark locks arose, meteor-like, a radiant diadem.

'Hail to our queen Eliza!' cried Tuiskoshirer and Dilbek, sinking upon their knees before her majestic form.

'The Spirit has decided,' said Eliza, giving them her hand to kiss. 'I have listened to its voice. Conduct me to my king and husband.'

'Eliza!' cried Alf, in boundless sorrow, stepping before the false fair one.

'Thou here, Alf?' said she, with some slight agitation. 'I would willingly have spared thee the pain of this parting.'

'Thou art my promised bride, my wife in the sight of God!' shrieked he, despairingly. 'Thou canst not, thou darest not leave me!'

'Before the great affairs of the world, the little interests of private and humble life must yield,' answered Eliza pathetically. 'The king of Zion needs me, that my kiss may sweeten the wearisomeness of governing. How then can I be so selfish as to regard the bands which previously connected me with thee? The people of Israel have a claim upon me paramount to thine, and joyfully I go to fulfil my exalted duties in obedience to the voice of the Spirit.'

'No, thou hast never loved me!' exclaimed Alf.

'I was always well disposed towards thee,' stammered the new queen, affected by sudden emotion. Soon however recovering herself, she said to him in the tone of a mistress, 'when I am seated upon Zion's throne you may safely rely upon my favor.'

She now quickly took Dilbek's proffered arm and hastened forth with him, without giving a single glance backward. Tuiskoshirer, however, stopped long enough to ask the astonished and bewildered Alf, 'dost thou not now repent, my brother, that thou rejectedst my proposition?'--and then followed the pair.

'Woman's love and woman's truth!' indignantly, exclaimed the unhappy youth, seizing his dark brown locks with powerless rage.

CHAPTER XV

At Clara's request the previously arranged marriage was postponed. Alf's baptism, also, for which his desire daily decreased, had not yet taken place. The pretext for the delay of both ceremonies was the changes which had been occasioned in Trutlinger's house by Eliza's sudden elevation. In consequence of the daily increasing disorder and confusion in Munster these omissions were not noticed by any body; and half the city, who, since the polygamy ordinance of the twelve judges, were living unrestrainedly with their newly selected partners, saw nothing amiss in Alf and the little Clara's following the general example. They lived together, quiet and retired, like orphan brother and sister; and it became for Alf quite a soothing custom to extract consolation and encouragement, under his bitter disappointment, from the mild and friendly eyes of Clara. The maiden also, now that she no longer felt the yoke of her proud sister, and no longer saw the beloved youth in the arms of another, began to recover herself, and gradually resumed her florid complexion, so that Alf contemplated her with increasing pleasure from day to day; but the maiden kept her love for him deeply buried in her own chaste bosom, and closely guarded her eyes and lips lest they should betray her heart. Her deportment towards Alf, however, was always kind and affectionate, and she assiduously endeavored to anticipate all his wants. This peaceful mode of life, also restored to her mind a portion of that serenity which had gladdened her earlier and happier days. Already were her softly tinged cheeks graced by frequent smiles; her fine blue eyes, which formerly always looked through a veil of tears towards heaven or upon the ground, now often sparkled with a playful archness which rendered the thoughtful maiden doubly charming; and from her lips escaped many a pleasing lighthearted jest. Alf, wondering at the change which had taken place, could hardly turn his eyes away from her; and, as a natural consequence, the wound which Eliza's unfaithfulness had made in his heart was daily less and less felt.

While the storm of wild passions began to subside in the narrow circle in which Alf and Clara moved, the whirlwind which menaced the state was rushing and roaring constantly nearer and nearer. The frivolities and horrors, which the anabaptists had up to this period enacted under the shield of a fanatical schism, had excited the indignation of the virtuous and intelligent portion of the people throughout Germany. Disregarding all existing differences upon other subjects, catholics and protestants united in the determination that their misrule should no longer be suffered; and that if neither the deceivers nor deceived would listen to christian instruction and mild admonition, there was no other course left but to root them out with the sword. The Rhenish provinces held a convention at Coblentz, at which John Frederick, the Lutheran electoral prince of Saxony, voluntarily appeared. At this convention it was agreed to furnish the bishop of Munster three hundred cavalry and three thousand foot soldiers, as auxiliaries against his rebellious subjects. The brave Ulrich, count Oberstein, held the command of the forces and directed the siege.

Yet Munster's walls, towers and ditches were, through the providence of the prophets (who, in this, acted with great foresight,) in such excellent condition, and the fanatical garrison exhibited every where so much watchfulness and spirit, that Oberstein was convinced, that a storm attempted under these circumstances might indeed conduct his soldiers to butchery but would not accomplish his object. Accordingly, after the attempt to enter the city by treason from within had been frustrated, the commander contented himself with closely investing it on all sides and cutting off its supplies. The light minded people troubled themselves very little about this investment of their city, at first, as the consequences were not immediately felt; but no sooner did the scarcity of provisions become so pressing that the public tables spread by order of the king could no longer be supplied, and the people actually began to feel hunger, than their spirits began to sink, and here and there murmurings and complaints were heard. These complaints, to be sure, were made covertly, from fear of the iron sceptre which weighed upon the necks of the free and privileged anabaptists; but nevertheless they reached the ears of the king, who saw that something must be done, however unwillingly, in conformity with the example of his bold predecessor; and he therefore determined to try how far fanaticism and cunning, without courage, would answer the purpose. Besides, he was desirous of ridding himself of some of the prophets, who were disposed to play the Samuel to his Saul, and sought to relieve him of the cares of government. To reach all these objects with one blow, he devised a new piece of jugglery, which did honor at least to his practical knowledge of stage effect.

CHAPTER XVI

While from the cathedral yard the trumpet blasts sounded through the streets as if they were blowing for the last judgment, Hanslein rushed into Alf's shop in complete armor. 'How, comrade, not yet in armor?' cried he. 'Arm thyself and thy people quickly. The whole community is called together to-day, and none should fail to be present.'

'Is the enemy already at the gates?' asked Alf, busily equipping himself.

'Not quite, this time,' answered Hanslein. 'I hope, too, that the ceremonies of to-day will go off peaceably. We may, however, expect important occurrences. The prophet Tuiskoshirer has commanded the king to hold the sacrament of the Lord's supper at the cathedral, and then send out his apostles to all parts of the world. The last thought is not so bad; for the bishop has us enclosed within such narrow limits, that if the eloquence of our orators does not succeed in bringing us speedy help from without, it will soon be time to be thinking of a decent capitulation.'

'As long as our walls stand,' said Alf, 'and we are able to use our weapons, I do not fear for the city.'

'That is bravely spoken,' said Hanslein, 'but I have already perceived evidences that the people begin to grow hungry. When starvation once commences, it will be easy to calculate how long we can keep the city, and when the strong hands in which you trust will become powerless. So much do I know of the state of affairs, that I am determined this very day to cut off my connection with this place, and seek an opportunity to save myself quietly before the closing of the gates. A good cat always finds a loop-hole, and, if I may take the liberty, I wish to give you a friendly invitation to accompany me in my evasion. By heavens, it is surely better to be off in time, than to stay and starve here, or in the end to become too intimately acquainted with the tender mercies of his reverence's bailiff.'

During this conversation Hanslein, with Alf and his men had arrived at the church yard, through the whole of which were placed immensely long tables, covered with white cloths. Upon these tables the royal pages were serving up smoking flesh to the great satisfaction of the men of Munster, who, to the number of four thousand stout hearts, in complete armor, their hungry stomachs tightly compressed under their coats of mail, were standing by.

The king now appeared in majestic dignity, wearing a short silk body coat instead of his royal robes. At a signal from him the servants placed the people at the tables. After a short prayer, full of unction, he nodded graciously to the multitude and the repast began.

After the first course had been consumed, the roasted meats were removed, and the flagons began to circulate.

'This is a strange sort of a holy supper,' whispered Alf to Hanslein, as he passed a full jug to him.

'It appears to be only the introduction,' whispered Hanslein in answer. 'It is a sort of love feast, such as was customary with the old christians. Have but a little patience, the best is yet to come.'

No sooner were the meats gone, than the king again approached the assembly. He was accompanied by two pages of honor, who brought the holy bread upon golden plates. 'Take and eat,' said he, with earnest solemnity, 'in commemoration of the Lord's death!' Thus saying, he went through the long ranks, breaking the bread to every man, who received it with great devotion. Hanslein, who best knew the worthiness of the new high priest, was not able to suppress a satirical laugh, when his turn came. After the king, followed the first queen, the beautiful widow of Matthias, in a simple white dress, the golden chalice in her hand, accompanied by the second and third queens, who brought golden vessels of wine after her.

As she came to Alf for the purpose of presenting the chalice to him, she started back in soft confusion, surprised at the beauty of the youth, whose dark curling locks contrasted finely with his blooming face and true German eyes. Alf, also, paralysed by the appearance of such wonderful beauty as he had never before seen, remained motionless. Here were more than Eliza's and Clara's united charms, and the *tout-ensemble* seemed to approach perfection. Large, full and voluptuous, an ideality in form, arose her stately figure. Her queenly bosom, upon which her brown locks were restlessly waving, shamed the whiteness of her dress; and her alabaster neck was surmounted by a cherub head, whose deep blue interrogating eyes spoke so plainly of soft wishes and glowing desires, that Alf's senses were wrapped in a flame.

'Take and drink!' murmured the sweet vision, presenting the chalice, with trembling hands. The youth eagerly drained it, while his eyes were immovably fixed upon the dispenser, who was so disturbed by his gaze that she forgot the last words of the ritual, and, covered with crimson blushes, proceeded to his next neighbor. As Eliza, who followed her, rustled by Alf's seat, she gave him a strange look with those eyes which in former times had made him so happy. There was much in that glance--repentance, grief, rage and jealousy--while through the whole was yet to be discerned a glimpse of her former love; but the impression, which that glance made upon Alf, was not strong enough to withdraw his attention from the first queen, and he followed her, as she went along the ranks, with gleaming eyes.

At that moment his friend Hanslein passed his hand over his eyes, and said in an under tone, 'forget not my brother, that it is the first queen after whom you are gazing, and that our lord the king allows no jesting in such affairs.'

'Let him come and call me to account!' blustered Alf. 'I will so defend myself, that of a thousand questions he shall not answer one. Already in possession of the masterpiece of the universe, and able to make his selection from all the beauty of Munster, he has yet torn my promised bride from my heart, like the merciless rich man in the bible, who, despite his numerous flocks, must rob his poor neighbor of his only lamb, to satisfy his wicked appetite.'

In the hymn of praise, with the singing of which by the whole assembly the festival was closed, the complaints of the youth were lost, until with much difficulty Hanslein finally succeeded in assuaging his anger.

The king now once more presented himself before the multitude; this time in full regal attire, with all the insignia of his high office, and surrounded by his insignia bearers and guards. With a loud voice he asked the people whether they were prepared to fulfil the will of God, and to live and die for the faith. Like the murmuring of the ocean before a storm, a loud awful 'Aye!' roared through the human mass standing there.

Then from behind the king, pressed forward a new prophet, named Wahrendorf. 'Thus saith the Lord,' cried he with a glowing fanatical enthusiasm: 'choose a number from among my people of Zion, and let them go out to all the ends of the earth, to work miracles and do my work publicly before all people. Whoever receives this command and obeys it not, shall die the death.'

The prophet then drew forth a scroll from his bosom, and hastened to read the names of the new missionaries. The prophet Tuiskoshirer drew near to the reader with his usual knavish smile, to listen; nodding his head exultingly as the names of some of his opponents were read; but when he heard Wahrendorf cry, 'John Tuiskoshirer!' as if astounded by a clap of thunder the little withered man shrunk within himself and turned his red glowing eyes upon the king. 'I, also, deceived!' murmured he to himself. 'The villain shall not obtain his victory easily.'

'Thou errest, my brother!' howled he to Wahrendorf: 'and mistakest the word of man for the voice of the Spirit. The night before the last I had a vision, in which I was commanded to remain in Zion to guard these flocks from their adversaries.'

'Silence!' thundered the king. 'At this moment has the father entrusted to me an important duty, for the execution of which I must prepare,' and, beckoning to his guards, they dragged before him a mercenary soldier in chains.

'This unhappy man,' said the king solemnly and significantly, 'has, like a second Judas, been planning treason against Zion, and has publicly manifested his wicked intentions through disobedience to the commandments of the Spirit. His blood be upon his own head.'

The king's sword swung, the head of the victim fell, and the horrible man stepped directly before Tuiskoshirer with the bloody sword in his hand and asked him, 'what hast thou particularly to say to this assembly, my brother?'

'That I bow myself under the hand of the Lord,' tremblingly answered Tuiskoshirer, and Wahrendorf proceeded to read the list of names to the end.

There were named, in the whole, eight and twenty missionaries. The king dispersed them toward Osnabruck, Coesfeld, Warendorf and Soest. 'Forsake every thing,' he admonished them, 'fear nothing, and promulgate the faith.' 'Amen!' cried the multitude, as they departed from the cathedral.

CHAPTER XVII

Alf was sitting in the twilight near the good Clara, narrating to her at full length the singular proceedings at the cathedral, at which he had been present, when his friend Hanslein entered in a state of great excitement.

'How much can be made of a good-for-nothing fellow!' cried he. 'Would you ever have thought, brother, that I was a block out of which a duke could have been carved?'

'Duke!' asked Alf in astonishment, supposing that he must have heard falsely.

'A duke! nothing less!' laughingly answered Hanslein. 'The king's majesty has become a little anxious about his personal safety in the midst of his trusty subjects; and he no longer considers his dear life entirely secure among them. He has therefore divided Zion into twelve districts and appointed a duke for each, from among his trustiest supporters; and he, with an adequate military force, is to watch over the order and repose of his district and smother every disturbance at its birth. Having become such a thing, I beg of you to show me all proper respect.'

'What new experiment will not this wicked king try in my poor native city?' sighed Alf.

'This lamentation comes from sheer envy,' said Hanslein, jestingly, 'because you are not created a duke. Make yourself easy, however; for you also are raised to high honors. The king has named you commander of the life guards, and I bring you his gracious commands that you forthwith appear before him. You will commence duty even to-day, that the timid tailor may this night sleep under the safeguard of your good sword.'

'I commander of the life guards!' repeated Alf, moodily. 'How can it have happened that the king selected me?'

'That has happened as many other things do in this world,' answered Hanslein, with a significant smile. 'I can explain all these things satisfactorily to myself, and I consider that you, with the command of the guards, have drawn a much better prize than I with my dukedom. Enjoy your good fortune with circumspection.' So saying he departed.

'Strange!' said Alf, buckling on again his scarcely laid aside coat of mail. 'Strange!' cried he again, as he girded on his sword, when his eye fell upon a small fresh wine spot on the neck-piece of his armor. The charming queen with the chalice instantly stood before his mind's eye, and an obscure suspicion of a connection between the recent occurrence and his present elevation sent a burning blush to his face. To conceal it, he pressed the knight's helmet low down upon his forehead, which he had sought out as becoming his new office, extended his hand to the good Clara for a hasty farewell, and with winged strides proceeded toward the royal palace.

A royal page conducted him immediately to the king, who advanced to meet him as graciously as if he had been born to a throne.

'The affair of the bishop's camp has proved thee to be an able warrior,' said the king, with a dignity becoming his station; 'I owe thee some recompense for a great loss; and thou hast moreover been so much commended on all sides, that I have determined to bring thee nearer to my person. Thou shalt henceforth lead my body guard as its commander; so that the head upon which the welfare of Zion depends may at least sleep in safety.'

Alf suggested some doubts of his fitness for the office.

'No qualifications are needed,' replied the king, 'but watchfulness, courage and truth. I desire no oath from you. Christ says, 'Let your communication be yea, yea; nay, nay: for whatsoever is more than these cometh of evil.' Give me therefore the hand grip of an honest man, that you will be my faithful guard.'

Alf reluctantly gave his right hand to the king, for he shuddered at the idea of connecting himself personally with this man--he shuddered at touching a hand that had shed so much blood.

'The yeomen of the guard are already assigned to you,' proceeded the king; 'but now it is fitting that you be introduced to the first queen; 'and he signified to him by a gracious nod that the audience was over. Alf proceeded with a beating heart towards the apartments of the queen.

'Walk in! walk in!' cried a silvery voice in the room, at the door of which Alf's name and dignity had been announced by the lady in waiting. He stepped in. Upon an elevated and gilded chair, in full dignity, sat the queen. He was so much dazzled by her beauty that he scarcely observed the other two queens, who were sitting upon less elevated seats on each side of her.

'It is you, young man,' said the enchantress, in the sweetest tones, 'whom henceforth we shall have to thank for the safety of our days and the tranquillity of our nights.'

Alf bowed in silence.

'Only be careful continued the queen, with an alluring smile, 'that you do not rob the ladies of the palace of their repose, whom it is your duty to guard.'

The embarrassed Alf could not find presence of mind to enable him to answer, and queen Eliza sprang from her seat and hastened to the window.

'You are already married?' asked the queen.

'Only engaged--I am--I was--and am half way so yet,' stammered Alf, very unintelligibly.

'And the other half?' asked the queen, mischievously. Eliza turned her burning glance upon the floor.

'Permit me to be silent upon that point,' said Alf, with becoming modesty.

The charming woman extended her hand to him to kiss.

Alf seized it hastily, and impressed upon the warm, yielding, velvet skin an almost endless kiss, believing at the same time that he felt a slight pressure from her taper fingers. Heading the confirmation of his suspicions, as he looked up, in the melting eyes of the lady, and forgetting every thing in the momentary transport, he spread out his arms as if he would have fallen upon her neck.

He was rebuked however by a severe look; but in contradiction to that look, the queen said to him in the tenderest and most friendly manner, 'we shall see each other again soon,'--and dismissed him.

Intoxicated, confused, and entirely incapable of connected thought, the youth withdrew.

CHAPTER XVIII

On the following night Alf, installed in his new office and fully equipped, sat in an arm chair before the door of the royal sleeping apartments. He was even lightly slumbering, and a well known trio of beautiful women led by the god of dreams were dancing around him, when he was dazzled by a ray of light which fell suddenly upon his face. He awoke, sprang upon his feet and drew his sword.

'Put up your sword, brother,' whispered a hoarse voice to him; and the worthy Tuiskoshirer, in his traveling cloak, with his bundle swung over his back and a dark lantern in his hand, stood before him.

'What do you want here?' quickly asked Alf. 'Ought you not, according to the king's command, to have been already on your way to Osnabruck with your companion?'

'Yes,' answered Tuiskoshirer, with a bitter smile, 'so has the great king who has become a severe and mighty lord over our heads commanded; and the leaders who faithfully placed him upon the summit, he scornfully thrusts from him, now that he no longer needs their aid. Luckily, he has allowed me to delay my departure a few hours, and a skilful head can accomplish much in that time.'

'Tell me briefly what you want of me,' said Alf, 'and then take yourself hence, that your chattering may not awaken the king.'

'God forbid!' hissed Tuiskoshirer. 'Who would awaken the sleeping tiger? While he sleeps, at least, he murders not. Rather would I prolong his sleep into eternity.'

'Man, what is your design?' exclaimed Alf, partly guessing his horrible intentions.

'Thou hast already once rejected my good will,' answered Tuiskoshirer; and, since this ungrateful bedlamite has been placed upon the throne to which I would have raised thee, thou must more than once have regretted thy folly. I have this day closely watched thee, and know the magnet with which thy apparently insensible and rugged nature is to be moved. Wherefore I have taken my life in my hand, and once more ventured into this den of murderers, to offer to thee life's sweetest blossoms, which none but a fool would leave unplucked when they fell in his path radiant with exhaling beauty. Oppose me not now,' begged he, as Alf was about to reply. 'Thou shalt go with me, and see and hear for thyself, and then decide as may seem good to thee.'

'Whither wouldst thou lead me?' asked Alf, drawing back.

'Do you not suspect?' asked Tuiskoshirer, smiling; and Alf, on whom a light suddenly began to dawn, delightedly followed the tempter, who led him through the dark, silent passage toward the apartments of the queen.

'We have attained our object,' said Tuiskoshirer, on arriving before a room the door of which he opened with a false key. They entered and passed through the anti-chamber, where the waiting women were sleeping, to the bed-chamber of the first queen.

'Behold!' said Tuiskoshirer, impressively, as he directed the rays from his lantern upon the bed in which the beauteous woman was sleeping.

Alf drew nearer. A heavenly smile played upon the sweet face of the queen, to which a sound sleep gave a yet lovelier tint of rose. Alf was about to rush forward, when Tuiskoshirer forcibly dragged him back. 'Wilt thou mar all?' whispered the prophet to him; 'and deprive thyself of the greatest earthly happiness through thy impetuosity? That beauteous woman shall indeed be thine; but now is not the time. Such ware is to be purchased only at a price about which we must have some conversation. As yet you have only seen, now I must be heard; and when you have decided, act with the speed and energy which become a man about to attain the accomplishment of all his dearest wishes.'

During this conversation he drew the youth through the rooms, closed the last with his false key, and they went both together back to the royal anti-chamber. Tuiskoshirer, in whose little dull eyes twinkled a hellish triumph, bolted the outer door on the inner side, motioned to Alf to walk softly, and cautiously opening the door of the king's bed-chamber entered on tiptoe, making a sign to Alf to follow.

Alf obeyed, and both now stood before the bed of the king, near which, upon velvet cushions, lay the crown and other emblems of royalty. Tuiskoshirer drew aside the heavy, purple, gold-embroidered silk curtains, and disclosed the sleeper lying there with open staring eyes, large drops of sweat upon his forehead, froth about his mouth, and clenched fists,--a shocking sight.

'The king is ill and must soon awaken,' said Alf, apprehensively.

'Oh no,' said Tuiskoshirer, calmly. 'Since sleep always flies the night couch of the murderer, he never goes to bed without his sleeping draught. He cannot escape the dreams which then torment him undisturbedly; and it is well, that in this life he should learn something of that world of spirits, which darkly and heavily rules over him with arm already outstretched for his terrible reward.'

'Kneel down!' the slumberer now cried. 'Down! I must see blood, blood!' and he swung his right arm as if his death-dealing sword was at its usual occupation.

'I have first shown you the reward,' said Tuiskoshirer, to Alf,--'here is the deed which is to merit it. Here sleeps the cowardly, sensual, cold, murderous, inhuman monster. Thousands more will he yet destroy, if life and power remain to him. Can another word be necessary to determine your course? Reject not again, for the third time, the good fortune which twice you have thrust from you. Here lies the king's sword drunk with innocent blood,--one determined thrust therewith,--we can bruit it abroad that he has committed suicide,--Munster will be relieved from his tyranny,--thou wilt mount the vacant throne, thine will be the glorious Gertrude, the false Eliza, and the other beauteous wives,--and that the crown shall stand firmly upon thy head, leave to the care of old Tuiskoshirer, who will give it to thee in the presence of the assembled multitude.'

Alf stood there upon the narrow passage way, glanced with flashing eyes upon the sleeping tyrant, and his hand already moved towards the weapon.

'Now strike!' urged Tuiskoshirer. 'Every moment's delay will be at the expense of human life. Thou wilt take upon thyself all the crimes which this wretch may in future commit, if now thou sparest him, through foolish tenderness.'

The true German honesty had soon conquered in the pure mind of the youth. 'He has my pledge,' said he to himself. 'Confiding in my faith he laid him down to sleep.' Then Alf turned to the venomous little man with all the fury which the latter, to satisfy his own revenge, had kindled in his breast; suddenly seizing him by the nape of his neck, he dragged him sprawling through all the apartments and down the stairs, until he reached the outer door of the palace, when he roughly sat him down. 'Go thy ways thither!' cried the youth, pointing the way towards Osnabruck, 'and if thou art in Munster at sunrise, I will expose thee to the king, that he may execute justice upon thee.'

Gasping for breath and groaning with anguish, the foiled tempter staggered forth into the midnight darkness of the streets.

CHAPTER XIX

Munster continued to sustain herself with a resolution worthy of a better cause. At the imperial diet at Worms, which the Romish king Ferdinand opened in April, 1536, great sums were granted to the besieging bishop, to enable him to support the war; but as the payments were made very irregularly, the scarcity of money kindled a revolt among the mercenary soldiery in the bishop's camp, who would no longer serve without pay. Nor was it without great trouble and peril to the commander that the insurrection could be suppressed. With such troublesome troops, offensive warfare was not deemed prudent. Consequently, the besiegers confined themselves to the continuance of the blockade, and to drawing their lines closer and closer, so as completely to shut up the unfortunate city and deprive it of supplies and assistance.

Constantly increasing suffering in the city, was the consequence of this course. The poorer classes, obliged to subsist upon roots, herbs, bark, and leaves, swarmed about the king with sunken eyes and haggard faces, whenever he passed through the streets in lordly dignity, and howled for bread. The royal courtiers themselves were compelled to accept such small portions as could be spared from the table where sat the king with his fourteen wives and principal officers.

In vain did the bishop call upon the citizens to surrender the city, under promise of full pardon for all except the king and a few of his principal accomplices. The fear of the terrible Johannes was stronger than the ardent desire for deliverance which had now arisen in many hearts. In vain did the landgrave of Hesse, by a special embassy to his brother in the faith, endeavor to bring him to reason. The king, to prove how much greater a man he was than the landgrave, refused to give audience to his ambassadors, and thus compelled them to leave their business unaccomplished.

Meanwhile the eight and twenty prophets had arrived at the cities of their destination, and had preached their customary fanatical nonsense with frantic zeal. The magistrates, warned by the example of Munster, were vigilant and energetic. The brawlers were every where arrested and questioned as to their doctrines; and, as they stubbornly maintained their faith, were immediately beheaded. Only one of them, Heinrich Hilversum, obtained deliverance. He was imprisoned by the bishop of Munster, bought his liberty with the promise that he would act as a spy in the rebel city, and returned back to the king. He related how an angel had delivered him from imprisonment and commanded him to announce to the king that Amsterdam, Wesel, and Deventer would come under his sceptre if he would send more prophets there.

These were sweet sounds to the ears of the king. He immediately sent out prophets, among whom were Johann von Seelen and Johann von Kempen, to those beautiful and important cities, to convert and win them for himself. The smooth-tongued Hilversum, however, he took into his own palace, clothed him in his ash-grey and green court-livery, charged the officers of the court to attend him, entrusted him with considerable sums, and, in short, confided to him the duty of negotiating with those from whom aid and assistance were expected from without.

With these presents Hilversum went over to the bishop on the first convenient opportunity; leaving a letter in Munster exhorting the citizens to desert the impostor and return to their old religion and their rightful lord.

This event touched the king in the tenderest point; as it tended to destroy the belief in the infallibility of his inspiration with those who were yet able to see. To a portion of the inhabitants of the distressed city it now appeared clear, that they had become the slaves of a wicked impostor, who was leading them to destruction; but the fear of the monster was stronger than this just conviction, and the king, comprehending that fear was the only lever now remaining to him, made the utmost use of it, and thenceforth, like Draco, he wrote his laws in blood. No punishment milder than death awaited disobedience to the least of his commands. Alf, notwithstanding, in his new situation, strove to shield, defend, and rescue the sufferers; yet new victims fell daily, and the slavish population daily trembled more and more before their cowardly and tyrannical tailor-king.

CHAPTER XX

Meanwhile Alf went on, truly and honorably discharging the duties of his office, although, after the first arrangement had been effected he had given up the personal guard of the royal bedchamber to other officers, reserving to himself only a general nightly superintendance; and the cruel Johannes passed his nights under as good a defence as if angels with flaming swords had guarded him. His office, however, daily called the youth to the palace, and he could not but perceive that the magnificent Gertrude often threw herself in his way. She evidently loved the beautiful youth as only an unprincipled woman can love,--and her passion had nothing to combat but the fear of the sultan of the harem, whose discovery of the least infidelity would have brought instant death upon the guilty. Yet so powerful was her passion that it conquered even this fear.

At one of those intoxicating court festivals with which the king sought to stupify himself and those about him, Alf was standing to take breath after a brisk dance, with his hands behind him, when suddenly he felt a warm soft pressure of his right hand, a piece of paper being simultaneously slipped into it, and a moment afterwards the first queen stepped forward from behind him, giving him a significant glance as she passed. He left the room immediately, and by the nearest lamp in the corridor read the following words:--

'An hour after midnight, in the upper passage on the left; the first door.'

Hastening back to the dancing-hall, his glowing cheeks and triumphant carriage immediately betrayed to the beauteous syren, that he had read and comprehended her billet.

Meanwhile the midnight hour struck. Gertrude was suddenly attacked by a headache and suffered her attendants to lead her to her chamber. The king smilingly whispered a word to Eliza, which caused a flush to pass over her cheeks, and which she answered with downcast eyes. The assembly gradually departed, and Alf, lost in pleasing dreams, proceeded to his dwelling.

He found the devoted little Clara yet patiently waiting for him, occupying herself at the spinning wheel; her now constantly bright eyes a little dimmed; but whether from late watching, or weeping, or from both together, he could not exactly decide.

'I began to think you were not coming home tonight,' said the maiden in a friendly tone, which yet had something of sadness in it.

'The dancing to-night continued unusually late,' replied Alf; casting a glance at the mirror, and coming to the conclusion that he was right worthy of the beauteous queen, he proudly pressed his richly plumed cap over his eyes.

Meanwhile Clara had lighted his chamber lamp and handed it to him.

'I am going out again immediately, dear Clara,' said Alf, with some little embarrassment. 'I came merely to tell you, that you might not sit up all night waiting for me.'

'You are going out again?' asked Clara, looking intently at him. 'This is not your time for guard duty.'

'The feast of to-day has disturbed all our arrangements,' stammered Alf with embarrassment. 'I must actually go to the palace once more to-night.'

Clara seized his hand with both of hers, and with her mild honest eyes gave him a piercing look. His guilty conscience deprived him of the power to meet her gaze. 'Kippenbrock,' cried she, suddenly alarmed, 'are you not going for some wicked purpose?'

'You are already dreaming, from having watched so long, my child. Go to bed, pretty one,' said Alf, bending down to kiss the maiden as he wished her good night; a friendly habit in which he had for some time indulged. But Clara avoided his embrace, saying earnestly to him, 'not this evening, dear Kippenbrock, all is not as it should be.'

'You are a little simpleton!' cried he half indignantly, and hastened forth as if he wished to run away from the 'unpleasant feelings her suspicions had given him. As the third quarter after midnight struck, he stood by the stove, closely wrapped in his mantle, in the upper passage way of the palace, watching with anxious eyes, by the dim light of the almost expiring lamps, the first door on the left. Finally, the hour struck, and still no door was opened.

'It is in reality a great wrong for me to be standing here,' said Alf to himself. 'Let the king now be what he may, and do what he will, yet I have once for all acknowledged him as my lord, and this Gertrude is his wife. It is the duty of my office to preserve order and propriety in the royal palace, which I in intention am so vile as to violate. Moreover, I encroach upon the rights of the good Clara, who so secretly and tenderly loves me, and whom I should look upon as my affianced bride. Did she but know that I was standing here waiting for the creaking of that door, she would weep her eyes out of her head; and she even appeared to suspect some intrigue. Her manner toward me appeared very strange at my departure. Good God! with what face shall I appear before her in the morning! No! it is settled,-- the beautiful Gertrude shall wait for me in vain, and thus shall we both be spared a sin.'

CHAPTER XXI

On the subsequent morning Alf was standing in the king's anti-chamber awaiting his commands for the day. There came the high bailiff Krechting, a raging fanatic, a true second Johannes, with some soldiers who were dragging along two of the royal pages, bound. Alf perceived by their faces, which hunger and affliction had paled and emaciated, that they were the two whom he had rescued from the hands of Matthias, and compassionately asked the bailiff what crime the poor children had committed.

'We caught them in the outworks,' answered the bailiff fiercely, 'as they were attempting to escape to their old lord, the bishop. Announce us to the king, brother officer.'

'Alas! dear lord,' said one of the boys, weeping; 'we have certainly done nothing; but we could no longer hold out for hunger.'

'This affair might well be overlooked,' said Alf. 'To announce the children to the king is to lead them to death,--and I do not wish to take upon ray conscience such bloodguiltiness.'

The bailiff gave him a venomous look and hastily stepped into the royal apartment. He soon made a signal at the door, and the soldiers dragged the boys in after him. Immediately a loud noise was heard within,--the king stormed, the boys wept and plead pitifully, and amidst all arose Eliza's supplicating voice. 'For our love's sake, Johannes, only for this time let mercy take the place of justice!' Simultaneously were heard the lamentations of the two boys. Alf heard two hard falls upon the floor, and, as if drawn by some irresistible power, he pushed into the apartment.

What horrors had been perpetrated! The two boys lay dead upon the floor, the king strode before them with his sword drawn, and at his feet lay Eliza, who loosed her arms from his knees and sprang up. Excited by the cruelty of her husband, and by her having pleaded in vain against what he had done, the proud woman now exclaimed in the bitterest tone, 'I do not believe, Johannes, that our God is served by the calamities you have brought upon this people.'

Krechting absolutely screamed with amazement at the audacious speech. The king, however, merely gave Eliza a cold, satanic glance, and quietly said to her, 'in the market-place will I answer thee upon that matter.' Turning then to Alf, 'let my wives and my whole court be summoned hither!' commanded he him. 'Also let my trumpeters and fifers assemble,--we would move to the market-place, where I have to-day to exercise my judicial office before the whole people. Thou wilt accompany me, Kippenbrock, with thy whole band.'

This strange solemnity excited various evil forebodings in the mind of Alf, and with a heavy heart he proceeded to execute the king's commands.

CHAPTER XXII

The multitude crowded the market-place, waiting to see what new thing was to be done there. Then sounded in the distance a solemn funeral march from the trumpets and horns, and duke Hanslein with his soldiers formed a wide circle to admit the king and his household.

Next came the procession. After the music followed Alf, with a division of his guards; then the king, and then the high bailiff; between them, yet in her night-gown, pale and tottering, with streaming hair and folded hands, Eliza. After these followed the stately Gertrude, the other wives, and the persons connected with the court. Another division of the guards closed.

At a signal from the king, Krechting stepped reverently back and the thirteen wives formed a circle about their lord and Eliza. 'Kneel down, ye pure!' thundered the king, and the circle of women fell upon their knees; in an instant the king's sword glistened in the air and Eliza's head flew from its bloody trunk!

'Accursed murderer,' screamed Alf, frantic with grief and terror at the wholly unexpected death of the once so well beloved woman, and sprang forward with high waving sword to hew down the king where he stood. The faithful Hanslein caught his upraised arm. 'Good colonel,' cried he, 'it was only yesterday that you were sick with a fever, and now the paroxysms have returned again. Help me, friends, to overpower him and bear him to his house where he can be taken care of.'

He was seized by the guards from all sides, and notwithstanding his furious opposition, was soon disarmed and carried away.

'The person who has been judged has blasphemed the Spirit as manifested through her king and husband,' said Johannes, to the people. 'She had in a spiritual sense broken her marriage vows, and well deserved her punishment. Give to God the glory!'

The remaining thirteen wives rose up and with clear voices sang, 'Glory to God in the highest!' The horns and the trumpets triumphantly fell in. The king seized Gertrude's hand and commenced a merry dance with her upon the open market-place. The other wives and the courtiers followed the high example. The poor infatuated people likewise joined in the dance and sprang actively about, notwithstanding their empty stomachs; and from all mouths arose the cry of jubilee; 'glory be to God in the highest!'

CHAPTER XXIII

The disease which Hanslein had invented, in his well intended eagerness to save Alf, had seized him in good earnest. The disquiet of mind in which the youth had been kept through the most diverse and almost always terrible occurrences,--the storm, so every way affecting, which had lacerated the deepest recesses of his heart,--above all, the daily increasing conviction of the flagitiousness of the new doctrines to which he had adhered so strongly,--and the remorse of conscience for the part which he had acted,--all this had destroyed the freshness of his youthful vigor; and only the tension in which his mind was kept by the constantly recurring horrors of every succeeding day, gave him the artificial support, which had hitherto kept him up. The last act of Johannes, the tender interest which Alf still felt for the fair victim, and the frustration of his just vengeance upon the infamous murderer, had weighed down the poor youth with resistless power, and he lay many weeks in Trutlinger's house in a high fever, carefully waited upon and nursed by the pale and pensive Clara.

The energies of youth finally prevailed over the fever. When once the crisis had passed, his strength returned as quickly as it had flown; and Alf had even left his room for the first time, to enjoy the mild air and warm sun of summer, when he encountered his friend Hanslein, who, in spite of all resistance, cordially embraced and congratulated him on his recovery.

'Go thy way!' said Alf, angrily. 'With the defender of tyrants I have no more to do in this life.'

'Always precipitate,' laughed Hanslein; 'and always letting your heart run away with your head. It was ever your way when a boy. I considered for you better than you considered for yourself. The poor queen once dead, we could do nothing more to help her. You might indeed have destroyed the king, but the fanatical people would have torn you to pieces for it on the spot; that would have been paying a greater price than his majesty's life was worth. Nor would Munster have gained any thing. Knipperdolling & Co. would have possessed themselves of the government, and it would thereby have remained the executioner's head quarters as before. I have therefore preserved you for greater things, which, now that you are so well upon your legs again, we may soon see.'

Alf looked inquiringly at his friend, and suffered himself to be led by him back to his own sitting room and to be seated upon a stool.

'The affairs of Munster stand badly,' said Hanslein. 'The famine increases, and I see the moment very near when the unhappy people will be driven to despair. Succor is not to be expected. At Bolswart in Friesland, the strongest power of the anabaptists had been collected, and would soon have marched to our aid; but the governor of Friesland surrounded the place with his forces, and after four assaults forced it, putting almost the whole population to the sword. In Amsterdam, von Kempen and von Seelen have done their best to bring us aid. As the council and chief burghers of the cross-guild retired from the council-room, our people stormed the city hall, overpowered all who opposed them, and the burgomasters, Peter Colyn and Simon Bute, were left dead upon the spot; but the burgomaster Goswin Rekalf collected the citizens, a severely contested battle ensued, and our people were slain, or taken and executed, including poor Kempen, who had caused himself to be declared bishop of Amsterdam. Seelen exposed himself upon the tower of the city hall, where he was afterwards shot down and fell dead upon the market place. With him expired our last hope.'

'Oh God, will these horrors never end?' sighed Alf, casting his eyes toward heaven.

'Here probably soon,' said Hanslein; 'but it will be a fearful end. The city must shortly surrender, and then the lord bishop Franciscus may not treat us more mildly than king Johannes has hitherto done. I have least reason to hope for pardon then, and have therefore determined to go back to my old master immediately. I have discovered a place through which an escape from the city can be made. By the same way I trust I can lead the troops of the enemy into Munster, and with this secret I intend to purchase my peace with the bishop. Will you make the experiment with me this night? The sentinels now upon the night posts sleep away their hunger and will not hinder us.'

'My father's house is a house of prayer,' said Alf, after musing a long time; 'but you have made it a den of murderers. Yes, the originally pure doctrine of the anabaptists might perhaps have been a glorious gift from the merciful hand of God;--but the monsters, who preach it to us, have so perverted it according to their own wicked purposes, and shed so much blood in its name, that its noble image can no longer be recognized. A doctrine which empowers a Johannes to rage among mankind like a famished wolf among defenceless lambs, cannot come from God. I disclaim it. May God forgive me that I also have labored and fought for a cause which must have been wicked, since it elevated the bad and destroyed the good.'

'Thou wilt accompany me then!' asked Hanslein, giving his hand a friendly pressure.

'If Clara can and will go with us,' answered Alf. 'I have loved her uncle, whom they shot, and cannot leave her behind in a city upon which all the horrors of war are soon to fall.'

At that moment Clara entered the room to set before the guest what the house afforded at a time when provisions outweighed gold,--a cup of water and a slice of bread with salt.

'You come to us too confidingly, young lady,' said Hanslein jestingly, while he helped himself. 'We have evil thoughts concerning you,--we have an idea of taking you out of Munster.'

'Ah, would to God!' sighed the maiden.

'The jest is earnest,' said Alf. 'This night I and my friend intend to leave Munster, if you will accompany us, my little Clara.'

'Through the whole world!' cried Clara with heartfelt fervor. 'Whom have I on earth beside you?'

'So then the thing is settled,' cried Hanslein. 'Prepare yourselves for the journey; but do not encumber yourselves with needless baggage. No armor, Alf. A short sword will be sufficient for all emergencies. Clara had better put on male attire--there will be some places difficult to climb, and I cannot allow any thing that might prove an obstacle to the rapidity of our movements. Hold yourselves in readiness; for I shall come for you precisely at midnight.' He departed. Intoxicated with joy at the near approach of her deliverance, Clara threw her arms affectionately around the youth and cried, 'with you out of this place of torment, dear Alf! Now for the first time I have reason to hope that there is earthly happiness in store for me yet.'

CHAPTER XXIV

Softly creeping by the sleeping sentinels, climbing walls and wading through ditches, the three fugitives proceeded in the dead of the night, until they finally found themselves in freedom; and then with fresh confidence they moved onward toward the besiegers' camp fires.

Soon a clattering of arms was heard near them, and a rough voice cried, 'Who goes there?'

'I have no desire to be caught here,' whispered Hanslein to Alf; 'for in that case I should get no credit for my voluntary return, which I particularly need on account of old scores. Wherefore I must endeavor to reach the bishop through indirect paths, while you boldly go straight forward.'

'Who goes there?' cried the challenger much louder.

'A friend!' answered Alf, whilst Hanslein went off to the right with great rapidity; 'deserters from Munster!' and in a moment he and the trembling Clara were surrounded by a squad of soldiers.

'Deserters?' asked the serjeant who led the squad. 'It is a question whether that title will save your lives. In these days a thousand Munsterers have come out, men, women and children, and a good part of the men were cut down as they came in, by the bishop's command.'

'It is the curse of these combats for opinion,' said Alf, sorrowfully, 'that even those, who are on the right side, are provoked to do wrong by the crimes of their opponents--and then other crimes are the consequence, until the horrible chain of wickedness is closed by the conversion of men into relentless destroyers, in whose breasts the voice of religion and mercy is stifled.'

'You talk it as solemnly,' sneered the serjeant, 'as if you were one of the prophets of Munster. First of all give up your sword and follow us into the camp, together with your boy. The bishop must decide upon your case.'

'I wish previously to be conducted to your field captain,' said Alf in a decided tone.

'You speak as if you were our captain instead of our prisoner,' snarled the serjeant. 'It will be necessary first to ascertain, whether the lord general will permit you to be brought to him. For the present, forward, march!'

'God preserve us!' softly murmured the timid Clara, clinging closely to her protector.

'Do not be alarmed, my little Clara,' said Alf, consolingly. 'All will go well.' They proceeded with the soldiers rapidly towards the camp.

CHAPTER XXV

A fine June morning was shining upon the camp, as Alf and Clara stood waiting with their escort before the tent of the commander in chief. There came out of the tent a tall, meagre clergyman, in his black clerical dress. He started when he saw the youth, and asked the serjeant, 'who are these people?'

'Deserters from Munster,' answered the serjeant, 'whom we found last night. They insist upon seeing the general.'

The preacher having closely scrutinized Alf, who stood there absorbed in his own reflections, approached and spoke to him, taking his hand in the most friendly manner. 'Do I see you again as a deserter? Now, God be praised, my prophecy is fulfilled!'

'Reverend doctor!' cried Alf in joyful surprise, as he recognised the good Fabricius.

'So, the disorders in the new Zion have become too great for you?' asked the latter. 'I only wonder that you had not come to the conclusion long ago,--that with your heart and head you could for so long a time have been a contented observer of their pagan cruelty.'

'When Germans have once become united with a ruler chosen by themselves, worthy sir,' answered Alf, 'they can be disunited only by hard blows, else they will hang fast to him until death.'

'The hard blows, I perceive, have been given and received,' said Fabricius. 'So you have again become one of us.'

'With all my heart and soul,' answered Alf with great ardor.

'We will leave the remainder of this for the confessional, where I may soon expect you,' said Fabricius. 'At present I must exert myself to prepare for you a good reception from the commanding general.'

Again most cordially shaking Alf's hand, he passed into the tent. Shortly afterward the youth and his girl-boy were bid to enter. Lord Oberstein was sitting with the doctor at the field table, taking his morning draught.

'Come nearer!' commanded the general, sternly.

'What have you to disclose to me?'

The voice of the questioner satisfied Alf, that it was the commander in chief whom he had caught and released on a former night; he however concealed this recognition.

'To make an end of the calamities of the city,' answered he, 'I am prepared to show your soldiers a way to enter Munster--the same way by which I have myself quitted it.'

'I recognise that voice!' cried Oberstein, springing up, and stepping directly in front of the youth. 'We have met before,' said he; 'it surely was in the outworks before the new gate, by moonlight. You were the officer who took me prisoner and then let me run? Is it not so?'

'I was very glad,' answered Alf, 'that it was in my power to save so old and merry a warrior.'

'And now are you willing to deliver the city to me?' proceeded Oberstein; 'to make a short ending to her long sufferings? You make me doubly your debtor; your reward shall be great.'

'Of myself little need be said,' answered Alf. 'My conditions are only pardon for myself and my companion, and that the conqueror of the city shall distinguish between the miscreants who have wilfully erred, and those who with honest intentions have been led astray, and spare the latter.'

'We must act according to the instructions of the diet of Worms,' said Oberstein. 'Whoever has not belonged to the leaders, and come not against us in arms, to them is given life and freedom.'

'Then should the lord bishop,' boldly replied Alf, 'have extended mercy to the unhappy refugees who have lately been fleeing from the city.'

'The bishop was exceedingly exasperated by events which accompanied the revolution!' answered the general, shrugging his shoulders; 'and an angry man does not always what is right in the sight of God.'

His eyes now fell upon Clara, who had timidly placed herself in an angle of the tent near the door.

'Who is that pretty boy?' asked he. 'Some one of the bishop's pages? It is to be hoped so. Two pages were made prisoners by the anabaptists and carried off at the time they attacked our camp at the beginning of the siege. To one of them particularly the worthy bishop was attached by a truly paternal affection.'

'Those boys have also fallen a sacrifice to the barbarity of the king,' answered Alf. 'This maiden is the sister of the queen Eliza, who paid with her head for having lamented the murder of the innocents.'

'Great God, what an accumulation of crime!' cried Oberstein, while Fabricius with upraised finger reprovingly asked, 'have you brought with you a maiden in man's attire? Must there not yet remain something of the old anabaptist leaven in you, which may in time again leaven the whole lump, destroying your morals for time and eternity?'

'All in honor, dear doctor,' protested Alf; 'and I shall have to request you, as soon as may be convenient, to unite me in honorable marriage with this blameless maiden, who is my beloved and betrothed bride.'

'That alters the case,' said Fabricius, affectionately patting Clara's velvet cheeks. 'May God keep us in the good old order.'

'The lord bishop's reverend and princely grace,' said an episcopalian officer, stepping in, 'sends his compliments to the lord general and politely requests him to repair immediately to his presence. An anabaptist prisoner has brought before him some matters of consequence, which demand a sudden meeting of the council.'

'Yon shall accompany me there,' said Oberstein to Alf.

'But where shall I remain?' anxiously whispered Clara to her betrothed.

'May I be permitted to confide the maiden to your care, worthy sir?' asked Alf of the doctor.

'I will foster and protect her like a beloved daughter,' answered Fabricius, taking Clara by the hand, and with a light heart the youth then followed the general.

CHAPTER XXVI

Glowing with anger and sorrow, Graf von Waldeck, bishop of Munster, strode up and down in his gilded tent. At the door, with a pale malefactor face, stood poor Hanslein, in chains, and surrounded by guards. Oberstein and Alf entered.

'This wretch,' cried the bishop to the general, 'proposes to purchase his forfeited life by betraying the city. He has, however, three times forfeited his life,--formerly a rider in my cavalry, he wounded his superior officer and went over to the enemy, swearing allegiance and adopting their faith. I am half inclined to compel him to show us the way to Munster and then hang him; for it would be contrary to all right, human and divine, to allow him to escape punishment by such an act.'

'The greatest right is often the greatest wrong,' said the general soothingly. 'Too much severity is often injurious, and with your grace's permission, if the spiritual lords had not formerly held so rigidly to their notions of right and wrong, and had not wielded the rod of authority too vigorously, much of the mischief against which the assembled christians of Germany of all denominations now appeal to heaven, would have been avoided. My voice is for mildness.'

'You have lost none who were dear to you, through these monsters!' cried the bishop, making great efforts to suppress his tears. 'I have just learned, that the reprobate tailor has murdered both of my pages, for making an effort to rescue themselves from his paws.'

'That is sad news,' said Oberstein, sympathisingly; 'but if you should outdo all these horrors by committing greater, you might thereby bring a stain upon your princely reputation; but you would remedy no evil. My advice is, that you grant a free pardon to the deserter, and thereby obtain a faithful guide into the city, the speedy surrender of which is yet nearest your heart. A resort to the rack, is, in my mind, as it must be in that of every man, highly objectionable, beside being a very unsafe means of accomplishing our purpose.'

'You may be right,' said the bishop, after a pause, somewhat softened by the decided tone and plain good sense of the old warrior.

'I bring you another individual who may be trusted to guide our forces to the attack of Munster,' proceeded Oberstein, pointing to Alf, 'and we shall be able by this means to divide and direct our troops.'

'Is this he?' cried the bishop with suddenly rekindled rage. 'Wretch! thank God--that I have you in my power. You shall learn to your sorrow what it is to fall into my hands.'

'What mean you, sir bishop?' asked the general.

'What harm can have been done to you by a youth, whom you probably now see for the first time in your life?'

'Oh I know him but too well,' raved the bishop. 'When the lying prophet Matthias surprised our camp last year, this villain led the anabaptists as their commander. I saw him rushing onward at the head of his troops, as I was mounting my horse to escape the danger of capture.'

'Heigh! you are again strangely severe!' cried Oberstein. 'Misled, like thousands of others in the city, to whom you long ago offered a general pardon, the young man only fulfilled what at that time he considered his duty as a christian and a soldier. Now, however, he has become disgusted with the tailor's government, and has voluntarily come out to us.'

'At that onslaught was my unhappy----pupil taken prisoner with his companion!' cried the bishop. 'Who was it, moreover, who dragged him to his death, but the profligate leader of that frantic host? Matthias is already judged. This one has the Most High given into my hands, and if God from heaven should cry mercy! he should die.'

'Such a speech little becomes a prince, much less a spiritual lord,' said Oberstein with melancholy earnestness. 'As for the rest, the duty of gratitude at this time compels me to spare you the commission of a crime. This youth has saved my life. I will never deliver him up to your revenge.'

'Forget not, sir earl,' cried the bishop angrily, 'that I am a prince upon this ground, and that you are only general of the forces!'

'The forces of the empire!' vehemently exclaimed Oberstein,--'not yours, and I am expressly commanded to execute the decrees of the Diet of Worms,--of which, as you appear to have forgotten it, it is my duty to remind you.'

'Unheard of insolence!' growled the bishop. 'It may be worth while to inquire whether I am yet sovereign of Munster.' With fury in his rolling eyes, he beckoned to the door an officer who stood near him, as if he desired to confide to him an order of serious consequence:

'Spare yourself steps, your princely grace, which you will be compelled to retrace,' said Oberstein; and at that moment the bishop's body servant, a pious, blameless, silver haired old man, entered with his master's morning meal.

'Jesus Maria!' screamed the servant the moment he saw Alf; and, letting fall the smoking platter, threw himself at the youth's feet and clasped his knees. 'God in his mercy has granted me an opportunity to thank the preserver of my life!' cried he, sobbing.

'Preserver of your life!' cried the bishop wonderingly.

'You are mistaken, father,' said Alf, gently putting aside the old man, 'I do not know you at all.'

'I am not more certain of future bliss,' said the old servant.--'Know you not, sir colonel, or whatever else you may have been, when you fell upon our camp, with the terrible Matthias, and his princely grace had fled, and Matthias had broken into this tent, and had already cut down the cook and two lacqueys, and the pages were kneeling before him, and the Goliath-spear was already raised to destroy them. I stood in a corner tremblingly awaiting the moment when my turn would come. Then you rushed into the tent and valiantly stayed the monster's upraised arm, although he was your superior, and commanded him and gave him hard words, and compelled him to spare their lives and take them with him prisoners to Munster. And then you dragged him away, together with the boys; I, however, slipped out of my corner, and in this place I kneeled down and prayed a devout Ave Maria for myself, and two for the salvation of your poor soul, that God might rescue you from eternal death, as you had rescued me from the murderous prophet.'

'How now, sir bishop?' said Oberstein, in an upbraiding tone. 'It appears that the youth saved the lives of those whose blood you would avenge on him. His crime is, that he could not be about them every moment to guard them against the beasts of prey who constantly beset their path.'

'Can you swear upon the Host,' asked the bishop of the servant, 'that this is the man who saved the lives of the boys?'

'As God may help me to a good dying moment!' answered the servant with his hand upon his heart.

The traits of passion disappeared from the bishop's features. He advanced towards Alf and said sorrowing, 'thou hast meant well, my son, but God has willed it otherwise.' Then, turning to Oberstein, he proceeded, 'I leave both the deserters to your unfettered disposal, and shall expect from you some indication of what I can do for the youths. I trust you will forget our little misunderstanding, when you recollect in how many ways and how deeply I have been injured by all these enormities, as a man, as a father, as a temporal prince, and as a dignitary of the church.'

Oberstein took the freely offered hand of the bishop, with a reverential bow; after which the latter, with an humble air, passed to an inner apartment of the tent. At the nod of the general, Hanslein's chains fell from him.

'It was hard clearing the gallows this time,' cried Hanslein, shaking himself. 'It shall be a warning to me forever to avoid the spiritual lords. I feared to make myself known to the general, who I supposed would not be able to comprehend my position; and therefore I went to the lord bishop;--but the crook, under which I had hoped safely to repose, had very nearly broken my brain-pan.'

'That also must be an old acquaintance,' said Oberstein, smilingly contemplating the chatterer.

'I now recognise his features. Anxiety about his fate had lengthened them a little.'

'Sure enough,' cried Hanslein, kissing his hand; 'and you, my prince of warriors, have spoken like a man in behalf of an unknown anabaptist, without suspecting that you were under obligations to him for a former service.'

'Follow me now, children,' said the good general, 'and forget in my tent all the trouble you have just experienced, and so put an end to the anxiety of the trembling little bride.'

'With a thousand pleasures!' cried Hanslein; 'besides, it is not good to set up our tabernacle here.' With a few vigorous leaps he found himself before the general's tent. The others followed.

'Perhaps you would like to be married to your little maiden to-day?' Oberstein affectionately asked of Alf, while on their way to the tent. 'There is no lack of monks and preachers in the camp. I will furnish forth the marriage feast, and you may safely reckon upon a magnificent wedding present from the bishop.'

'Until the city is gained,' answered Alf, 'I must postpone the consummation of that holy act. If I should fall in the attack, then would my wife become an early widow, and more unhappy than if she mourned her promised bridegroom only as one betrothed. Besides, I cannot be married with any satisfaction, or really enjoy the greatest festival of my life, until my poor native city is freed from the domination of the devil who now lacerates her with his infernal claws. When good old Munster has found peace and safety I will seek the consummation of my own domestic happiness.'

'Thou hast a good faith, my son,' cried Oberstein, pleased with the self-denial of the youth.

By this time they stood before the general's tent, when they were met by Fabricius holding by the hand the amiable and sweetly smiling Clara, already modestly clad in the dress of her sex.

CHAPTER XXVII

Yielding to the voice of clemency, the worthy Oberstein sent messengers into the city to admonish them to surrender and save the lives of the starving people; but the answer which orator Rothman gave in the presence of the king, was, like the preceding one, the sending back of the messengers with a paraphrase of the passage in the prophet Daniel of the four ferocious beasts, in the description of which, he said, the bishop might easily learn to know himself.

The last of mercy's sands had finally run, and the next night was determined on for the attack. It was on the 13th of June, 1533, an hour before midnight, that Hanslein, in perfect silence, led five hundred volunteers through the shallow place in the ditch and thence upon the walls. The sleeping sentinels were cut down, and the detachment reached the little gate without hindrance. This was broken down and the soldiers rushed into the city. The alarm was, however, now given. The armed burghers, who had hastily collected, beat back the last of the entering troops, closed, and occupied the gate, and then attacked with redoubled rage those who had already entered. An hour and a half they endured the bloody onslaught in the dark, until Hanslein with the rest of his band broke through the nearest weakly guarded gate. The commander in chief, guided by Alf, waited for this event with the main force; and, as the gate was burst open from within and its wings flew asunder, the bishop's troops poured with loud cries into the city. The victory was not, however, yet won. Each footstep in advance was at the expense of much blood of the half starved fanatics; and when finally Oberstein with resistless power forced them back, they retired only towards the market-place at St. Lambert's church; there once more to make a stand. Here was the king, who had suddenly sprung from his bed, with the best of his people, and this availed to renew the fight. Bloodily the red morning rose upward over the promiscuous slaughter; and the battle, now that friends and enemies could rightly discern each other, became regular; by which the anabaptists gained nothing. Alf kept himself constantly at the side of the general, only defending himself when necessary, as he did not like to draw his sword against his fellow citizens; but now, amid the tumult, he caught a glimpse of the infamous Johannes as he was stimulating his troops to the fight. Then the wrath of the youth kindled into a mightier flame. 'Eliza!' cried he, urging his horse to the place occupied by the king. Right and left the foot-soldiers were overthrown before the hoofs of his springing charger, and he soon approached the spot. 'Eliza!' cried he once again, as he reached the king,--and, as if he did not hold the monster worthy a soldier's blade, he struck him so heavily on his mailed breast with the hilt of his sword, that he shrunk almost double. Then, with a strong hand, he lifted the swooning king from his horse, and taking him like a stolen maiden before himself on the pummel of his saddle, darted back to the commander in chief. 'I bring you here the torch of this unrighteous war,' said he. 'Dispose of him as you deem proper.'

'The bishop has expressly reserved to himself,' answered Oberstein, with sad earnestness, 'the duty of deciding on the fate of the leaders. Therefore take a sufficient number of men; let the wretch be strongly chained, and hold him in close custody. I shall require him at your hands when the proper time arrives. You may safely count upon your reward.'

The battle had continued until now. Orator Rothman, observing the capture of the king, and despairing of the fortune of the day, precipitated himself, sword in hand, upon the thickest crowds of the enemy, that he might not fall into their hands alive; and fell, bravely fighting, more honorably than he had lived. Knipperdolling and Krechting having disappeared, the rest of the anabaptists, deprived of their frantic leaders, and terrified by the universal massacre, threw away their arms and begged for quarter, which the commander in chief immediately granted. The worthy old general gazed sorrowfully upon the dead and dying, who deluged the marketplace with their blood, and upon the pale, meagre countenances, distorted by the sufferings they had experienced, of those who were left; and observed with heartfelt compassion, 'poor fools, you might have obtained pardon at a cheaper rate!'

CHAPTER XXVIII

The next morning the bishop entered the tranquilized city at the head of fifteen hundred horsemen. All the houses had been strictly searched; during which operation many a mad fanatical spirit was found, and the exasperated soldiery did not always respect the general pardon which had been granted. Among others Knipperdolling and Krechting were drawn from their lurking holes; but their lives, with a cruel, calculating forbearance were spared for a future and more solemn execution. Alf's testimony as to the total inactivity and inoffensiveness of his kinsman, the butcher-burgomaster-treasurer, and also of the tailor-duodecemvir-lord-steward, Dilbek, rescued both from imprisonment and death. The first, Alf charged with the duty of collecting his little property, as well as that of Trutlinger's niece, converting it into money and sending it after him, by the first convenient opportunity, to the place where he might thereafter take up his abode; he not feeling disposed to remain in his native city after what he had experienced there,--and besides, the bishop, notwithstanding the favor he shewed him during the audience, had not gained his approbation to such a degree as to induce him to wish to dwell under his sceptre.

Nor was the bishop yet quite disposed to make his home at the episcopal residence. He drove out to castle Dulmen, three miles from Munster, on the day of his entrance; thereby giving to Oberstein a fine opportunity to execute the decisions of the Diet of Worms in relation to the unfortunate city without the interference of its irritable master. He did every thing in his power to mitigate the measureless distress of the citizens. Plentiful supplies of provisions put an end to the torments of hunger. A general pardon, which the bishop himself could not avoid signing, relieved the Munsterers from their incessant and excessive fears of being yet reached by the sword of judicial power. Only the king, Knipperdolling and Krechting were excepted from this pardon. Every one, protestant or catholic, besieged or emigrant, was allowed to take his property out of the public repository where the prophet had sequestered it. The refugees returned again; particularly the expelled burgomaster and aldermen, who immediately resumed their functions, and every thing appeared as if the city was well pleased to find itself returning to the old order of things.

Three days had thus passed away. Early on the fourth, Oberstein sent for Alf. 'I have caused St. Lambert's church to be repaired and embellished a little,' said the general to him. 'It looked as drear and desolate in its large plundered interior, as if the Zihim and Ohim 2 were to rule in it--and the poor people must truly have some external show with their public worship. We must in some measure provide for an impression upon their senses, because their thoughts and feelings are confined within a narrow circle. If you please my young friend, we will go together and observe what great things the painters and garnishers have accomplished in so short a time.'

Alf proceeded to the church with the old hero, and could not refrain from expressing his surprise when he found the lateral walks wholly desolate and untrimmed.

'Only be patient, the best is yet to come,' said the smiling Oberstein, consolingly, and passed into the next lateral walk, where, turning suddenly, they found themselves before the freshly gilded and well adorned high altar. Before it, with the church service in his hand, stood doctor Fabricius in his priestly robes. With a myrtle wreath in her blond hair, in a simple white dress, her eyes cast down, her cheeks glowing with love, joy and shame, stood the faithful little Clara, opposite the youth; while his kinsman Gerhard, Hanslein, and the old body servant of the bishop, as witnesses of the marriage ceremony, approached to wish him joy.

'Oh my God!' cried Alf, surprised and enraptured,--and the worthy Oberstein himself accompanied the pair before the clergyman.

The YES was spoken--the benediction pronounced--and Alf had seized the hand of his young wife to lead her out of church--when an episcopalian officer entered and delivered to the general a letter of which he was the bearer.

Oberstein opened, read, and angrily stamped his foot. 'No joy without interruption,' cried he. 'More than a year have we been detained before these rascally walls without any interruption of the everlasting sameness. This is the first day which I had thought to spend happily here, and now this is to be marred by such a bum-bailiff commission! I cannot help you, my dear bridegroom,' proceeded he, turning to Alf; 'the bishop here commands that you immediately bring to Dulmen, under a strong guard, the tailor-king whom you took prisoner.'

'Is not my marriage a sufficient excuse?' asked Alf dejectedly.

'With the bishop, hardly,' whispered Oberstein to him. 'Man-service goes before God-service with these proud prelates--and we have already, on account of the poor Munsterers, every motive to keep him in as good a humor as possible. It will be fortunate if he satiate his anger upon the wretch whom you are about to conduct to him.'

'Poor little Clara,' sighed Alf, printing a passionate and sorrowful kiss upon the lips of the maiden.

'He named you and thought of himself,' said Oberstein, jestingly; 'but in order that the happy couple may not be separated on this first day of their espousal, I will ride out to Dulmen and endeavor to get you excused by the lord bishop.'

'You are very good!' said the little bride, bending over the hand of the gray old general and pressing it to her lips.

CHAPTER XXIX

At Dulmen, in the hall of state, sat the prince-bishop upon his gilded throne. On each side of him were placed his counsellors and field officers. At a table covered with rich red cloth, sat two secretaries with ready pens. Oberstein had announced the tailor-king, and after a short conversation with the bishop resumed his place. The bishop made a signal--the guards opened the door, and, accompanied by Alf, Johannes entered, loaded with chains and very pale; but with a proud and solemn bearing, casting round upon the assembly his wild, impudent and bold glance.

'That is the murderer of my son,' sighed the bishop in a suppressed tone to Oberstein, covering his face with his hands from grief and horror.

'Remember that you are here as a prince and judge, and not as a party,' whispered Oberstein in return.

The bishop recovered himself with difficulty. 'Wretched man,' cried he vehemently to the criminal: 'wherefore hast thou ruined my defenceless people?'

'I have not done less than you deserve, priest!' answered Johannes, as proudly as if Zion's crown had yet stood upon his head. 'I have given into thy hand a strong city which can stand against every power. Nevertheless if I have injured you I have sufficient means to make you reparation, in case you will but follow my counsels.'

'Wretch!' growled the bishop, 'how wilt thou compensate for a single drop of the innocent blood which thou hast caused to flow in streams?'

'Human blood,' said Johannes, scornfully, 'comes not into the account in the reckoning of kings. Here we can only speak respecting the restitution of money. Therefore shut me up in an iron cage as Tamerlane did Bajazet, take me through the neighboring countries and show me for money--you will make more out of me in that way than the whole siege has cost.'

The whole assembly broke out into a loud cry of astonishment and displeasure at the unparalleled insolence of the criminal, whose life hung upon the nod of his judge.

The latter was paralyzed by the extent of the monster's profligacy. He soon however recovered himself, and silently viewed him for a long time with a horrible smile upon his countenance.

'My God!' murmured Alf, when he saw that smile; 'this will end tragically.'

'Thou hast advised well, wise Solomon,' said the bishop with great calmness. 'Be it done to thee according to thy words. Deliver up your prisoner to the constable of the castle,' he commanded Alf. 'Let him be confined in the murderer's cell until further orders--and do you convey to the smiths of Munster my command that they immediately make three iron cages of a man's height. Therein shall this man and his coadjutors be conducted round the land as he himself has desired, and be shown to the people as they are accustomed to show wild beasts. What further is to be done with the worthy trio, shall be duly pronounced at the proper time in the criminal court.'

With unaltered pride Johannes suffered himself to be led forth by Alf. The bishop dismissed the assembly. Only Oberstein remained with him, and now Alf returned to announce that he had deposited his prisoner in his dungeon.

'It was you who captured the hyæna who butchered my children for me,' cried the bishop with horrible joy. 'I thank you for the opportunity to avenge on him the blood of all his victims! Oh that he had more than one life! Say, what reward do you desire for the deed!'

'Such a reward would be the price of blood,' thought Alf, 'and therefore God preserve me from it.'

'Would you like a good military or civil office at my court?' asked the bishop in his desire to express his gratitude.

'I am a protestant, most reverend sir,' answered Alf: 'and hope to die in the evangelical faith; but if I may prefer a petition to you, I have to request that you will permit me without ceremony or hindrance to take my own and my wife's property to the place where I am to settle myself.'

'Are you determined absolutely not to remain in my territories?' asked the bishop resentfully.

'I think of procuring for him a captaincy from the elector of Saxony,' said Oberstein, with a view of softening the effect of Alf's short and ungracious reply.

'Pardon me sir earl,' said Alf, 'for respectfully declining that favor also. I have lately seen so many people commanded, and so many evils have been caused by the orders given--and I myself in my simplicity have done so much mischief by my own commands, that I have become utterly disgusted with the whole business. Wherefore I have solicited the reverend doctor Fabricius to seek me out a quiet little place in Hesse Cassel, were I may honorably employ myself as an armorer and enjoy the society of my wife and the children with which God may bless our union, until my happy end.'

'Do you not think he has chosen the wisest part?' asked Oberstein of the bishop, at the same time leaving the room.

'O that I could find in Munster a hundred burghers like this who now deserts me!' said the bishop, through forgetfulness, laying his hand in blessing upon the heretic's head.

'Think well of my request, reverend sir,' said Alf, bowing low and following his friend and protector.

CHAPTER XXX

When the happy Clara opened her blue eyes on the first morning after her marriage, she saw that her young husband was already awake and sitting upright in bed as if in deep and earnest meditation upon some important matter. She threw her arms about his neck, kissed him tenderly and asked him what he was meditating upon so intently.

'Upon my future destiny, and the decision I must make as to what business I shall hereafter pursue, my dear wife,' answered he with seeming earnestness. 'So many offers were made to me yesterday that I hardly know which of them to embrace. The lord bishop wishes to retain me with him, either in a military capacity or as an officer of his court, as I may choose; for the latter of which I suppose I am more particularly well qualified. I can also at any moment become a captain in the service of the elector of Saxony.'

'You surely will not accept of either of them?' cried Clara, anxiously. 'Leave those high honors and dignities to others, and be satisfied with the quiet domestic happiness which awaits you, and which your unambitious disposition is best calculated to enjoy. Remain what you are, a good armorer! As such only have I joined hands with you, before God's altar, in the holy bands of matrimony. If now you wish the captaincy, or a seat in the royal council, then have you deceived me, even at the moment of marriage, and that would be very wrong in a bridegroom.'

'God be praised!' joyfully exclaimed Alf, pressing her to his bosom. 'That is precisely what I desired to hear from you, my dear Clara. I only wished to ascertain whether you agreed with me upon a most important question; and behold, our wishes and opinions are as similar as if we had been made for each other.'

'Ah, that was always clear to me from the first moment I saw you,' stammered Clara, blushing; 'and it used to render me truly miserable to see that you had eyes only for my unfortunate sister.'

'Peace to her ashes!' said Alf with emotion; 'but I now perceive quite clearly that she would have been no wife for me. What God brings to pass is intended for our good.'

At that moment began under the windows, arranged by the wedding guests, an excellent morning serenade; and the vocalists, falling in, sang to the bridal pair, in Martin Luther's words: 3

'Oh happy man, whose soul is fill'd

With zeal and reverend awe!

His lips to God their honors yield,

His life adorns the law.

'A careful Providence shall stand

And ever guard thy head,

Shall on the labors of thy hand,

Its kindly blessings shed.'

'Shall on the labors of thy hand,'--said the young couple joyfully to each other at the same moment, and Alf smilingly remarked; 'now we shall be sure to live together at least a year, my Clara, since we both had the same thought at the same time.'

Again sang the choir:

'Thy wife shall be a fruitful vine;

Thy children round thy board,

Each like an olive-plant shall shine,

And learn to fear the Lord.

'The Lord shall thy best hopes fulfil

For months and years to come;

The Lord who dwells on Zion's hill,

Shall send thee blessings home.'

Reminded of the pleasures of paternity, Alf pressed his beloved wife yet closer, while she hid her blushing face in his bosom. They listened with delighted attention to the remainder of the hymn, and when the last verse came they joined in with a pious ecstasy, and in thankful remembrance of all that God had done for them:

'To Father, Son, and Holy Ghost,

The God whom we adore,

Be everlasting honors paid

Henceforth, forevermore.'

CHAPTER XXXI

Having obtained an honorable discharge from the army of the Diet, Alf settled himself with his young wife under the shadow of Fabricius's wing at Cassel, as a respectable armorer. The property which he took with him from Munster, together with the rich marriage presents which he received from the bishop and count Oberstein, rendered him a well conditioned burgher. He enjoyed the blessings of a middle station in society, in an unusual measure, and the painful remembrance of what he had experienced, performed, and suffered, was merged by degrees in the feeling of repose, and in the quiet enjoyment of well merited prosperity.

Meanwhile the timid and exasperated bishop began to bring poor Munster fully under the yoke; so that it should never again be able to raise its head in rebellion. Two castles arose towering over the city, with the aid of which he hoped easily to suppress every disturbance, and occasionally to curtail some of the ancient privileges of the people; but the ambassadors of the Circle, who suddenly appeared in Munster, efficaciously remedied this fault and many others. The peaceable citizens of Munster, whom he had compelled to perform all sorts of labor, were protected; the fortifications of the anabaptists as well as the castles of the bishop were razed; and the latter was compelled to permit a decision, by a trial and sentence, upon the fate of the tailor-king and his companions, who, until then, had been, in mockery and scorn, dragged through all the neighboring parts of Germany in their cages. In February of the year 1536, the three criminals were finally led to the scaffold. However great was their guilt, the cruelty of their punishment seemed unworthy the mercy which should have been exercised by the spiritual lords, from whom alone a mitigation of their sentence could emanate; but who commanded its execution with unrelenting severity.

'Holy God!' exclaimed Alf, when he heard of their unhappy end; 'whither will not fanaticism lead its unhappy devotees! Happy is he who confines his attention to the narrow circle of his household and his business, and who does not forget that prayer and labor are the best antidotes to vain imaginings. Thrice happy is the man to whom God grants a good wife, who, with gentle power, draws him from the wild impulses of the world, and with flowery chains binds him to his own hearth. Under that hearth lies buried the true treasure of life, which so few have the desire and happiness to raise. We have disinterred it, have we not, my Clara? When the olive plants stand around us, which Dr. Luther has promised, what shall we then lack?' Saying this, he laid his hand affectionately upon his young wife, who was most assiduously spinning at the opposite side of the table. At first, with a sweet smile, she clasped her beloved husband's hand, and then passing quickly round the table, she fell upon his neck. 'Lord God, we thank thee!' cried the superlatively happy husband, glowing with love and gratitude.

FOOTNOTES

Footnote 1 : The name of one of the imperial regiments, composed of catholics.

Footnote 2 : Evil spirits.

Footnote 3 : We use the version of Dr. Watts.--Tr.